Praise for LIA MATERA and DESIGNER CRIMES

"One of the most articulate and surely one of the wittiest of women sleuths at large in the genre . . . [Matera] writes with intelligence and feelings about issues that still hurt and people who still care."
—Marilyn Stasio, *New York Times Book Review*

"This is a winner."
—Patricia Holt, *San Francisco Chronicle*

"Resonant with dark and cynical undertones, this novel also shines with a fresh plot premise, strong action scenes, and entirely credible characters."
—Mary C. Trone, Minneapolis *Star Tribune*

"Two knotty cases, some fine detection, a satisfying explosion when Laura puts all the pieces together, and an unusually honest meditation on going home again."
—*Kirkus Reviews*

"Lia Matera brings back her feisty heroine, Laura Di Palma, in a story that immediately plunges the reader into a heady mix of politics, intrigue, romance, and murder. . . . swift and beguiling. . . ."

—Shirley Krichmar Murray, *Mostly Murder*

"Lia Matera is often compared with Sue Grafton and Sara Paretsky. However, Matera has her own distinctive voice. Her offbeat plots, quirky style, and hard-to-pin-down characters make for a novel both unique and entertaining."

—*San Diego Union*

"Gutsy, grown-up crime writing from one of the best practitioners around."

—*Newsday*

"Tragedy catapults Di Palma into a wild roller-coaster ride of a plot that . . . held my attention. . . . I was hooked until the end."

—Kathleen A. Carlson, Nashville *Banner*

"Matera demonstrates that she is one of today's best mystery writers."

—*Publishers Weekly*

Books by Lia Matera

*Designer Crimes
*Face Value
*A Hard Bargain
Prior Convictions
*The Good Fight
Hidden Agenda
*The Smart Money
A Radical Departure
Where Lawyers Fear to Tread

*A Laura Di Palma Mystery

Published by POCKET BOOKS

LIA MATERA

DESIGNER CRIMES

A LAURA DI PALMA MYSTERY

POCKET STAR BOOKS
New York   London   Toronto   Sydney   Tokyo   Singapore

A Pocket Star Book published by
POCKET BOOKS, a division of Simon & Schuster Inc.
1230 Avenue of the Americas, New York, NY 10020

ISBN: 0-671-00196-5

First Pocket Books printing July 1996

10 9 8 7 6 5 4 3 2 1

POCKET STAR BOOKS and colophon are registered
trademarks of Simon & Schuster Inc.

Cover photo by Barnaby Hall/Photonica

Printed in the U.S.A.

To Kevin Lewis and Robert Irvine
for perfect suggestions, again;

And to Jim Aschbacher and Lisa Jensen,
Faye Augustine and Tom Derr,
Tom Maderos and Vicki Bolam,
Kent Benedict and Paula Gomez:
What a swell party this is.

PROLOGUE

HE WAS AN IMPOSING MAN, UPHOLSTERED IN PLAID WOOL. My porch light mantled him in fog. Two men faded in and out of view behind him.

"Laura Di Palma?" He didn't wait for me to respond; he knew me from the courtroom or the news. I knew he was a cop. It was in his voice. "I have a warrant for your arrest."

He brandished a document, its paper bright in the spotlight of my shock. "You are under arrest for conspiracy to murder Constance Gold. You have the right to remain silent."

Other rights, too. He recited them.

Beyond him, a car braked to a stop beneath a street lamp. A district attorney—not Connie Gold, but one of her underlings—erupted from it, leaving windshield wipers up, headlights on. Slick concrete glared like ice.

I had a sudden glimpse of chaos: my bills, my caseload, my dishes. My suitcase, still unpacked.

All I could think to say was, "I was shot at, too. Twice." But I hadn't been hit; maybe that aroused suspicion. "Someone's trying to kill me. In San Francisco, in Jocelyn Kinsley's office—you know about that.'' A masked man had burst into the office, missing me by inches when he shot Kinsley dead. "He's been after me ever since." The bullet that got Gold was certainly meant for me. I had to make them understand that.

"Can't you see—" I faltered: there was so much to explain, and much of it would rouse their ire. It would say to them, I don't trust you backwater cops, don't trust the DA to draw the right conclusions. And obviously I was right.

"I'm unpopular with the DA's office, that's all this is about." I had waged war on Connie Gold, fighting for the privacy of my wrongly accused client. But way up here, three hundred miles from the nearest city, it was a short step from logging town to banana republic. I mastered a desire to rail against the ugly provincialism of it.

The deputy DA stood before me, her hair sugared with mist, her heavy-browed face harsh in the lamplight. She shook her head.

I felt a fresh and slicing fear: maybe there was more to it. Maybe they had evidence I didn't know about. Maybe they could make a case.

One of the plainclothesmen began patting me, searching for weapons. The DA stood by, tight-lipped and stiff-shouldered. I tried without success to remember her name.

"I need to call San Francisco." San Francisco, where my law practice was; where I'd be now if I hadn't agreed to defend a high school friend. "I need to speak to my lawyer."

The cop's expression said, No shit, Sherlock. "You'll be given that opportunity." He began walking me out. No handcuffs: small-town informality, perhaps; more likely a bow to my uncle, the mayor.

"You've hardly had time to investigate." I cast a wondering glance at the deputy DA. "You can't have any evidence."

"We can and we do." Her voice was smugly musical, full of querying lilts: an LA voice. One of many Southern Californians finding nature in the redwoods below Oregon? "We try to act quickly. We try to protect our citizens."

Unlike sleazy defense lawyers? I bit my tongue. No one could match the Hillsdale DA's office for politically selective enforcement.

Outside, the drizzle cooled my adrenaline-scalded skin. There had to be some pretext for my arrest. The DA had proffered *something* to get the warrant. What could it be?

In the back of the police car, I closed my eyes. Yesterday a man came out of nowhere, masked and supple, to shoot me. But this time I'd seen him coming. This time I hadn't fallen accidentally out of the way—I'd ducked. Connie Gold had been standing beside me. And now she was a wounded grizzly, out for blood.

Just last week, I'd told Sandy Arkelett he was crazy; that no one was after me.

Just last week, my biggest problem had been that I hated Steven Sayres.

CHAPTER

One

I HATED STEVE SAYRES THE WAY YOU'D HATE AN EX-husband. And I'd spent almost as much time with him. For six and a half years, we'd been two doors in a hallway, two stars in the too small firmament of White, Sayres & Speck.

And if I'd been the bigger star, well, he should have been glad. It was his partnership share of the law firm that I'd swollen. He'd taken home the extra money—bought the sailboat, the wine cellar, the lathed mahogany wainscot—not me. He'd been able to leave at seven because I, a hungry associate determined to "make partner," could be trusted to toil fiercely till ten.

But his prosperity came at a price: I stood beside him in the mirror. And he was a doctor's pampered son, star of the corny-movie football team; if he shared the sunshine, it was supposed to be with other golden boys on a happy shortcut. Not with a woman who wouldn't cheerlead and wouldn't pass the ball if she could run with it herself.

Even now, with me out of the firm and out of Sayres's

(expensive) neighborhood, even now, he could only be-grudge me.

Worse, he couldn't let it go, he couldn't leave me alone. I'd tried to tell him: Yes, you won the pissing contest, Sayres; you can put it back in your pants now.

But I'd heard his slanderous spewings from a half-dozen sources. And now my only cash-cow client was firing me because of him.

I tried not to leap from my chair with an angry, "Fine! Lose your case the good-old-boy way!" I tried to remember it might not be too late to pull this chestnut out of the fire.

"I think you'd be making a mistake to go elsewhere, Perry. There's an enormous learning curve in a case like this." Though the intricacies of custom robotics had justi-fied my retainer, it hadn't been a fun study. "Why pay for someone else to become acquainted with the details of your operation? Plus"—I spoke hastily, seeing he wanted to put an end to an embarrassing situation—"you won't find a better-suited attorney. I have years of experience in corpo-rate litigation."

"Well," he shifted his ample posterior. "You've taken on this criminal case"—his tone implied I'd jilted him for a mere servant—"and as I said, with the ins and outs of that . . ." He trailed off, as if there were no need to reprise his reasoning. As if he'd already explained.

"You've heard that I back-burner civil cases, haven't you? That I concentrate on my criminal clients and short-change my corporate." I forced myself to swallow Steve's name. "It's not true."

Perry, and the multimillion-dollar business he repre-sented, stood up, preparing to leave. "It's just, you know, Laura. With so much money at stake . . ." His jaw tightened visibly. "The shareholders pay me to be cautious. You're a one-person firm. And you now have this big criminal case."

I looked up at his well-fed, petulant face. He had the

spoiled-husband air of a wealthy man in his fifties. He appeared unused to contradiction.

How many times had his corporation been sued, I wondered. Often enough for him to realize the judge in his months-away-from-trial suit would allow me court days off to defend another case.

"Be honest," I urged. "Steve Sayres came to you, didn't he? He told you I'd ignore you because of this other case."

But even as I said it, I knew it hadn't happened quite that way. Steve was a master of the small needle, a jab here and a jab there, until the inflammation set in.

He'd have made a comment or two over drinks, another over lunch, a friendly hint, a sad shake of the head. Sayres was easy to see through, but most eyes stopped at the crinkly smile and gorgeous suit.

My client—former client now, I could see—frowned slightly, pursing his lips in dismissive distaste. I sometimes think our strongest cultural bias is against accusers: no matter the accusation, we suspect it of tacky paranoia, silly conspiracy theory, strident bad sportsmanship. Maybe we hate to have to deal with other people's problems; it's easier to think ill of the afflicted.

I watched Perry and took stock. He would believe Sayres over me because Sayres had convinced him they were the same: good guys in business. He wouldn't believe me because I fit a favorite stereotype: ballbreaker with a problem. I'd encountered this a thousand times in a thousand guises.

One day, you accept the familiar injustice with your usual resignation. The next, you know you've had enough.

CHAPTER

Two

I've had enough of Steve Sayres and his slimy innuendoes," I concluded. "I want to sue him."

The lawyer sitting opposite me toyed with a black metal tape dispenser. She'd been doing that the whole time I talked to her. It was a measure of my general irritation that I said, "Do you need some tape?"

She flushed, setting it back on her desk. "I'm sorry—I have been listening." She scooted the dispenser farther from her, across a litter of file folders and sheets of yellow legal pad turned upside down for privacy.

Damn, she looked young. Young, indecisive, and not quite completely with me. And yet I'd heard this was the most aggressive and cleverest labor law firm in town. I'd been told this firm played hardball. But you'd never guess it from the sweet Renaissance angels decorating the walls of Jocelyn Kinsley's office, nor from the pink angora sweater beneath her beige linen jacket. She looked like a woman with a big extended family in the Midwest and two cats at home. A woman who started her Christmas crafts in August.

Not a labor lawyer. Not a player. Perhaps it was her law partner, Maryanne More, most people thought of when they mentioned More & Kinsley. But More, it seemed, specialized in high-tech labor. And Kinsley, among other things, handled employment-related slander.

As if startled by some inner prompt, she picked up a pencil, touching the tip to her yellow pad. "Steven Sayres," she said, and wrote. "And who are some of the people you believe he talked to?"

I defused a small volley of anger. Hadn't she been listening? We were talking about my financial survival. "It got back to me first from—"

"What's that?" She looked like a pretty rabbit, big-eyed and twitchy.

"What?" I was only a few more irritations from walking out.

She had the dispenser in her hand again, sitting straight, staring past me at, I supposed, her closed door.

"Do you want the names?" I tried to bring her back to business. I was aware of a slight commotion somewhere in the outer office. I could hear someone shouting, a few loud cracks, as of party poppers or champagne corks.

Kinsley straightened, rolling back slightly in her high-back chair. She didn't look at me, didn't seem to hear me.

With a screw-this shake of the head, I started out of my chair. I'd find a lawyer with a normal attention span.

Because it happened so quickly, I didn't get a chance to analyze her shocked cry or the fact that she suddenly hurled the tape dispenser at me.

The metal object caught me in the forehead. The impact, perhaps coupled with the surprise, collapsed me sideways. I tried to use the chair for support, felt it slide backward, legs raking the gold carpet. I landed on my shoulder and face, in a turmoil of outrage.

I wanted to excoriate Jocelyn Kinsley for her stupid behavior, to turn a fire hose of rage on her, in fact—rage toward Steve Sayres and all the unfair obstacles and petty bullshit threatening to sink my law practice. I was too angry to feel pain, but quite ready to use the unfelt pain as an excuse to detonate.

I should have known something was terribly wrong: Kinsley had pitched a tape dispenser at me.

I heard explosions again, this time too loud to be distant corks. I could feel a cool shift of air: the office door was open. The explosions were almost deafening.

From somewhere behind me, somewhere out in the hall, came a staccato of screams and panicked voices. I inhaled a sharp stink like spent firecrackers. I looked up. The ceiling lights wavered like daylight through water.

I felt motion on the floor. On the other side of her curve-legged, antique desk, Jocelyn Kinsley lay crumpled on the carpet. Her face was turned toward me, pink foam gargling from her lips.

I screamed. I knew why I was on the floor—but why was she? Reality had done a sudden somersault.

Her eyes were half closed, her face was a sweating alabaster white with foam angling from her delicately painted mouth. I became aware of commotion around me, someone holding my shoulders when I tried to get up, a voice screaming, "He shot them!"

I tried to bat the person's hands away. I wanted to get up, get oriented, understand what had happened, make everything normal and within my control again. But pinned by worried hands, I was forced to remain down, staring through the arch of Kinsley's desk to her pale face.

There were people around her, too, but to me they were just sleeves and torsos, hastily ripping off jackets to cover her, talking about pressure points and keeping her warm.

Her eyes were half open; she seemed to stare at me across the meter of carpeted floor. Her lips moved, stopped. Her tongue came out to push bloody sputum away.

Her eyes opened wider, holding my gaze. For the first

time, I noticed they were yellow brown, similar in shade to her curls.

To me, directly and distinctly, she rasped, "Designer crimes."

Someone hovering over her, a woman in white silk, her jacket partly covering Kinsley, said, "What? What? Jocelyn?"

Above her, someone else replied, "A sign of the times. She said, 'a sign of the times.'"

"Oh, Joss, no," said the white-shirt woman. "No, it's not. It's not." As if Kinsley would be all right if the shooting weren't a sign of the times.

"Not what she said," I told the person hovering over me. But she was busy looking over the desktop, trying to learn from her coworkers' faces whether Jocelyn Kinsley would be all right.

My disorientation was fading. I struggled to a sitting position, unceremoniously pushing the woman away.

I could feel a crawling tickle on my forehead and reached up a frightened hand. It was blood. I stared at it on my fingertips for a cold-clutch second before I realized the tape dispenser had hit my forehead and broken the skin.

I hadn't been shot. The second I realized it, I knew Jocelyn Kinsley had.

And I knew the explosive sounds for what they had been. I recognized the firecracker smell in the air.

Someone had burst into this office carrying a gun. Kinsley, already startled by the sound of gunfire in the outer office—had she known it was gunfire?—had been watching the office door. When the person entered, she hurled the object in her hand, the tape dispenser. But I'd risen impatiently at that moment, catching it on the forehead and blundering down.

The gunshots that hit Jocelyn Kinsley might have hit me if I'd remained seated. But I was already on the floor when they blasted past, catching her once in the shoulder and once in the chest.

In the moment it took me to look around the room and understand what had happened, Jocelyn Kinsley died. The woman crouching over her began to tremble fiercely and to sob. And more than once, waiting for the paramedics to arrive, I heard the phrase "a sign of the times."

But those had not been Kinsley's last words.

Designer crimes. I could close my eyes and hear Kinsley. It seemed to me she'd offered the words like a journal or a diary, expecting me to understand her by them.

Merely because I had been in her range of focus? Or because I had been the only relative stranger in the room?

I backed into a corner and hugged myself, watching the grieving women. Within seconds, the police burst in, guns drawn to make sure the scene was secure. They were followed by frantic paramedics, pulling open Kinsley's shirt and muttering about "tubing" her.

I must have spoken to the police, assuring them I'd stand by for their questions. I must have told the paramedics I'd suffered nothing worse than a nick in the forehead. But all I actually remember was huddling alone, watching and thinking.

Designer crimes, her dying words. They had to mean something. You wouldn't utter nonsense before you died. You'd want to say as much as you could about whatever was topmost in your mind.

Designer crimes. The phrase would become my mantra.

CHAPTER

Three

WHAT MIGHT ONCE HAVE SEEMED A NORMAL REACTION on Sandy Arkelett's part I now freighted with connotations. We were growing close again.

He turned away, running his hand over thinning, sand-colored hair. From the back, he might have been Gary Cooper, tall and lanky in an almost baggy suit.

He paced the length of his office, then turned.

"I don't care." His tone said otherwise. "I don't care what you say about it, what you put on it, where you think it comes from."

"A good man takes care of his own."

"Pretty much." His long legs brought him swiftly back to hover over me. Behind him, streaked windows framed gray buildings. The city looked grimy. It had been too long since the last rain. "Why not, Laura? Who's going to do it any better?"

"That attitude usually means a lot of posturing and bluster. A lot of noise and not much listening." If I could keep honest, I stood a chance. If I had to tiptoe around his ego, all I had was a replay of my last relationship.

"Well, that might usually be true," he conceded. "But what's it got to do with you and me?"

I looked up at him. Before I could stop it, my feeling for him caught me in a pouncing ambush. I'd left him—foolishly, it turned out—for my cousin Hal. We were friends again now that Hal was gone, but it had taken time. I wasn't sure what else might be salvaged.

"Seriously," he continued. "What does any of this have to do with you getting shot at?"

"I don't know that I *was* shot at."

He knelt, grabbing the arms of his office rocker, stopping my comforting movement. "We've been over this. If you hadn't stood up and gotten knocked down—for which I bless Kinsley no end—those bullets would have ripped through your back somewhere right about here." He touched my collarbone and my chest. "You'd have a hole in your heart, most likely."

"Maybe if I'd still been sitting, he wouldn't have fired from that spot. If he was after Kinsley—"

"We're talking about a couple of seconds. Question if he'd register you falling out of the way that quick."

"But he didn't fire until I fell."

"Don't be fooled. The sound takes a while. Shots happen sooner than your ears hear them." As if in agreement, horns popped on the street below.

I'd spent hours with the police. I'd been taken to the hospital for a checkup I didn't need at the insistence of some insurance company and of the district attorney. I'd been reliving the incident since it happened. I was sick of it.

Sandy repeated, "I'm going to find out who did it, Laura. Guaranteed. I don't care if you think that's macho bullshit. You tell me it had nothing to do with you. But you don't have that on anybody's authority. We need to know for sure." He watched me assessingly. I suppose he knew I'd overdose on my emotions soon. "Tell me again. 'Designer crimes'—you're sure that's what she said?"

"Yes. The police have three other witnesses swearing it was 'a sign of the times.' But I was looking right at her, eye level. I know what I heard."

He nodded. "Who suggested 'a sign of the times'?"

"Her law partner, I think. Maryanne More."

"It's easy enough to mishear something like that, I guess." He sat back on his haunches. "But we can't rule out misdirection. This could be a professional hit. Only one person shot, killer wearing gloves and a ski mask, drops the gun and walks away like a pro. Or it could be a One oh one California thing."

One oh one California. The address had become associated with a crazy client bursting in and shooting eight people in the law office he felt had done him wrong.

"Well, Kinsley definitely didn't say 'a sign of the times,' " I insisted. "She said 'designer crimes.' Whatever that means."

"Almost sounds like a service for bored yuppies. 'Tired of weekend kayaking? How about a fun little felony tailored to your individual needs and skills? Come to the Designer Crimes boutique.' " His Louisiana boyhood could be heard in the word "boo-teek."

"More specializes in clients who design computer hardware and software. Maybe it has to do with that." But I gave his suggestion points for flair. "We could open a crime boutique, Sandy. With your knowledge of surveillance and lock picking—"

"And your criminal-defense credentials?" He had a Will Rogers grin and long dimples. "I think it's time to put the new kid to work."

The new kid in Sandy's private investigation agency was a computer specialist—at least, that's what his freshly printed business cards said. He was really a hacker with an insatiable thirst for raw, unprocessed information.

Sandy rose. "We're going to sneak a peek at Kinsley's E-mail, do the grand tour of the office files."

I considered questioning the ethics and legality of this. But Jocelyn Kinsley was beyond objecting. And Sandy liked to run things his way when they were his to run. As did I, when they were mine. We usually respected that about each other.

He crossed to the telephone. "I just hope we can get in."

By "get in," he meant crawling through some electronic mousehole connecting More & Kinsley's computers to a network service. If they had old-fashioned unmodemed computers, that would be impossible. But most firms subscribed to on-line case-law libraries, at the very least. Many could access public records, news stories, and a rich menu of other services as well. Lexis-Nexis, ATT's Easy-Link, and the Internet were cyberspace low roads for a new generation of information bandits.

I still wore the cement shoes of an older technology—telephone calls, paper files, handwritten notes on yellow pads. But working for Perry Verhoeven had forced me to learn the basics of electronic communication.

I watched Sandy make the call, admiring his undertailored length.

He muttered into the mouthpiece. "You heard me, Ozzy. However you need to."

Sandy usually reigned his newest employee in, reminding him they could get their information by legal means, if they were patient enough. Certainly their lawyer clients preferred admissible evidence to the ill-gotten lowdown. "Especially look for anything around the phrase 'designer crimes.' Doesn't have to be those words, but anything that could fit under that umbrella. Focus on clients who design computer systems or do graphic design. See if the firm handles any criminal cases or even if the word 'crime' pops up in the files.''

When he hung up, I commented, ''You're picking a hell of a time to break into their computer system. You leave a trace and the police will nail you to the wall.''

He turned back to face me. ''Could be someone's after you.'' As if that justified any risk.

''No.'' I resumed rocking. ''I'd have some clue or worry. There'd be some area of my life it could come out of. I'd know what it was about, even if I didn't know who.''

I reviewed the months since my return to San Francisco. I'd angered a few people, certainly—I was a lawyer, it went with the territory. But I could think of nothing likely to generate an attempt on my life. Not down here, anyway.

''I've got the Rommel thing up in Hillsdale.'' I'd returned to my hometown to help my Uncle Henry with the sad business of probating my father's will. I'd ended up agreeing to defend my high school friend Brad Rommel against a murder charge. ''But there's nothing in that case to send someone gunning for me.''

''Connie Gold.'' Sandy offered the name jokingly.

Hillsdale's DA had written a teleplay based on her prosecution of the county's only serial rapist. She'd spent months winning the victims' trust and eliciting confidences no one else could have. Then she'd put them on the witness stand, dragging out humiliating details arguably irrelevant to the case but necessary for a teleplay. There were ethical rules prohibiting defense lawyers from doing that. But prosecutors could cash in on the public's hatred of criminals even if it meant revictimizing the victims.

I'd handled some very high-profile cases, too; as near as I could figure, Gold hated me for being as famous as she was. Her rage mounted when Rommel was granted bail despite a statute disallowing it in capital crimes. Even I'd been surprised the judge accepted my argument: that the lack of a dead body made the statute inapplicable. Gold had

17

been too smart to accuse the judge of foolishness or favoritism. Instead, she'd cast aspersions on me, equating me with past clients.

I'd been forced to retaliate; Brad Rommel deserved a fair fight. If I was going to enter the arena spattered with mud, Gold would have to appear soiled, too. It made extra work for me—depressingly cynical work—but the jury couldn't be allowed to see me as less upright than the opposition.

I'd gone to the State Bar to protest in advance Gold's sale of rights to the Rommel story—though as far as I knew, she wasn't planning a sale. I'd made a media splash about the commercial exploitation of victims, and the DA's obligation to provide closure rather than seek personal enrichment. What if victims stopped revealing "embarrassing" details to DAs because they didn't want them featured in a movie of the week?

My public statements convinced two of the serial rapist's victims to sue Gold. I hadn't intended that to happen.

"I'm not so sure I'm kidding," Sandy added.

"No," I repeated, "it's crazy, Sandy. The whole idea of someone being after me is crazy." I said it with such authority.

"When do you go back up to Hillsdale?"

"I've got a motion to suppress evidence tomorrow. Win or lose, I'm back here the day after. If I do lose, I'll go up again on the weekend. Can you come?" One of Brad's better qualities was his affluence. He owned a fishing boat, an airplane, and a mountain cabin. He could afford an out-of-town investigator. And Sandy was worth the extra money.

His grin told me he planned to stick close to me for a while. "Looking forward to the sunshine," he replied.

Again I glanced out his window. Sometimes I found myself fantasizing about the savage chill and smothering wetness of the Pacific north coast. There was an animal sensuality to being battered by wind and flogged by rain.

Maybe I'd spent too much of my adulthood in the temperate city.

Or maybe I'd finally noticed that San Francisco was changing. Mission neighborhoods that a few years ago enjoyed a colorful renaissance now cowered in fear of gang violence. AIDS lent a plague-year leer to the Castro Street carnivals. Everywhere stunned throwaways shivered in doorways. On a gray day, without bay sparkle or views, the city could be downright ugly.

And somehow it was gray days I missed most.

CHAPTER

Four

ONLY ONE RESTAURANT IN HILLSDALE MADE A PRETENSE of city elegance. I shared a table with my client, Brad Rommel. The aroma of roasted garlic and olive oil wafted over us. He looked around as if wanting me to look, too. But I was used to sponge-painted walls and huge abstract canvases; I couldn't muster the requisite appreciation. And the view—a downtown blighted with soaped windows and FOR LEASE signs—was depressing.

It appeared I'd taken losing the motion to suppress evidence harder than Brad Rommel had. But then, some clients harbored the misconception they could prove their innocence at trial, that failure to go to trial would blemish their reputations. Unfortunately, few reputations could survive the negative publicity of a trial. A mere arrest, on the other hand, might eventually be forgotten.

"Hillsdale's changed a lot, hasn't it?" Brad's face reddened beneath white-gold hair, setting off the blue of his eyes. There was a high-intensity virility in his coloring, his burliness, the way he sat too far forward and talked too loud, as if demanding agreement.

"Mmm." Every acquaintance I saw seemed to need my reassurance that Hillsdale had improved in the last two decades. Considering it once offered only a roaring highway of drive-in burger joints and bad coffee shops for entertainment, of course the restored waterfront and Victorian bed-and-breakfasts helped. On the other hand, downtown, paltry as it had been, was dying like a gangrenous limb. And the renovated Old Town district looked like an untrafficked stage set.

"Even the weather's better," he continued.

Everyone I encountered made a point of telling me so. It seemed to disturb them that I'd left—or maybe that they'd stayed.

I looked out the window at the cold white sky. The watersheds of my youth—losing my mother, battling the matriarchal relative who'd "taken her place," making a disastrous teenage marriage, and having an even more disastrous love affair—were mere memories now, without the power to torment me. I'd been forced to relive them on previous visits, and I'd found them surprisingly life-sized. Only my youth had made them huge; perspective—and physical distance—had shortened their shadows. I could finally see Hillsdale for what it was, not what it had done to me.

"I like it here, Brad," I reassured him. "I like how green and overgrown it is, I like the old Victorians, I love the wild, empty beaches and woods." But the new shops and restaurants couldn't hold a candle to city life, not even close. The things people bragged about were the things that mattered least about Hillsdale, as far as I was concerned.

"It'd be a great town if the mall hadn't cut the heart out of it."

To roaring fanfare, a mere eight years ago, Hillsdale got its first real mall, as plastic and predictable as any other, with the same stores and multiplex theater. I'd nixed several invitations to eat in its "food court." No chance Brad would suggest going there.

His longtime lover, the woman he was accused of killing, had been driven out of business by it. A sign reading FIX- TURES FOR SALE was all that remained of her downtown boutique.

"So let's talk about the next step, Brad."

He seemed chagrined, whether at the return to matters at hand or my reluctance to discuss the mall, I didn't know.

"We'll have to go to trial—unless we can find some exculpating evidence." In this case more than any other I'd tried, it seemed a possibility. "Next time I come to town, I'd like to bring the detective I generally use. You need some- one really good."

"What's wrong with our local guys?"

If I could understand the Hillsdale inferiority complex, maybe I could move Brad beyond silly boosterism. "This isn't a buy-local situation, Brad. You need someone that I trust and know how to work with. Not a pig in a poke."

He scowled, his Nordic brows several shades paler than his fisherman's skin. "I don't see the good in taking bread out of a local person's mouth, not with the area hurting like it is. Bad enough the chain stores at the mall killed the downtown." His eyes brimmed. "Bad enough its restau- rants buy frozen from Mexico when they could get hours- old fish from their own bay."

"I know." And he knew the mall had been my Uncle Henry's pet project, Hillsdale's "ticket to modern times." But the mall wasn't the issue.

Brad could end up on death row. Surely that was suffi- cient reason to import the best. Or did he think mere inno- cence was enough?

"All I'm saying, Brad: this is a factually complicated case. We're talking about a woman disappearing. She has to have left some trace somewhere. The police and sheriff have

already done their best to find her''—her body, anyway—
''and now we need to do ours.''

A bucket of her blood had been discovered beside a trail
near Dungeness Head, not far from Rommel's fishing boat.
A fisherman's bucket, still contaminated with traces of fish
guts, a bucket like the ones on his vessel. ''I wouldn't tell
you how to fish. Please let me do the best job for you that
I can.''

He rubbed a rough hand over his brow as if massaging a
headache. He seemed reluctant to speak.

A chipper waitress brought long twists of bread and recited the day's specials, most involving deep-sea fish. She
looked back over her shoulder at Brad when she left.

''We'll be checking more places Cathy Piatti might have
gone,'' I told him, as if it were settled I'd bring Sandy along.
''I know the police have looked everywhere she said she
was going. But''—he always hated this suggestion—''it is
possible she lied, faked her death and ran off.''

''Why would she do that to me?''

''Maybe not to you. We don't know what she was running from, Brad. If she was.''

All we knew was that one and a half liters of her DNA-
matched blood, partly decomposed, was frozen in the sheriff's evidence locker. A woman losing a third of her blood
would be disoriented, possibly in shock, but probably not
dead. But this wasn't necessarily all the blood Piatti had
lost, merely all that had been captured in a bucket.

Because she'd been missing for weeks, Piatti was pre-
sumed dead by misadventure. And the misadventure was
easily blamed on the boyfriend she'd been ready to abandon
after a seven-year affair.

''We'll also need to concentrate on how and where she
might have died. We've struck out so far on motive, on
finding out who her enemies were. But where the blood was
drawn will tell us a lot. We'll check mortuaries. They're set
up to pump blood out of bodies; maybe some employee

played Igor. And we'll talk to people at local hospitals. Any paramedic, nurse, or doctor would know how to bleed someone. We'll also get a list of places that slaughter animals."

I watched Brad shudder. It was repulsive to imagine a person hung upside down, blood pouring from her jugular into a bucket. Worse than imagining her with catheters in her veins. But there was simply no way to bleed into a bucket from some accidental wound—not one and a half liters' worth. Whoever put the bucket beside the trail collected the blood in a systematic way, perhaps to make some point.

Brad buffed his shirt as if his chest ached. Hearing me argue the motion had been hard on him. He'd hated the "mere technicality" aspect of my argument—that the sheriff hadn't had sufficient grounds for the warrant to search his boat and cabin. He'd nearly simmered to a verbal boil over statements seeming to assume his guilt.

But it was essential to throw out as much physical evidence as possible. They'd found buckets on Brad's boat. They'd found a skirt caught in truck tires lashed to the boat to keep it from smacking into the dock.

It was known Cathy Piatti had had enough of Hillsdale. Her business had failed, and, to hear her neighbors tell it, she'd grown tired of Brad. They'd quarreled frequently. He'd grown furious when she packed her things, made a blustering scene her neighbors kept embellishing. Then Piatti surprised everyone by leaving without saying good-bye.

No one had heard from her for almost three weeks when the sheriff was persuaded to investigate. Because Brad had grown belligerent when questioned, the sheriff had gotten a warrant to search his boat and cabin.

En route to the boat, a deputy discovered a bucket containing a congealed, moldy, insect-infested substance resembling old liver. It had turned out to be nineteen-day-old blood. Cathy Piatti's blood—one and a half liters' worth, once it was reconstituted.

Today I'd argued that Brad's belligerence—if it could be characterized as such—hadn't been sufficient grounds for the search warrant; that the empty buckets and skirt must therefore be excluded as evidence. The skirt might not matter—it could be anyone's, washed in any time; it had yet to be identified as Piatti's. It didn't support the DA's contention that Brad, after inexplicably bleeding Piatti to death, sailed out to sea and dumped her body and belongings overboard. Without the buckets, the DA didn't have much of a case.

But Connie Gold put everything she had into her defense of my motion. None of the state's evidence was excluded.

Now I'd have to argue that the bucket might have come from any boat, and that, besides, other people had access to Brad's. I'd have to argue that the trapped debris of strangers, including clothing, proved nothing; or, if the skirt was Piatti's, that it had fallen overboard during some recent date. If the case went to trial, that is.

With luck, I'd be able to clear Rommel long before then—either by finding Piatti or figuring out what had happened to her.

I'd known Brad since high school. He'd been an earnest, nose-to-the-grindstone kid who didn't trust shortcuts and didn't shirk blame. From what I could see, he hadn't changed. He'd grown into a forthright, hard-working man, willing to fish all day and spend his evenings helping staff his girlfriend's boutique. He was no killer. And the evidence against him didn't amount to a hill of beans.

That didn't mean the DA couldn't make life hell for him. Not knowing what had happened to Cathy Piatti seemed torture enough.

"The other thing, Brad . . . I think Connie Gold might get in touch with the cable-network people who produced her teleplay last year."

He shook his head, shrugging slightly.

"Two years ago, Gold prosecuted a serial rapist . . ." I

cut my explanation short, seeing from his curt nod that he recalled the case. "She signed the contract with the production company before the rapist's trial. She sold 'her,' quote-unquote, story. It was on television a few months ago."

"I knew there was a TV movie about the DA here." His tone said, What does it have to do with the price of fish?

"The point is, she approached that trial with the idea of turning it into a good movie." I couldn't prove it, but how could it not become a major consideration? "She stage-managed her witnesses. Two of them are suing her now." After I insisted on an investigation by the State Bar. "To keep her from doing the same thing in this case, I've made a preemptive stink."

I'd contacted reporters from *California Lawyer,* the *ABA Journal,* and the *Recorder.* Articles dissecting Gold's ethics in the rape case had appeared in each. *Entertainment Weekly* had picked up the story. And Hillsdale's media had taken a gratifying interest.

I'd had to do it. Gold had hinted—on camera—that I'd condoned the politics of Wallace Bean, my craziest client, assassin of two conservative U.S. senators. She'd implied I had no commitment to justice, only to enhancing my reputation by freeing dangerous criminals. In a society that worships fame, however achieved, it seemed useless to bemoan the publicity I'd gotten. It seemed useless to canonize privacy when the man on the street longed for attention.

But I couldn't let Gold tarnish my reputation, not before a trial. I had to make sure her pot looked as black as my kettle. I'd shown her how it felt to have the press on her heels instead of in her corner.

"I think I've stopped her, Brad."

"I don't know why you bothered," he said through tight lips. "It sounds like a lot of trouble for no reason." His chest heaved as if it were difficult to breathe. "It won't make much of a movie when I get acquitted."

"That's true." If an unconvicted man was presented as

guilty, he could sue. And without suggesting guilt, the story would lack interest. "They won't make a movie unless there's a conviction."

"Then I don't see what difference it makes." He broke a breadstick. "I don't see why you're making trouble."

"It won't hurt your case," I assured him. Did he think Gold would come down harder if she was angered? She'd try to get him executed regardless. "It affects how the DA's case is structured," I insisted. "As defense counsel, I'm prohibited from selling your story. That's so I'll focus on doing what's best for you instead of heightening the drama to get a better movie or book deal out of it. The DA should have to play by the same rules."

"It won't matter in the end," he reiterated.

With his cold, blue-eyed stare, he looked, at that moment, almost crazy enough to have killed Piatti, after all.

CHAPTER

Five

I FLEW HOME THINKING ABOUT THE BUCKET OF BLOOD, A dented, fishy bucket holding the remains of a liter and a half of blood—about two champagne bottles' worth. I flew home wondering what kind of statement it makes to drain a third of the blood from a person and leave it in a bucket beside a trail. Leave it to dehydrate and decompose, to get rained on and insect-infested, maybe tipped over, maybe even consumed by animals.

But when I reached my apartment, my consciousness filled with other matters.

Sandy had left me an urgent message to call him. When I did, he told me I was coming to his office right away.

Sander Arkelett, Private Investigation Services, was on a sunless street of warehouses between the bustle of the financial district and the black-water commercial corridor of the bay. Sandy was close to his clients and his rent was reasonable, and it would never occur to him to find the neighborhood dreary. He was surprised I felt that way about my south-of-Market office.

His secretary, Janette, her hair ribboned with thin strands of blue and burgundy, continued a phone conversation as she motioned me into what had once been Sandy's conference room, but had lately become a computer room. The room could no longer do double duty because Sandy's new "op," Osmil Pelo, was a cyclone of electronic litter. The once spartan room—a table, a bit of warehouse view, and not much else—now looked like a teenage nerd's room. There were wires and cables and computer parts all over the table, along with Osmil's detritus—Coke cans, candy wrappers, *Mondo 2000* magazine. Between Osmil—an unkempt whippet who looked about sixteen—and Janette, a cynical twenty-seven-year-old who'd taken lately to dressing like a biker slut, Sandy's office was becoming a Generation X stronghold.

And Sandy, a traditional-values ex-cop pushing fifty, liked it that way. They were smart, was his analysis; and there was no bullshit about them. Not like Reagan-era kids, on the hustle and full of hype.

He was squatting beside Osmil's chair now, staring beetle-browed at one of two computer screens. He said, "Laura, come and look at this."

Osmil didn't glance up. His posture was reminiscent of a curled rind. But his face, olive-skinned and large-eyed, was sweet, almost demure in its frame of dark curls. I knew little about him except that he'd set off on a tire raft from Havana to Miami on his thirteenth birthday. A couple of years later, he fled the macho exile community for the same reason he'd left Cuba: he was a homosexual. In San Francisco, he'd taken to sneaking into computer labs at State, at USF, at Golden Gate, at Cal Berkeley. It turned out he had a genius for navigating the canals and cybermazes of computer networks. Within months, he was the talk of the net.

Sandy, who hated the increasing amount of time he needed to spend on his computer, heard about the new whiz kid. Uncharacteristically (I thought), he offered the talented but unknown quantity a keyboard-jockey job.

If Sandy had ever traveled to Cuba, I'd have suspected a secret relationship—that Osmil was his love child or reminded him of a bittersweet time there.

But Sandy only laughed when I hinted at some hidden motive. "He's the boy wonder of hackers. Doesn't everybody want one? Didn't you see *War Games*? *Revenge of the Nerds*? *Sneakers*?"

The few times I'd spoken with Osmil, he'd seemed skittish and self-protective; I supposed life had given him reason. But he relaxed into a near-meditative trance when his fingers touched the keyboard. Only his eyes retained intensity, as if vacuuming information from the screen.

I walked around behind the two men, squinting at the black letters on the pearl screen. I saw a list with Roman numeral headings, preceded by some text:

I can't believe I've opened this file. But I've got to begin documenting this. I started worrying after what happened at SunSource—because something had happened earlier [something with the Precorp case? or was it the Christmas singers? Look up]. It's too much to be a coincidence. Months ago, I thought I overheard a phrase that might explain it. I'm going to have to bring it up. Before Super Prime starts spraying!!!!

I. SunSource: Mario Calas appointment with Maryanne 1/14; Calas could have/should have gotten an individual patent; instead his boss took credit, stole the idea; targeted Calas for layoff. But the contract governs re the patent—no case; and Calas can't prove animus behind layoff. 1/24 Maryanne meets with SunSource public info officer at plant—WHY? 1/25 Merc-News headline "Sabotage Closes SunSource" Hardware Calas invented broke down, costing them hundreds of thousands. Calas not in plant, no access beforehand.

II. Nova Tech: Systematic refusal to advance women employees or acknowledge their contributions to program refinement/tech support. Common knowledge but no documentation, no way to prove; no case. False predictions by fictitious stockbroker on Internet causes plunge in value of stock. Undercapitalization may cause closure. Check office Internet bill.

III. Thefts: At Tulliman Gallery, aborting their main show of year; restitution made anonymously afterward. (Consultation with Maryanne three weeks earlier; no case.) At Hilltop Cannery, of machinery needed to can perishables; entire stock perishes; machinery returned. (Maryanne, no case, ten days before.) At Dataphile. Headline today, restitution. Check Maryanne's calendar.

IV. Super Prime lays off most of quality-control dept.—one by one after harassing and hassling each about trumped-up things. But no direct evidence of illegal motive for firings; no case for rehire. Maryanne warns fired workers not to say it's so SP can save money using cheap antioxidants (commercial slander). Machine parts spraying next week. If sabotaged, SP loses biggest contract.

"Is this what I think it is?" I wondered. I scrolled back to the beginning of the document.

"It's one of Jocelyn Kinsley's files."

"Where was it?" It read like an accusation; why would she leave it where prying eyes could see it? "How did you find it?"

Osmil, his inflections still foreign, replied, "They got remote terminal access."

"That's what lets you break in in the first place," Sandy explained. "They're set up to access their work computers from home or on the road or wherever. Basically, we pretended we were them and sneaked in.''

''Encrypted password—that's no problem,'' Osmil continued. ''But stuck in a strange place.''

I glanced at Sandy.

He grinned. ''Meaning Kinsley had a program that took her password and turned it into mumbo-jumbo—encrypted it. So even if you found her password, it would look like nonsense. You'd have to unencrypt it to use it. But Ozzy's got the same encryption software. Awhile back, he encrypted the whole dictionary; has it on disk. He matched the encrypted word against everything in his encrypted dictionary—well, up into the Ds, that's as far as he had to go. Turns out the password was 'designer.' ''

''As in, 'designer crimes.' ''

''Bingo. And this''—he waved at the screen—''wasn't filed anywhere you'd think to look for a memo. It was in a systems folder for some shovelware utilities no one in an office would care much about.''

I shook my head. ''Shovelware?''

''Junk,'' he said. ''Imagine the top shelf of an attic closet. Imagine a box of crap that came with the house. One of them is labeled 'canning jars.' There's a box inside one of the jars. There's an envelope in the box. That's where this memo was. In an electronic kind of way.''

Osmil all but snorted at Sandy's kindergarten explanation, but it suited me. Explained that way, I got it.

''Not easy to find.'' Sandy patted Osmil's shoulder as if to say, That's my kid. ''Usually you can retrieve a file by its date of creation—get recent entries no matter where they're hidden. But in this case Kinsley changed the date on the computer, making the date on the memo match the one on the shovelware.''

''Everybody hides files that way,'' Osmil scoffed.

Sandy nodded. ''Ozzy looked to see if a modification was made to the system—if the date was changed, then changed back. He found it was, just last Friday, so he started rum-maging.''

"And he found a list of crimes involving software de-signers and artists. In a box in the attic closet." I was impressed.

"One software designer and one art gallery. It's hard to say what 'program refinement/tech support' is. And what about the cannery? Or the paint primer place?" He shook his head, squatting beside Osmil. " 'Designer' might not refer to the kind of client. It might mean the kind of crime, a custom-designed crime. Think what the cases have in common: A guy gets ripped off on a patent idea, but he can't do anything about it legally; next thing you know, the ma-chine breaks down. A company treats its women like shit, and it gets sunk by rumors on the Internet. Three other places, we have no details except somebody stole something crucial and returned it later, after the damage was done. And all those places except maybe the last one, More had a powwow with an angry employee first."

"She talks to angry employees for a living, Sandy."

"Granted. But Kinsley didn't just list clients who got fired. She hid the list, hid it pretty damn well. She obviously didn't believe their employers' bad luck was coincidence."

"Maybe she thought the clients were committing crimes because More couldn't help them."

"Then why question More's business meetings? Why check the Internet bill? I'd say Kinsley was worried her partner did help the clients—in ways she shouldn't."

"Designing crimes for them?" I shook my head.

"Looks to me like a possibility."

"More could be arrested, disbarred for that. It's too risky, Sandy."

"Risky, sure. But a person could charge big bucks for a service like that. Sabotage the son-of-a-bitch who fired you; bankrupt the sleaze who wouldn't promote you; embarrass the jerk who stole your ideas. No question about the demand.''

"Fired workers don't have big bucks—they don't have money to waste on revenge."

"Revenge is never cost effective. But it's a basic human drive. People are going to get it even if they go broke. Even if it's crazy and it tears their life apart." He made a sweeping gesture. "I wouldn't have this office if that wasn't true. And who'd need lawyers?"

I felt a sudden rush, a mingling of hatred and glee: "I wish I could hire someone to mess with Steve Sayres."

Sandy's brows rose slightly. "Maybe the clients with money were overcharged to subsidize the ones without. I already looked at More's bank accounts, the ones under her name. There's plenty of money there—in four different banks, two checking, one savings, some short-term CD accounts. More than three hundred thousand."

"That is a lot for a labor lawyer. But for all we know, she was born rich." And yet part of me wanted her to be below-board, wanted there to be a Robin Hood for the working person. "I wonder what it would take to sabotage Steve?"

"Her salary's only sixty-one a year." Sandy remained on point. "Senior partner in her own firm—that's not very damn much."

"They don't have any big union clients." The Teamsters, the Hotel & Restaurant Workers, the public-employee unions, they were with the cigar-chomping old-boy firms. "Still, they're supposed to be *the* hot new labor firm. I'd have guessed they were doing a little better." But maybe they didn't have to do better. Maybe some of their income was undeclared. "It's a hell of a concept, Sandy. Custom revenge on your ex-boss."

"Get that look off your face. You're an officer of the court, remember?"

"But, Sandy," I put my hand on his shoulder. I could feel his body warmth like an electric charge. "If someone thought of a perfect way to make Steve eat crow, I'd pay—god, in a minute. You know what it'll cost me to sue him for slander? And I wouldn't have to wait years for some ambiguous resolution!"

He cast a surprised glance at my hand, still on his shoulder. "Yeah, well, you could also drop the whole thing. Cut your losses now."

"What were you just saying about revenge being a basic drive?"

He started to respond, then seemed to think better of it. "Maryanne More specializes in high-tech labor. I'd have thought that was a strong base, that she'd draw a decent salary."

"It's hard staying afloat without the cushion of a big established firm. Or a major client; I don't know if I can make it without Perry Verhoeven." I tried to stanch my rage; Sayres had put a hell of a hole in my boat. "I'm not kidding, Sandy: If there really was a designer-crimes employee revenge service, I'd go wait in line this minute."

"We've got, what"—Sandy checked his watch—"two hours till the close of business? Let's go see if More's at work."

"Wait a minute. This"—I nodded at the computer screen—"doesn't mean Maryanne More did anything illegal."

"True enough. It could all be coincidence. Or Kinsley could have been way off about who was behind it. It could have been a client. Somebody who got canned and latched onto an idea. Kept informed about who was being fired where and for what." He rose. "Don't worry—we'll be doing plenty more research before we go accusing anybody."

"Then why bother Maryanne More? They probably don't even have the coroner's seal off the door yet."

"Nope, it came off this afternoon. More insisted they get done in there. She's got hearings she can't put off, that's what I heard." Sandy had friends in Homicide. Sandy had friends anywhere there were cops. "That's why I think we might find her there. Be interesting to see the office."

"Actually," Osmil put in shyly, "she's there right now."

Sandy, in the act of rising into a tall stretch, paused. "What do you mean?"

"She's looking through everything."

Sandy dropped back down to a squat, checking the computer screen.

"What do you see?" I wondered.

"Somebody going through the folders."

"Could be the cops."

"No. She's got passwords." Osmil spent a while watching. "Unless she's taking the police for a tour. No, wait wait." He squinted intently at the screen. "Ay! She's in the attic. In the closet."

"Whoever it is," Sandy interjected, "are they going to find the memo?"

"Up to you," Osmil said cheerfully.

Sandy glanced at me. "Leave it or erase it?"

"You have a copy?"

"Of course."

"Can the person open the file?"

"Not unless she unencrypted the password."

"Ha!" Osmil's laugh began as an explosion and subsided to a titter. "She's trying to open it, trying passwords. Trying 'Joss,' 'Jocelyn,' 'Kinsley,' 'Puff'—bet that's her pet's name."

I stared at the screen, seeing the words appear beneath a list of file names, a few of them highlighted.

"Guess she's giving up for now. She's making a copy onto a diskette. Whoa!" He twisted in his chair to face Sandy. He looked like a happy kid about to dive off the tall board. "She's burning the file."

I could tell by Sandy's expression this was significant. I nudged him. "Tell me."

"There's a program called Norton Utilities," Sandy said absently, his attention on the screen. "It can bring up a file even after it's been erased."

"Unless you write a new file to that exact place on the hard drive." Osmil spoke with adolescent triumph.

"Usually if you erase something by mistake, you can get it back because you haven't done enough in the meantime to use that exact same spot on the disk. The old file doesn't show on your menu anymore. But it's still sitting there, under the command Write over me. It's like taping movies on your VCR. If you've got a cupboard full of tapes, your chances of taping over a bit you want are slim, at least initially."

"But if you *want* to erase something you've taped, you tape over it right away." I endeavored to prove I followed.

Osmil grinned up at me. As happy as he looked, as intelligent as he was, it seemed a great pity he had no mother to feel proud of him. "You can write over it with random strings, one zero zero one, like that. If you write over it three times not even an electron microscope can pull the old file off the hard drive!"

"That's called burning a file," Sandy added absently. "Well, we know the cops aren't there. No way they'd be burning anything." Sandy grinned. "Let's go check her out."

To my surprise, Osmil said, "Can I come?"

"Too many cooks."

Osmil looked bewildered.

"I'll tell you about the hardware when we get back," Sandy promised.

He nodded, dark brows dropping a sullen fraction. "Want me to catch her phone bills?" He began tapping the computer keys.

Sandy grinned at me. Subpoenas? Privacy? The laws of the state of California? "I didn't hear what you just said, Ozzy." To me, he added, "He's just going to play a few

37

computer games while we're gone. No harm in that. I can't be in here supervising him every minute.''

I turned away, choosing not to show my comprehension. This didn't involve any case or client of mine. It was none of my business.

Just once I'd like to say that to myself and have it turn out to be true.

CHAPTER

Six

THE LAST TIME I VISITED MORE & KINSLEY, ANGER AT Steve Sayres kept me from noticing the outer office decor. Now I saw that the artwork, which I recalled as too sweet, was simply classic. The walls were hung with Renaissance-style oil paintings, the largest showing a golden-haired pregnant woman beside a man tending vines. Smaller ones depicted women spinning thread or washing marble floors or wet-nursing a wealthy couple's baby.

The carpets were gold, the furniture a muted white-gold, the receptionist's desk bow-drawered, with pale fruit and flowers painted on it.

Nothing could have suited the receptionist less. She was tall and square-faced, muscles bulging the arms of her knit sheath. In contrast to the filigree curls of the Renaissance women, her hair was blunt cut and dark, threaded with gray. Her eyes were smart and hard beneath thick, straight brows. Sitting at her desk, she was the only thing in the room that was blatantly, undemurely of this century.

Sandy tried again to engage her in conversation. "So you were here two days ago? Must have been awful."

She glanced at him. Her expression said, What do you think?

"You have my card there," Sandy continued, his tone as pleasant as if she'd offered a chipper reply. "I'm investigating the shooting."

"Ms. More," she said carefully, "should be free to see you soon. As I said."

"You were here, though? When it happened?"

The look she tossed me—Can't you keep your dog quiet?—almost made me laugh.

"The police have asked us not to discuss it." She picked up the telephone receiver, pointedly dialing a number.

It proved useless as an avoidance technique. Her party apparently didn't pick up.

After she replaced the receiver, Sandy continued, "So you heard her say, 'A sign of the times.' What do you think she meant?"

The receptionist folded her arms across her chest, regarding him steadily. "I've been asked not to discuss the matter."

"But you heard it yourself? You're sure? Not just that's what someone else said?" Sandy's tone remained light, as if she hadn't already refused to answer, not once, but twice.

His persistence paid off. Her shoulders slumped and her eyes welled. "I heard her myself. I was standing near her."

" 'A sign of the times'?"

"That's exactly right." Again she picked up the receiver. "I'm not supposed to talk about this. And I don't want to talk about it."

"Kind of hard you have to work today." Sandy's tone was tinged with mild outrage. It was a voice to encourage complaints.

"Kind of hard to do without the day's wages." She nearly smiled.

"A good labor firm can't give you paid time off? Situation like this?"

"A management firm could afford to give me the whole damn month off." Her cheeks suffused with color. "But virtue has to be its own reward."

"Not always," said a quiet voice.

Maryanne More stood at the entrance to the inner office hall. She wore a dark brown suit that buttoned up the throat. Her light brown hair was full and glossy, but tied back. She looked midfortyish, unwrinkled and unpainted, her brows and lashes pale, her lips barely glossed. She wasn't beautiful, not nearly, but I found myself admiring her looks. She showed more taste than vanity.

The receptionist cracked a private-joke smile.

"We like to think we work longer and harder than the other side," More continued, "because the vanguard never rests."

"By definition, I guess." Sandy rose, crossing to her with his arm extended. "Thanks for seeing us." He pumped her hand. "You remember Laura."

I stepped up beside him. He was taking imperious control of this visit. I supposed that was fair—it was his idea. But was there some agenda? Were we here to learn something in particular?

I greeted Maryanne More, but didn't renew my condolences. I wanted to distance memories of our last encounter. Up close, I could see her eyelids were swollen, almost lavender.

"Well," she said, once the amenities were observed, "come on back to my office."

"Actually," Sandy's gesture swept the reception area, "comfortable enough out here, and I was thinking if Ms. . . ." He smiled at the receptionist. "I didn't get your name." When she didn't offer it, he rolled on. "It might be useful if we all sat down together."

The two women exchanged surprised glances.

"I was only speaking for myself when I agreed to talk to you today," More pointed out.

"Oh, I know," Sandy hastened to assure them. "And I'm not meaning to pressure anybody, but look . . ." An apologetic glance at me, maybe a little too theatrical. "Let me put my cards on the table. Laura is my fiancée." He didn't check my reaction. I hoped no one else had. "I'm trying to find out if someone was shooting at her out of craziness, or on purpose, or not at all because their aim's that good."

"We can't possibly tell you that," the receptionist said firmly. "And really, I'm sorry, but I'm not, I don't want to talk—"

"Look," Sandy turned toward her, stepping closer. "Someone might be trying to kill Laura. I need to know everything I can. I really need to know." He invested the last words with slow weight. "I can't do less than that. Imagine, God forbid, I take 'no' for an answer and something you know could have helped me."

His face wasn't visible to me. Whatever was on it, the receptionist caught her breath. She even took a slight step back.

But she shook her head. "I just can't talk about it, I'm sorry." The words came out in an uninflected rush, as if she'd rehearsed them.

"I can't force you," he conceded. "I *can* beg."

"Sorry," she repeated.

Maryanne More said pleasantly, "Why don't you follow me back to my office. I'll heat water, if you'd care for tea?"

I hung back, leaving the next move to Sandy. When More turned, he had no choice but to follow. But his backward glance told me he hadn't given up.

More's office lacked the angelic warmth of Kinsley's. Though it echoed Renaissance themes of the outer office, it was a darker room, with moody chiaroscuro portraits and carved mahogany furniture. The carpets were deep green and the walls a mere shade lighter. With its built-in bookcases, it resembled a manor house library but for a corner of computer equipment and a clutter of file folders.

Sandy complimented her on it.

She looked around, almost wistfully. "So much of my work involves new technology—squabbling over patents and copyrights, getting licenses in place, defining the rights of employee-developers. I have to learn the technology in every case, the way the chips work, the fiberoptics, how the software and hardware interact and how you decide which is which. It gets so that, however much I respect and admire the technological advances, I long to touch real paper, real bindings. Books are becoming antiques, to be fondled and treasured. And magazines, especially arts and graphics magazines, with their luxuriously thick paper—" She grinned wistfully. "To have an image exist independent of a glowing screen, to have it fixed indelibly on a matte surface, seems a fleeting miracle. It can't last much longer. We'll read everything on our TV and computer screens one day, and books will be curios. Maybe then they'll get the respect they deserve."

Sandy seemed a bit off balance.

"You have quite an art collection," I observed. I sat down, freeing her to cross to the other side of a low table and do the same.

"My father left me some marvelous pieces. And I've been adding to the collection," she told me. "I hoped at one time to become an artist—I studied at the Sorbonne. But . . ."

Sandy joined me on the green leather couch. "Not much of a living?"

"No." Her pale brows pinched. "That wasn't it. Certainly it wasn't a factor for my contemporaries—many of them forged ahead. I suppose I just couldn't find my voice. I could study and copy, but either I didn't have a statement to make or I couldn't quiet the background chatter. Technique is never enough, is it? I've heard software-developer clients say they suddenly—often briefly—acquire a kind of enlightenment. It lights their path to creation. Whereas I was a Xerox machine with a brush, my classmates were seeing something entirely new. They were dipping their brushes into some internal well I couldn't find.''

To my surprise, tears filled her eyes.

"I'm sorry." She blinked them away impatiently. "Every conversation since Jocelyn . . . I end up crying. Everything takes a sad turn. Maybe two days ago I'd have told you how enchanting it was to live in Paris, and how lucky I am now to work for people who make art from electrons. But my grief spills over.''

"How could it not?" I was miles behind her in reacting to what had happened. I had that luxury, having barely met Jocelyn Kinsley.

"You know," she sat straighter, "Hester's right: we were asked by the police not to discuss the shooting with anybody." Her eyes searched Sandy's face. "I do understand your need." A glance at me. "And I can't pretend you have no right. But frankly, I'm not comfortable. My emotions aside, I don't want to do anything that could possibly impede this investigation. I want to cooperate totally with the police—including honoring my word.''

"I was a peace officer myself for eighteen years," Sandy told her. "I respect how you feel, believe me. But completely honestly, the homicide detectives on this case aren't the best in the city, not even close. I've known them for a long time." Sandy's face crimped with worry. "Anybody could get a good break and solve a case. But if it takes something extra . . ." He shook his head. "Let me put it to you this way: Check me out, check my references, my track record, my back taxes, if you want. If you're satisfied I'm good at what I do, share your information with me. I can't do squat if I don't have a connection inside, do you see what I mean? If I don't have access to inside information, to things about this office only you—you and the receptionist, let's say—know, then I'm going to miss something, maybe the most important damn thing of all.''

She watched him carefully. I could see by her face that she was considering his offer. And I knew what she'd find if she checked up on him: stellar references, an impressive track record.

I also knew he wasn't being quite as cards-on-the-table as he seemed. Whatever this "something important" might be, if it was in Maryanne More's private E-mail, her phone bills, or any other place Sandy could snoop without permission or conscience, he would find it.

I'd also heard him make this offer, in full-pitch sincerity, to witnesses and clients. In fact, it was his best and favorite tool.

"All right," she said at last. "That seems fair. I'll check your references. Because I do understand your motives." She looked at me again. "And I don't see the harm in it, not if what you say about the homicide detectives is true."

"Good. Good." Sandy sounded relieved. "So let me ask how much you're comfortable telling me in the meantime? Are you willing to show me her office? They've unsealed the door, haven't they?"

"Yes. They took away some of her files, and of course the forensics people took everything they thought might be evidence. But the office is unlocked again." She frowned, sitting very still, obviously having no wish to go in there.

"When you say the police took her files, do you mean you gave them access to your office computers?"

"Oh, no—I meant her personal files, her date book. I can't have them invade the privacy of my clients. There's a lot of privileged information in the computer files, not to mention trade secrets, patents in the works, things I absolutely would not make available without a subpoena."

"Really? How do you protect all that stuff?" Sandy sounded merely curious.

"Passwords, mainly." She looked a little confused. "I leave the configuration of the directories and most of the computer security measures to Hester."

"Encrypted passwords?"

"No. We have encryption software somewhere, but this is such a small, secure office. Neither of us ever bothered with it."

For a woman who learned the technology applicable to each of her cases, she was suddenly quite the computer bimbo. It didn't jibe with Kinsley's memo being erased beyond the reach of utility programs.

"Did you handle cases together usually, you and Ms. Kinsley?" Sandy's tone showed he knew it was a difficult subject.

"No. We discussed cases oftentimes. Sometimes, if one of us had an emergency, we'd cover for the other." Again her eyes brimmed. "But we had separate caseloads. I hope this isn't going to lead to questions about the cases themselves. My willingness to consider talking to you again really will depend on my checking your references. But no matter what, I can't discuss our clients."

"I'm grateful you're willing to keep an open mind. May I see her office? Since the police have been through it?"

She bowed her head. Clearly she didn't want to go in there.

"We could show ourselves around, if that's okay. Laura could show me where she was sitting and all. Or if the receptionist would take us in?"

"Receptionist?" She seemed bewildered. "Hester is our office manager. And executive secretary. And paralegal. But no, no, I'll let you in. I just hate to go in myself, I suppose. But I'll wait by the door. Someone should stay with you."

Damn right, I thought. She'd be crazy to let us mill around alone. Bad enough we could ransack her computers.

She stood, taking a reluctant step toward the door. Sandy sprang up, beating her to it and holding it open. He grinned at me when I followed her out.

Maybe he had cause to be pleased. It was hard to imagine two women less willing to go into a room.

Kinsley's office wasn't quite as I'd remembered it. I'd disdained its pretty angel paintings and pastel color scheme. Later, under police scrutiny, the room had become a place of shocking parts: the chair I'd risen out of, the portion of carpet I'd fallen onto, the tunnel of French Provincial legs I'd looked through watching Kinsley die.

Now, the angel paintings seemed less sweet, their smiles ironic. The carpet had pieces cut out of it, the centers of blood splotches that had dried brown. The desktop had a rummaged and rearranged look. Traces of black fingerprint powder remained, a testament to the cops' by-the-book thoroughness, since her killer hadn't reached the desk and had worn gloves.

Maryanne More leaned against the door frame, looking rather stunned.

I walked to the chair I'd occupied two days earlier. "This is where I was, Sandy." I spoke quietly, conscious of the terrible grief across the room.

"Okay, take the chair. I'll be Kinsley. Walk me through it second by second." He examined Kinsley's high-back chair minutely before sitting. Something about the arm seemed to catch his attention, but he made no remark.

I waited while he examined the desktop, the computer table to his left, and, with a rather mystified expression, a power strip on the floor.

Maryanne More advanced into the room. She stopped a few feet behind my chair, possibly wavering on the brink of asking us to leave.

I jumped in quickly. "I was sitting here watching her play with a tape dispenser."

"The police took it," More said, her voice low. "Jocelyn used to tear tiny pieces of tape off and ball them up. We used to laugh about how much tape she went through, how the piles of tape balls looked like frog eggs.'' She turned away.

I waited a moment before continuing. "I was getting testy because she didn't seem to be listening to me," I admitted. "She took her hand off the dispenser and picked up a pencil to jot down some names, but then there were noises out in the reception area or the hall. When she heard them, she grabbed the dispenser again. That really annoyed me. I was standing up to leave when she threw it." I stood, touching my head where it hit me. The tiniest scab remained. "The sharp edge with the teeth, the tape-cutting part, caught me in the forehead." I did my best to scoot the chair backward and drop to the spot I'd occupied two days ago.

"You didn't catch even a glimpse of the person with the gun?"

"No."

"Stay down on the floor a second."

He leaped up, walking past me and past More. From my low vantage, I tried to recall what I'd seen, where I'd looked.

Sandy's police sources had offered their reconstruction, but they might have missed something.

"How funny," I said. "From down here if you look out the window . . ."

Sandy trotted back, then crouched, trying to align himself with my line of sight. When he did, he laughed.

"What?" Maryanne More sounded frightened.

"I'm sorry," Sandy said, rising. "Just a coincidence. You can see Laura's old office from down there on the floor."

"I came here that day to talk about my ex-boss, Steve Sayres. It's just strange . . ." I stared at the lighted square that used to be my space. For a moment, I was back there, I could see it all: my scarlet leather furniture, my bright collages, my tiny beverage bar.

Sandy, maybe worrying More had had enough, moved

swiftly back to the door, determined to gauge how far in the killer had come.

"Tell me when you can see me in your peripheral vision."

A second later, I said, "Stop."

"Really?"

I turned my head to see exactly how far in he'd come. He was barely past the door.

"Unless your eyes were closed or you were actually looking at something else . . . you should have seen him, some part of him, a pant leg, the color of his shoes. Something."

I stood, addressing Maryanne More. "How far in do the police think he came? Or didn't they say?"

"They didn't, but—" She bit the sentence in half.

"Please tell us." Sandy was beside her now. "It's no use Laura racking her brain if you know for a fact he didn't get past the door frame."

"I didn't see that part. But Hester saw him come out."

"Stepping backward or facing front?"

"Backward."

"So he didn't come far enough inside to turn around." He looked fretfully back at me. "Too bad you didn't get a glance at him."

"There were other witnesses in the building, Sandy. People who saw him charge out of this office, take the elevator. People who saw him hustle through the lobby. What could I add? A blurry idea of his shoe color?"

"That's right. If you don't know what's important, better know everything you can."

"If you don't mind, I should get back to work." More sounded too weary to work. But I could easily believe she needed to be alone.

CHAPTER

Seven

SANDY STOOD ON THE SIDEWALK STARING UP AT MORE & Kinsley's tenth-floor office. Occasionally, he loped to the lobby door and back. Then he turned toward the building across the street, a finer, newer, pricier palazzo.

"Let's go say hi to Sayres," he suggested, as if it were just a thought.

I was able to turn a snort into a merely noticeable exhalation. But he heard it.

"I'm not kiddin'."

It didn't take me but a second to believe him. He liked to charge in and barge around: be a guy, be an ex-cop. The quality had, at times, endeared him to me. It could also be damned inconvenient.

"Talk to Sayres? No way! I'll go—"

"No." He took my elbow. "Don't go marching off, Laura. I want you to come with me."

"Oh, right. I'm about to sue him, Sandy." He knew that meant no contact, no way, except with a lawyer present.

"We need to talk about that." His hand slid up my arm, gripping for real. "You're just going to mess yourself up. Yourself and me both. Steve's my main client; he's most of the money I've got in the bank."

I didn't want to think about that. "He's got enough money to pay me damages and still pay your retainer."

"But he won't." Sandy was right; Steve would enjoy playing guilt by association. It would give him a chance to be a spoiled, angry tyrant—his favorite and best role.

I looked up at Sandy, torn between wanting to accommodate him—he'd done his share of that for me—and wanting Sayres to get what he deserved. All I could think to say was "I can't be guided by what Steve might do."

"Of course you can!" He squared off against me, face inches from mine as foot traffic flowed around us.

"Sandy, he turned Doron against me, he got me fired, now he's crippled my—"

"I know Steve's a dickhead; I know he got you fired—"

"I could put that behind me." I backed up enough to gesture, chopping down from the elbow. "But he's chasing away my clients. Perry Verhoeven dropped me like a hot rock because Steve told him I bungle civil cases so I can focus on criminal."

"I know that, too, but it's no damn use suing him." Sandy's brows crimped. "You're just thinking like a lawyer. You're going to waste a lot of money and a lot of energy on something that's going to come to no good anyway, just for some damn settlement that doesn't put any money in your pocket once you back out costs—"

"It'll cost *him* money, too! And it'll shut him up."

"No, it won't. It'll just get all his friends—and he's got a townful—talking bad about you!" He frowned so hard his head tilted forward. If that weren't enough, he shook it. "And I'll have to rustle up a bunch of new clients, which I'm too damn old to deal with."

"No, you're not! You're not too old. And you can't ask

me to forgo the only legal remedy to what I consider my biggest problem. Just because you and I are, are . . .''

''Friends'' didn't cover it, not as far as I was concerned. ''I won't just roll over and take it from Sayres. Not for anything!''

He backed up, to the irritation of people trying to walk around him. ''That's the least you should be willing to do for me. You know that, Laura? The absolute least.''

This was the first time it had come out into the open. I'd left him for Hal, and yet he'd stuck by me, settling for friendship. Even when I rebounded into another affair, when we quarreled and grew distant, even then I'd been able to count on his professional help.

I tried to shake my head.

''You are coming with me to see Sayres,'' he insisted. ''Not to prove your damn loyalty; that was out of line—I'm sorry. But because I can talk to him alone any time. And I can't know what he'll say with you there unless you're there.'' His eyes were narrow with anger, but his voice was calm.

''What do you even need to ask him? What's Steve got to do with anything?''

Sandy almost got his arm dislocated waving it in front of a rushing teenager. ''Ouch. Because that's Steve's office two windows over from your old one.''

''So?''

''So he could have seen you go into Kinsley's office two days ago.''

''With what, Sandy? A telescope he keeps trained on More and Kinsley in case—just on the off chance—I walk in there to sue him? And you're not too old to get new clients!''

''I am going to calm completely down now, Laura, because I have got to do a better job''—his jaw was too tight, he had to stop and work it a second—''of explaining this to you. Steve Sayres can see into Jocelyn Kinsley's office, where you were sitting when you got shot at.''

''Talking in a Mr. Rogers voice doesn't make you sound reasonable, Sandy. This is the heart of the most lawyer-intensive neighborhood in the most lawyer-intensive city in the world, probably. A whole cliff of windows looks into Kinsley's office. And only if you're lying on Kinsley's carpet do you see Steve Sayres's window. Probably if you crawled around her office, or walked through it on stilts, you would see the offices of many other people we know because so goddamn many lawyers have offices right here.''

I thought I was speaking with professorial calm. But the people walking by jostled one another to keep from coming too close.

''I don't care if you can see a holy vision of Elvis from Kinsley's window,'' was Sandy's response. ''All I care about is that the one person you'd probably call your biggest enemy on the planet can see into the office where you got shot at. I'm not going to assume that's a coincidence because I never got anywhere by assuming anything.''

We stood there, a stationary monument to stubbornness in a flowing river of suits and briefcases.

''Laura, look. So what, so you have to see Steve Sayres for five minutes. It won't hurt you—you're a big girl. It won't even keep you from suing him. At the worst, you'll get a lawyer who says, Why'd you go and do that? And you'll explain—''

''That I wanted to be obedient?''

It was his turn to snort. ''You'll explain that a private detective you trust to do his job with something approaching thoroughness and logic told you it was the only way he could get the reading he needed on Steve Sayres! Okay? Because it don't cost you diddley and it buys me information.''

And because he was absolutely right: in matters of loyalty, I owed him. This *was* the least I could do.

"I would never, because of this," his tone contained a promise, "think or tell anyone that you were obedient."

"I doubt anyone would believe you, anyway."

His smile made me want to turn back the clock a few years.

CHAPTER

Eight

IT WAS AS BAD AN IDEA AS I'D FEARED. RIDING UP IN THE elevator, I realized it wasn't just Steve Sayres I'd be seeing again. There were other attorneys at White, Sayres & Speck, not to mention paralegals and clerical help, with whom I'd worked six and a half years. My old secretary, Rose, might still be prone to sobbing sentimentality. I felt unprepared, antisocial, underdressed. Worst of all, I felt obedient.

When we entered the outer office, I was struck not by how familiar it looked, but by the gaps in my recollection. My memories didn't include a carpet this shade, yet this one didn't look new. Nor could I have described the walls, the furniture, the smells with anything approaching detail. My memories, I realized, focused on me, on my clients, my case files, my clothes, my movements, my conversations. I'd inhabited the office without truly noticing it. Because it had remained the same, day in and day out, I hadn't bothered tattooing it into my consciousness. Today, the small touches—the white-and-cream-striped wallpaper, the gunmetal frames around minor Hockneys and Kandinskys, the cast-glass tables—were familiar only because I was seeing them again.

The receptionist watched me look around. She tilted her head, working her jaw as if biting the inside of her cheek. "May I help you?" Her tone seemed to apologize for not being able to place me. She'd been new when I was fired. When Sandy walked in behind me, she broke into an easy smile.

Sandy said, "Steve in?"

She hit a button on a sleek machine, speaking toward it. "Mr. Sayres? Mr. Arkelett to see you."

"Arkelett?" the machine crackled back. "Well, okay. Send him in."

For me, the voice was a hit of ammonia, a sharp, shocking slap to my attention.

I didn't bother rubbernecking as we walked down the hall. The decor here, however elegant, however expensive, said nothing about the office itself. That was determined by the people in it; maybe that's why the physical details never fixed themselves in my memory. Now, as then, they faded behind my dislike for Steve Sayres.

We walked past the office that had once been Sayres's, past the office that had once been mine. I was relieved and disappointed that the doors were closed. At the end of the hall was the corner office that had once belonged to Doron White, the founding partner who'd been my mentor and protector until Sayres turned him against me.

Sandy tapped at the door. Without waiting, he pushed it open for me to precede him.

Sayres was fussing with sheets of yellow legal paper, rustling them as if looking for something. He grumbled a greeting without looking up.

The office, I saw, had been redone. Doron had decorated it with older-man conventionality, browns and tans and greens, dark woods and leathers. Steve, ever chichi, had replaced the wall-to-wall carpet with oak parquet and a huge kilim carpet. The desks and tables were antique Persian inlay. The chairs were carved wood thrones. Welcome to the seraglio.

Sandy stood to one side, making sure he wasn't between me and Sayres. He was slightly slumped, head forward, intent on studying Steve's face when he looked up and saw me on the other side of the sultan's desk.

We must have raised a flag in Steve's peripheral vision. His head jerked suddenly up, his brows lowered, his lips in a petulant twist.

The sight of me did not sweeten his mood. He flushed, nostrils flaring. "What the hell is this?" he demanded, as if I were some offensive package. He glared at Sandy. "What are you doing?"

"You heard about the shooting across the street?" Sandy's voice was calm.

"Of course I heard about it." He shook his head impatiently. "What's this about? What do you want?" This last was directed at me.

"You can see Kinsley's office from your window, Steve," Sandy continued. "I'm wondering if you saw or heard anything."

From across one of the busiest streets in the city? Steve looked justly derisive. "I didn't know I could see the window from here. Not that it makes a difference. I've got plenty to do without staring at other people's offices." He scooted his chair back from the desk, glowering at me. "I heard you were almost shot. What? Did you think I had a long-range rifle in here?" His upturned lips told me he appreciated his own wit. "I heard, of course, that you were fine." As if he'd have sent armloads of flowers otherwise.

"I went there to see Jocelyn Kinsley about suing you, Steve." Might as well give Sandy his money's worth. "For commercial and personal slander."

The initial flush of rage he'd managed to master regained

ascendancy. He stood, face aflame beneath silvered brown hair. "On what grounds?"

"You've been telling my clients and potential clients that I—" I stopped. "Never mind. You'll be contacted by my lawyer." Why commit to a generalized version of the facts when I could hit him with particulars later?

"Warning your clients? No." His eyelids drooped, making him look as cold and mean as a snake. "But when I'm asked to evaluate the work you did for this firm, I must in good conscience refer inquiry to Second Continental. And to some of the other clients who became of little concern to you during the Crosetti debacle."

Fury froze me. I loathed him beyond sensation or movement. "My cousin was missing from his hospital bed and my friend Dan Crosetti had just died in front of me. Do you tell them that? Do you tell them about the millions of dollars in legal fees you'd never have collected without me? About the cases your unimaginative, sloppy arguments would have lost if I hadn't stepped in? Do you tell them about the time Graystone Federal—"

"And you accuse *me* of slander?" he sneered. "You've got a nerve to come in here, to my own office, and say these things to me. And then turn around and tell me I'm slandering you because I refer people to your former clients!"

Smart son-of-a-bitch. Getting other people—coached to his point of view—to do his slandering for him.

"That's a whitewash, Steve. You don't refer people to the clients I won five-year cases for. You refer them to a handful of clients that got your side of the story when things went wrong." I'd lost one pinch-hit motion, and a few continuances cost other clients a few bucks. That was as bad a job as I'd ever done. Steve was a worse lawyer than that at the best of times. "And that's only part of it. You've done and said more than you let on."

I could see it in Perry's embarrassment the day before yesterday. I could see it in the frigid cordiality of bank lawyers I met in the street. I'd just have to find a way to document it.

Maybe I was kidding myself; maybe I'd never prove it. Or worse: my money would run out first.

"Is this your idea of a joke, Arkelett?" Sayres demanded.

"This is my idea of asking you if you saw anything from your window that day, Steve. Or if anyone else in the office did." Sandy dropped calmly into a carved minithrone.

"No, I did not." He turned back to me. "And you can do as you choose. But just remember that truth is a defense to slander. And it will be my pleasure to put a few facts into the public record that maybe not everybody knows."

"Ditto." I'd be happy to take out tongs and hold his trial record up to view. His lack of imagination had amounted to recurring sabotage. Every time I'd second-chaired him, I'd struggled to keep him out of court during crucial motions; when I couldn't, we lost. "You've never thought of an argument in your life that the opposition wasn't expecting and couldn't demolish. You've got no creativity and no guts."

Still Sandy made no move to rise. He seemed content to let us squabble. And yet he must have known Steve would retaliate, would withhold business from him.

Maybe he was growing used to the idea of canvassing for new business. Or maybe he was learning something from this—though what, I couldn't imagine.

"Well," Steve wore his pomposity comfortably, "you do what you think best, Laura. It's no secret you have a vendetta against this firm."

I was stupefied; felt my jaw drop. "I—*I*—have a vendetta?"

He brushed imaginary lint from a perfectly pressed blue suit. "Do you suppose your rantings don't get back to us?"

I could smell him now, his sporty post-workout cologne, the stiff starch of his shirt, the faint cedar of expensive closet. I took a backward step, repelled by the stink of rich city lawyer.

"We hear about it," he continued snidely, "when you interrogate people, insisting we've said negative things about you." He'd interpreted my withdrawal as his victory, not my disgust made manifest. "Our clients are loyal to us, you know. They have reason to be."

At that moment, surrounded by his pasha fittings, comfortable in his oneupmanship, he looked like some spoiled European count, like old money that couldn't spare a raise for the servants.

My God, I was lucky not to work for him anymore. Lucky and blessed to work for myself. Better the leanest year on my own than one moment of submission to this imperious, untalented little man.

"Your clients' loyalty," I said with careful anger, "is bought and paid for. You wine bank VPs and dine them and racquet-ball them. And they don't care that you overcharge them because the money comes out of their shareholders' pockets. They don't mind spending other people's money for services you can't even perform well. But, Steve, there's not a business in this town that wouldn't be stupid to hire you if they could get me. And I'll make sure that comes out in court if I have to discover every file in your office."

As I turned to leave, he said, with theatrical weariness, "Can't you grow up, Laura? How often do we have to play this little ego game of yours?"

I had thought my earlier resolve strong. But now I took the modern equivalent of a blood oath. I would get Steven Sayres. I would mop his reputation through the gutter of his own stupidity and moral slop.

I slammed the door behind me, leaving Sandy inside. Let him make nice to his boss. Let him ask whatever else he wanted to ask, guy to guy, sport to sport, serf to master.

Halfway down the hall, it occurred to me to wonder who

had told Steve—if he was telling the truth—that I'd accused him of maligning me.

At the front desk, I stopped. I looked down at the receptionist. She was as painted and prettily coifed as a Christmas doll. "They want to know"—I jerked my head back toward Steve's office—"if Perry Verhoeven has been here this week."

Perry was the only client to whom I'd vented, the only one to whom I'd actually voiced my accusation.

She nodded, not even looking at her computer date book. "Oh, yes. He was here when we heard about the shooting across the street. We sent someone down into the street because one of the other lawyers saw the commotion outside. We wanted to ask Mr. Sayres if we could look out his window, but Mr. Verhoeven was in with him."

I felt my fists clench. No sooner did Perry Verhoeven fire me than he came here to hire Sayres. And Sayres expected me to believe he hadn't been turning my clients against me.

Had he offered Perry bargain-basement rates? Just so he could crow that Perry had been dissatisfied with me?

I scowled at the receptionist until she began to look alarmed.

Sandy still hadn't come out to join me, so I left the office. Outside, I stared across the street at Jocelyn Kinsley's window, the third square on the left, tenth floor.

I was damp with rage, a cold city wind billowing my sleeves. Shivering, I tried to lock Kinsley's office in my memory: the angel paintings, the golden carpet, the oak-armed cloth chairs, the French Provincial desk. Maybe it would prove important. I didn't want to forget the details, as I'd forgotten the decor of White, Sayres & Speck.

I took refuge in memorization. I didn't want my anger vibrating so intensely it paralyzed normal motion, necessary thought. Anger was my least favorite hell, more bitter for me than sadness, harder than embarrassment. I'd never figured out what to do with it. Anything constructive took too long; nothing in the moment seemed to help. And an out-of-control lawyer was no use to anyone. If I couldn't remain good at my work, what was the point? What else could I do? Who else was I?

I walked on. Steve Sayres always brought out the worst in me. I wished I could shut him up before he killed my practice and wasted more of my emotional energy.

If there really was a Designer Crimes, I certainly understood its appeal.

CHAPTER

Nine

OSMIL PELO PRACTICALLY CAPERED TOWARD ME WHEN I appeared at the door of Sandy's office. His eyes were bright, his olive skin flushed, his curls finger-raked. He began singing the old Peter and Gordon hit "Where Have You Been?" I must have looked surprised he knew the song.

"I know everything, everything about fun," he explained. "I listen to songs on record players at the library so I know about old fun, historic fun. I eat something small at every restaurant, something I can afford, everywhere, man, all the time." Suddenly he wasn't capering. He stood still, looking blessed, the picture of beatific cheer. "In Cuba, we have nothing, nothing to do, not even a small thing. No clubs, no stores, no restaurants—except for tourists. Even the tourist places, old-person stuff. For the young there's only sex, sex sex sex, that's all they do." He looked disgusted. And well he might, since his kind of sex was illegal in Cuba.

Confused, I looked beyond him at Sandy, sitting splay-legged near the computer, frowning in concentration.

"What's up?" He'd made it sound like big news. He'd

made me rush right over, despite my continuing fury at Sayres—and my irritation with him for dragging me there. "Sandy?" Now he was spacing off while his computer pet pranced boyishly around me. "You summoned and I appeared. But I'm not in the best mood, okay?"

"You're not going to believe this." He straightened in his chair. No remorse or mention of Sayres—it must be something big to push the episode out of his mind. "Come over here."

Osmil trotted beside me. What was making the kid so happy, so outside himself?

Osmil said, "I don't know why I checked. I don't know if I had a feeling or what. Man, I'm always lucky, but this is Lucky."

I sat beside Sandy, in Osmil's still warm chair. "You've got my full attention."

"You don't know anything about listening devices." Sandy didn't make it a question. "Basically, if size didn't matter, you could use a walkie-talkie as a bug. Plunk one down where you want it and use its mate to listen. Smaller bugs operate on the same principle, but unless you're talking real expensive, they transmit within a much smaller radius."

"Okay."

"Well, one of the computers at More and Kinsley is set up to receive signals from a bug. That's as near as we can figure it. Ozzy was looking for new data in their system and he found something. There's not much in the file. But he lassoed it."

Osmil smiled broadly. He looked like the classic Boy Posed with Big Fish.

"And what did he get? Am I allowed to know?" I'd lied about my full attention. I was hungry, still cranky, worried about money.

"Listen." Sandy hit a button on his keyboard.

The computer made a loud noise, scaring me. Other sounds followed. In a few seconds, speech.

"God damn!" I responded.

The computer was playing my voice. I was saying, with a bit of buzz and crackle, "You have quite an art collection."

To which Maryanne More's voice, sharp and tinny in the computer speakers, replied, "My father left me some marvelous pieces. And I've been adding to the collection. I hoped at one time to become an artist. . . ."

"God damn!" I repeated. "That's our conversation in More's office!" I talked over More telling us she'd gone to the Sorbonne. "Her office has a bug in it?"

"Yup." Sandy tapped a button, turning the sound down but letting the conversation wind on. More was describing her classmates: "They were dipping their brushes into some internal well I couldn't find."

"Our whole conversation was bugged, Sandy?"

"Yes, ma'am," he nodded. "Kinsley's office, too." He tapped another button. On-screen graphics resembled the control panel of a VCR or a tape deck. The cursor lit a small panel with a forward arrow. However this data was stored, one could pretend to play it as if it were a video or cassette tape.

When Sandy hit the play icon again, his cowboy baritone could be heard: "Okay, take the chair. I'll be Kinsley. Walk me through it second by second."

"It wouldn't be the police, would it?" I asked him. "Bugging the murder scene?"

"No way. For starters, their listening devices are Jurassic; they'd have to be right in the building with a receiver. But what I've been trying to tell you: the receiver is inside one of More and Kinsley's computers—it's gotta be. If the computer weren't storing this, we wouldn't have access."

"How about the FBI, maybe an unrelated investigation? Maybe they bugged the office, and they're eavesdropping through More's computer." Out of the corner of my eye, I saw Osmil still jittering with excitement.

Sandy clicked off the sound as More said of Kinsley's tape dispenser, "The police took it."

"Not the Fibbie," Sandy replied. "Anybody sophisticated, anybody in the spying biz, would have put a scrambler on this. It would record as gibberish that had to be unscrambled to be understood. No, if I had to put money on who did it, I'd say either Kinsley was bugging More or More was bugging Kinsley."

"First the hidden file, now this." I let it sink in. "They've got to be doing something illegal over there."

"Designer crimes . . ." Sandy rubbed the spot between his eyes. "Let's assume Kinsley thought More was conspiring with clients against their employers—that's the obvious way to interpret her memo. Say she decided to listen in on More's consultations, see if they were kosher. Why bug her own office? More wouldn't be using Kinsley's office to talk to clients."

"Kinsley might have been trying to protect herself, prove More didn't let her in on it." Office bugging didn't match my recollection of Kinsley, sweet in angora and linen. But that didn't make my impression right.

"Or it could be More was listening in on Kinsley, seeing if any of her clients needed customized revenge."

"If More installed the bug, wouldn't she have taken it out by now? Why leave all those incriminating electrons lying around?"

"Probably doesn't think anyone knows about it. Whoever's doing it must keep on top of it," he mused. "Play the stuff back ASAP and erase it. We didn't find anything besides this afternoon's conversations."

"They know how to erase over there," Osmil put in. "Damn fine erasers."

"Or," he continued, "it could be More put the bugs in

today, just for our visit. Although"—a shake of the head—
"I can't think why."

"Hester," I said. "The executive secretary or whatever
More called her. It might have been her. She has a computer
out in the reception area."

Sandy nodded. "I'll have to find out what she's about—
strange lady." He flipped through a small notebook on the
table. "Hester Donne; BA from Berkeley; former union
organizer; one year of law school at Malhousie; paralegal
courses at Golden Gate; been with More since the office
opened."

"Have you checked her bank accounts?"

"Yup, just did. She looks about as broke as she should
be. But it's not hard to hide money. It could also have been
a client—someone with physical access to the equipment.
Maybe an industrial spy looking to eavesdrop on other
clients. Or someone trying to set More up—gathering proof
of illegal activity; maybe a client's employer. Top of the
agenda: we need more information about the cases in
Kinsley's memo. You want to help?"

"Who do I have to visit this time? My Aunt Diana?" My
least favorite person on the planet, as Sandy well knew.
"Charles Manson?"

He grinned. "I thought that went okay, at Sayres's office."

I could feel my jaw drop. "Went okay? As in what? I
didn't kill him? He didn't actually pull it out of his pants to
show me how big it is?"

I heard Osmil snicker.

"As in he told us your Mr. Perry Verhoeven is a turncoat,
at least, maybe even a spy from day one." A wry grin.
"Maybe even a co-conspirator in a botched attempt to murder you."

"I asked the receptionist about Perry." Gloom sapped
my excitement over Osmil's discovery.

Sandy nodded. "I guessed you would. That's why I kept

Sayres in there, wouldn't let him chase out after you shouting schoolyard insults." His tone told me he didn't think Sayres was the only one.

"You thought of Perry, too?"

"Of course. How else would it get back to Sayres you were accusing him of slandering you to clients? Number one, you haven't hardly got any clients."

"So glad you reminded me. I assume Perry went there Monday to hire him in my place."

"He was there on Monday?" Sandy sat up. "I figured he'd been there sometime, but damn! Monday! That ain't no coincidence."

"No. Obviously, he went straight to Steve's office after firing me." Just as I'd gone straight to Kinsley's.

"Right across the street from where you almost got—"

"Right across the street from thousands of other lawyers! We've been through this. You're talking about the heart of the financial district. Not that I wouldn't love to implicate Sayres in a felony!"

Sandy laughed. "What do I get if I put him in jail for you? Would you marry me?"

I froze, catching my breath. I didn't dare glance at him. Was he joking?

The tension was immediately unbearable. To break it, I blurted out, "I should plant some evidence against Steve. Scare the pompous bastard."

When I looked at Sandy, he was typing computer commands, the ghost of a smile still on his lips.

CHAPTER

Ten

SANDY HAD LEARNED, BY SETTING FREELANCE INVESTIGA-
tors to the task, more details of the incidents listed in Kinsley's memo. He'd also found out when Super Prime was
performing the "spraying" Kinsley worried would be sabotaged. And he'd become convinced, after a mere day of
research, that another of More's clients qualified for the
designer-crimes list.

He offered to tell all on the drive down to Santa Cruz—
including the reason for the trip. An hour and a half of
winding coast road seemed a long drive at the end of the
day. But he swore we'd be on our way home by midnight.

"And you can sleep in tomorrow," he'd coaxed. "No
reason you have to be in your office before noon."

He was right about that: I had no morning appointments.
No afternoon appointments, either, unfortunately.

So I relaxed into the velour of his passenger seat, trying
to ignore the dry-clean smell of new car.

Basically, he explained, Jocelyn Kinsley had been right:
In every instance she'd listed, a client had approached Mary-

anne More with a hard-luck tale the law could only ignore.

"I didn't know this till one of the researchers told me, but I guess it's pretty hard for an employee to get a grievance fixed." Sandy rounded a cliff curve so fast I clutched the door handle. "The law's on the employer's side. For one thing, employees can't strike without getting replaced, not anywhere anymore, not really. Did you know that?"

A no-strike clause had been "implied" by the Supreme Court for the duration of every employment contract. Workers could be permanently replaced if they tried to strike or picket, removing the only real leverage they had. "I'm afraid that's old news, Sandy."

"And the government body that's supposed to hear employee grievances," Sandy continued, "got packed with proemployer lawyers during Reagan and Bush."

"I know." Even the skeleton of old labor laws, picked clean by the "right-to-work" forces of the eighties, were rarely enforced by the National Labor Relations Board. Maybe the Democrats would change that. But so far their "probusiness" agenda had been merely promanagement.

"So here you have these folks, some of them with outrageous grievances—one guy's supervisor outright stole his idea and fired him so he wouldn't try to take credit. The Dataphile guy got blamed for something that was corporate policy; it messed up his work record so bad he probably can't even get a volunteer job in the field. Big-deal stuff, but none of them had a legal leg to stand on. No place to complain, and no chance of winning even if they did. That's what Maryanne More told them, and my researchers say she was right."

"But somehow, after these people saw More, things worked out so they got what they wanted?"

"Not if they wanted their jobs back." Sandy slowed behind a timid out-of-state driver crawling the cliffs of Devil's Slide. He blinked his lights: speed up. "But if they were looking to make the jerk who screwed them over look bad, then bingo. For instance, the case where the supervisor ripped off the new process, it suddenly went berserk and cost the company almost half a million in missed shipments and lost contracts—which got the supervisor fired.''

''Serves him right.'' The encounter with Steve Sayres was fresh in my mind.

''That seems to be the whole idea. The theft cases were maybe the slickest. An art gallery—terrible employment record—got a chance to get an impressive show in there, really hit the big leagues, and what happened? A couple of pieces got stolen. They were returned later, but by then it was pretty clear they didn't have the best security. Nobody was going to put any Matisses in there.''

''And you think Maryanne More said to these clients, The law can't help you but I can.'' She looked so orthodox, hardly a Scarlet Pimpernel.

''Yup.'' Sandy passed on the first straight stretch, enjoying his powerful engine. I wondered if the trip down to Santa Cruz wasn't an excuse to take his RX-7 on the road. ''That's definitely what I think. All but one of the clients had money. Their careers were maybe important to them, but they had some cash laid by, too— family money, a court settlement, one guy even had a golden parachute.''

''Do you have any idea what More charges—assuming you're right?''

''No. Are you comparison shopping?'' The dashboard light seemed to lengthen his dimples. ''Remember the last bit of Kinsley's memo? A company that primes mechanical equipment so it won't corrode or flake paint, it went and fired almost everyone in its quality-control department. They brought in a new supervisor who hassled them over every damn thing—fired people for taking an extra five at lunch, for a little cussing, for wearing dangly earrings, you name it. These were people who'd been there five, ten years. Within two weeks, the new supe was the only one left in quality control.''

"Presumably so the company can cut corners? The machine parts they prime will start rusting—"

"Right after the warranty date, most likely."

I expected him to say more; Kinsley had anticipated sabotage there.

Instead, he changed the subject: "The other thing my researchers found, the cherry on the cake: the most recent case More turned down for 'failure of remedy'—it fits the profile. The client's got bucks—"

"How do you know that? Did she put it in the file?"

"Nope. But he paid for the consultation with a check—that number's in there. So I called his bank. And I followed up a bit. He's got a good bit tucked away."

"What's his story?"

"He invents arcade and funhouse software. The company he works for put together a new pavilion at the Santa Cruz Boardwalk—independently run by them, not by the corporation that runs the rest of the Boardwalk. A lot of virtual reality and interactive games, some fancy puppets, too, to hear Ozzy tell. I guess it's nerd Mecca, in addition to catering to the backward-baseball-cap crowd. Laura?"

"I'm listening." I'd been staring out the passenger window at pounding waves, their white ridges dazzled by a three-quarter moon hanging low and huge. "I was just thinking the ocean's beautiful here, too."

"Too?"

"I've been missing the way-north coast."

"Oh." He was quiet. He'd thought I was crazy to walk away from city life last year, to bury myself in the countryside near Hillsdale. But he'd grown up in Louisiana; the craggy, rain-whipped majesty of the Pacific Northwest didn't speak to him. He liked wetlands and bayous, honky-tonks and heat. "I was saying: We think we figured out why Lovitz went to see More. Turns out everything that went into assembling the pavilion, every last chip, every scrap of plastic, every bit of cloth, comes from some country that's using forced labor, or close to it."

"Lovitz objected on political grounds?" I envisioned a buy-American purist or perhaps a green global warrior.

"Possibly. But in terms of his job, Lovitz was told it was the only way to turn a profit—this part's in his file. He was told it would be marginal anyway, more of a get-our-name-out-there kind of a thing, and that they were going to have to keep his salary low. That it would increase in future projects, once this one created demand."

"And that wasn't true?"

"They made a huge profit—money's pouring in. He thinks they lied to get him to take less than he's worth."

We were sailing over empty road now, strips of farmland between us and the sea, hills rising to the east like a Bruegel painting. "You guys got all this out of More's computer?"

"Nothin' to it."

I'd have to learn how to protect my files from all the punky little Osmils out there.

"And you think he's Designer Crimes' next client?"

"Computer types can't stand to believe they're powerless. That's why they tell themselves information is power; that's why they break into systems and poke around. The more information they access, whether they understand it or not, the more powerful they feel."

"What's More going to do for him?"

"We're on our way to find out."

"Right now?"

"This very blessed night. If me and Ozzy have it figured right."

This was a Thursday night in the tourist off-season. The Boardwalk would be closed down, dark, its rides creaking like dinosaur skeletons. A perfect time for sabotage and fireworks.

"Funniest thing, Laura: A person can be cautious in a

hundred ways, and then forget something very damn obvious. More called Lovitz on her car phone."

I waited for the punch line.

"We picked up the conversation—piece of cake, no scrambler. She's meeting Lovitz in Santa Cruz for a late dinner."

That was all? "And we'll, what? try to find a table near them at a restaurant and eavesdrop?"

"There's one other reason for the trip. You'll see."

PRESUMABLY, YOU KNOW WHERE THEY'RE MEETING?" I SAT
with Sandy on a lap rug on his car hood in the middle of an
empty parking lot facing the Santa Cruz Beach Boardwalk.
It was a clear night, cold only because I'd sat motionless in
a car for an hour and a half. "But you're choosing not to go
there?"

"Wouldn't want to invade their privacy," Sandy offered.

"God, no."

We were in a neighborhood of shabbily constructed motel
apartments, rows of them facing each other across short
strips of concrete. Here and there the monotony was broken
by a T-shirt shop or a minigrocery with barred windows. In
one, we'd bought rolls and cheese, their best Merlot (which
wasn't saying much) and some plastic glasses. We ate and
drank, our own little moonlight tailgate party.

"We could be equally respectful of their privacy from
across the street," I pointed out. "We could also watch the
ocean."

"We've been watching it the whole drive down."

Spanish-language television chattered out of a motel apartment. Down the block, a plump child rode his Big Wheel in the dark. A car full of bored-looking teenagers cruised toward the silent frame of the roller coaster.

"So much more interesting to be one with the parking lot," I agreed.

"Mmm," was Sandy's noncommittal reply.

"A person could get chilly and bored."

"A person could wait patiently."

I drank more wine. "You're lucky Aunt Diana is a bitch. You're lucky my childhood was stifling. It made me willing to do pointless, inappropriate things at night when a young lady should be at home."

"Well." His tone was measured. "I've never been with your Aunt Diana that I felt lucky she was a bitch. But I see your point."

He folded one leg to his chest, leaving the other dangling from the hood. He'd wolfed a few rolls and cheese, and was working on the wine more slowly than it deserved.

"So what would you do if your boss lied to you just to keep your pay low?"

"That's the name of the game, Sandy. That's Labor History One-oh-one."

"But say you have a unique skill. And the boss made a big point of using cheap foreign labor—screwed over a lot of other workers, too."

I tried not to think about Steve Sayres, about the money and prestige I'd earned him.

"Really, Laura, how smart are you? How would you fix him?"

"I'm not trained to be 'smart' the way you mean it. Clever, devious, yes, but within legal parameters." Which was bitterly annoying at times. "The Steve Sayreses of the world don't want another Reign of Terror."

"But without the parameters, throw all that away. What would you do?" He craned his neck, staring up at the three-quarter moon. "Say it's just you and Lady Justice. How would you put things right?"

I pulled my legs up, hugging them. It was quiet in the neighborhood now, no more kids on night tricycles, no more blaring television, no cars cruising the barren amusement park.

I was demoralized to find I couldn't think of anything. Hadn't I just accused Sayres of lack of imagination?

"I have to give her credit, Sandy. If she really comes up with ways to get revenge for her clients . . . Yesterday you said I was thinking like a lawyer; I guess that's true. If my employers screwed me over, wrecked my career, and I couldn't take them to court, I don't know what I'd do. Maybe murder."

"The direct approach."

The air smelled of sea salt and enchiladas. The surf pounded just loud enough to be heard beyond the amusement park and the wide beach I'd wanted to picnic on.

"Show time." Sandy sat up.

"Where?" My eyes were used to the semidarkness of street lamps and moon, but I didn't see anything I hadn't been looking at for the last thirty minutes.

"Down there."

A heavy man and a slender woman approached the biggest building of the Boardwalk complex, an Art Deco monstrosity with a garish sign reading COCONUT GROVE. They were on foot, probably coming from a wharf of restaurants and souvenir shops perpendicular to the Boardwalk buildings. We were parked across the street almost two blocks away, but they were closing the distance fast.

Sandy snatched up the bits of our tailgate picnic and slid off the hood. "Let's get in."

I grabbed the lap rug, glad to comply. It hadn't been the most comfortable perch.

"They were eating at the fish house where this street

meets the wharf." He pointed to a row of lighted windows. "It has a view of the beach."

Which explained why we'd picnicked in the parking lot. There was too much moonlight for us to sit within the restaurant's view.

"Lovitz told her on the car phone to meet him there. I figured, this close to the Boardwalk, they must be planning something."

They were standing in a well-lighted area in front of the Coconut Grove. Lovitz, a bear of a person in a dark sweater and watch cap, gesticulated passionately, while More, in slacks and sport coat, stood nodding.

"They're not what you'd call skulking," I observed.

"No. If they're looking to break in, they're being pretty conspicuous."

They continued past the Coconut Grove to a building labeled FUN CENTER. A gap between the buildings showed unlighted rides, their outlines traced in moonlight.

"If I had to guess, I'd say the new arcade's on the beach side of the old one. To keep the skateboard crowd localized."

"So this is the building they'd be breaking into if they wanted to mess with the equipment."

Sandy sighed. "He could mess with it much easier in the daytime. He has every right to be in there, nice and legit, during business hours. No point waiting till night and breaking in with your lawyer."

"Even I could have thought of that bad a plan," I agreed.

"It lacks the subtlety of false rumors on the Internet," Sandy conceded. "And it ain't as direct as murder. But who knows?"

We watched as the two of them stood in front of the arcade, talking, occasionally checking their watches.

I glanced at Sandy's dashboard clock. "It's nine-thirty. What are they waiting for?"

A moment later, a vehicle resembling a meter maid's one-seater zoomed down the sidewalk toward them.

"Where did that come from?"

"Probably a passel of them parked on the other side of the entrance. This one came out of there." He pointed to a dark gap between the arcade and the next building. "Security," he explained. "Boardwalk security."

A man in a light uniform jumped out of the one-person cab. He talked to Lovitz for a minute, shining his flashlight on a piece of paper Lovitz displayed.

A few minutes later, the guard unlocked the arcade door, holding it open for them. As they filed in, we glimpsed a bright room of outsized video games. The guard trotted in behind them, closing the door.

"Interesting," Sandy commented. "Very damn interesting."

"Very damn up-and-up, I'd say. He produced some kind of pass and went in with his lawyer. This is not the stuff of caper movies."

"But why go in at night—off season, too? Come on." Sandy hopped out of the car.

I followed. The wine and bread were making me tired. I longed for a warm room and a soft bed. I'd had a long day, a long week. And I felt guilty about not checking in with Brad Rommel, worried something might have developed in my absence.

I told myself there was no urgency—Rommel was out on bail, not sweating it in a jail cell. But he wasn't just a client; I'd known him a long time. It wasn't enough to mitigate his ordeal; I wanted it to end.

Sandy and I cut a diagonal across the parking lot and the street, avoiding the arcade. We hurried to the far end of the Boardwalk, to the last of its barred entrances. Behind iron gates we saw kiddie rides, concessions, carnival games. Rows of lamps caught wisps of sea mist tumbling and intertwining like otters. The glare reflected off hundreds of unlit bulbs filigreeing every ride and stand. But the most gorgeous attraction was the beach itself, absorbing the soft light of moon and wharf and boardwalk, and the crashing surf, glowing black-light white.

"You up for some climbing, Laura?"

The iron gate was less than ten feet tall. "Must we?"

"I was kidding. No need for you to tag along." He was already wiping two of the bars, making them less slick as far up as he could reach. "Security must be watching the beach. That's the usual way to get in here at night, I'm sure."

"What if more security people come by?"

"Wine on my breath. I've got it covered."

The old drunk tourist routine. Great. It had to work for somebody someday.

He hoisted himself up, then, with a grunt, clambered over the top. He dropped with a thud.

"You okay?" I whispered.

"Oh, man," was his reply. He sat on the ground for a minute. "Have you called me a dumbshit lately?"

"Not without contradiction." It wouldn't be the same by invitation. "Anything broken?"

"No." He stood. "I'm all right." He didn't sound all right. "I'll be back. Wait here, okay? If you get too close, More will make you when she comes out."

"And if she spots you?"

"I won't let her see me up close. I'll stay out of the light—I'll weave off like Peter Pan on a wine toot." With considerably less alacrity than a Lost Boy, he limped off.

I was borderline amused, for a while, peering through the gate at the rides. Without casino light bulbs and calliope music, without the smell of caramel and corn dogs, without the sound of kids running and roller coaster shrieks, it was not a less interesting, but only a different experience. Motionless and shrouded in mist, it was like some shrine to the fifties, a place in some Ray Bradbury story, not real, but asleep with quaint magic, dreaming of old America.

The romance of it carried me through ten or fifteen minutes. Then I tried to outwit my impatience. I walked to a spot where a snaking ride curved on steel rafters over the concrete. It dripped salt water on me. I walked a little further. A railway trestle—a real one—spanned a shallow stream eddying into the ocean.

I returned to the gate.

I waited.

I froze into a hunch-shouldered coma of boredom. I remembered other times Sandy had kept me waiting, other times he'd used his easy manner to soothe me into stupid situations. I had plenty of kindling to feed my displeasure. Instead, the memories reignited other feelings. We'd been a happy couple once, we'd been friends; I couldn't say that about my other relationships.

I was considering going back to the car when I heard shouting on the other side of the gate, somewhere inside the Boardwalk. A man cried, "Hey there, God damn! Stop!" He was too far away to be referring to me. He continued, "Stop! Stop!"

It could only mean Sandy had been spotted lurking.

I heard men running. Within seconds a meter-maid car came barreling out of nowhere toward me.

I stood motionless in its headlights. Two men in light uniforms ran behind it. I didn't know if they were even armed, but I found myself fearing they'd shoot—fallout from my encounter in Kinsley's office, perhaps. I didn't want to run from them, didn't want to turn my back.

As the cart stopped, the two pedestrians close behind, I felt my spine stiffen. It's no crime to stand outside an amusement park. They had no right to demand an explanation.

A man leaped out of the cart, saying, "What are you doing here?"

"Looking in." Anger leaked into my voice, giving it some steel. "What's the problem?"

"Are you waiting for someone?"

"Why are you hassling me? I'm just walking."

But their reason became apparent. Sounds of a scuffle came through the gate, grunts and oomphs as of men playing football. Then a loud silly tittering.

"Sorry, fellas." Some more tittering. "Ha ha ha, what a ... used to do this when I was a kid. Sneak in at night."

Sandy, playing drunk.

I heard the clip of high heels and two men's voices. Maryanne More and Karl Lovitz with their guard, approaching quickly.

Damn.

Sandy might have gotten away with his drunk nostalgia act if More hadn't come out of the arcade. But encountering him here, she would leap to the obvious truth: that we'd followed her to spy on her.

I could see Sandy now. The security guards had him pinned between them. They were scooting him on rubbery legs toward the entrance and their fellow guards. Sandy was looking over his shoulder, his expression in that instant all too sober. He looked at me and started kicking and wrestling, tossing out slurred exclamations. Clearly, he was trying to move the guards back. He was trying to hustle them out of my sight. He was trying to keep More away from where I stood.

I had only a few seconds to ponder. Sandy had resigned himself to More's seeing him, but he didn't want her to see me. Because he'd tell her something—something he saw as a better story—if she didn't know I was with him?

He'd play the headstrong lover, perhaps, acting out of manly protectiveness toward me. Following her because he couldn't bear the purgatory of doing nothing after my narrow escape. There were enough action-before-thought males out there that she might just chalk it up to macho excess.

Whereas my presence here meant we had a rational suspicion of particular wrongdoing. It meant we'd followed her for what we considered a good reason, not just because a guy's gotta do *something*.

I turned tail and ran. I ran under the loops of the dripping ride and onto the railway trestle. There was a wooden foot-path beside the tracks. There was no way a cart could follow.

The wood sounded like empty barrels beneath my feet. I soon heard footsteps join mine. At the end of the trestle, a hill rose steeply toward a city street with the train tracks beneath it. I continued along the tracks into the pitch darkness of the underpass.

The smell hit me first—dank, uriney, oily. I concentrated on getting through, pushing away fears of skulking men and rabid rats. My feet squelched over what I hoped was not fetid excrement or decomposing animal.

Moments after reaching the other side, I found myself beside a street streaming with cars.

I hoped I'd interpreted Sandy's behavior correctly because, damn, running in the dark in city shoes (probably spattered beyond cleaning) was not my idea of fun.

I finally slowed down and looked over my shoulder. My pursuer had vanished. He probably stopped chasing me when I reached the underpass. I hadn't been doing anything wrong, after all; he had no right or reason to detain me.

I'd started running and then somehow gotten spooked. Lately, my adrenaline pumped too readily.

I started back toward the Boardwalk, feeling a little foolish.

When More saw Sandy, she was bound to suspect that the woman waiting at the gate, the woman who'd taken all the trouble to flee from Boardwalk security, was me.

Who else could it be?

No matter how well Sandy presented it, if More was indeed masterminding Designer Crimes, she would be smart enough to see through his lie.

I walked back to Sandy's car, relieved to find the doors

unlocked. I could hear the loud bass of a cruising car's radio. I slid quickly into the passenger seat, shoving the picnic detritus into the back.

Ten minutes later, I watched Sandy lope across the parking lot toward the car. I'd been reading by the light of an open glove compartment.

"Good." His breathing was a little labored as he climbed in. "Glad I left it open for you. Why is it you never go wrong planning for the worst-case scenario?"

"What happened back there? Did they make you ride the Captain Hook ride till you got sick?"

"I look that bad?" He ran his hand over his hair and shrugged his jacket back to a nondrunk fit. "No. Maryanne More didn't rat me out; she looked plenty surprised, but she didn't let on she knew me. I just talked soused and promised to walk back to my motel."

He shifted in the seat to get a good look at me. "You're all right? I didn't know you could run that fast."

"He didn't chase me far. I've been sitting here reading *Man and His Symbols.*" I held up the book I'd found beneath the seat.

"You'd be surprised how useful it is in catching taggers—graffiti artists. Seems like a lot of images are hardwired into us." He sounded a little embarrassed to have been caught with Jung. He patted his pockets, extracting his keys.

"I'll be glad to get home."

His grin was sheepish. "One more stop."

I tried not to groan. "I won't have to elude security people again?"

"Qué será será." He started the car. "That Lovitz is too damn much, posturing and puffing about how they should check my ID and call the cops. The man could use a Valium mickey."

"Well, actually, you *were* lying."

"But I was doing it well." He swung out of the parking lot, driving past the Boardwalk toward the wharf.

We wound a few miles along a residential cliff drive. I cracked the window, enjoying the sea smell, the sound of surf against rock.

Eventually we turned right, into a district of small warehouses and night-shift industries. Farther on, vacant lots began the segue from town to roadside dunes and farmland.

"Here we are." He pulled up beside an acre or two of weeds.

"Are we on some kind of parking-lot tour?" There were empty lots to our left and right, small factories across the way.

"That's Super Prime right there." He pointed to what looked like a big square shed with a Quonset roof. Light poured from frosted windows onto a parking lot of company trucks. "See why I got jazzed when I heard Maryanne More was coming here for dinner? She's two minutes from Lovitz's arcade and less than ten from the factory Kinsley worried would get sabotaged." He modulated his voice to mimic a radio announcer's: "Coincidence or conspiracy?"

"We're just going to sit here and hope something happens?"

He leaned close, surprising me with a kiss. "We could neck."

I was spared—and deprived of—schoolgirlish turmoil by a sudden blare of sirens.

"Holy burglars, Batgirl! That's Super Prime." He pushed his car door open, calling over his shoulder. "Scram! Go!" He took off across the empty lot before I had a chance to get back on mental track.

His keys were still in the ignition, so I slid behind the wheel and started the car. Super Prime's alarm was deafening. Either it had gotten louder, or Sandy had temporarily addled me.

I drove off. Several blocks away, police cars began passing me, heading toward the factory.

I parked on the cliff drive, hoping I'd remember my way back. I'd have to outwait the police, but I didn't want to tarry any longer than I had to. Here at the northern tip of town, where bay met open sea, the wind and ocean chill would be hard on Sandy—assuming he lurked successfully and didn't get arrested.

I wondered what he was doing. It would be a neat trick learning anything without himself becoming a suspect. But I didn't doubt for a minute he could do it.

CHAPTER

Twelve

SANDY WAS TRUE TO HIS WORD; WE WERE ON OUR WAY home by midnight. The alarm at Super Prime had been written off as false: nothing in the plant appeared broken or tampered with. The police had come and gone without spotting Sandy. And Sandy hadn't spotted anyone, either. If sabotage had been the plan, the alarm must have delayed or aborted it.

I was back in my office by late morning. I spent an hour on the phone. I called Brad Rommel, called the sheriff's department, called the DA's office. I satisfied myself there were no new developments there.

I flipped through my phone messages. I'd been besieged by calls from reporters wanting to discuss Kinsley's death, to add my voice to their breathless buzz. I tossed the message slips into the trash.

With little else to do, I stared out my office window. Traffic crept toward the freeway, shadowed by dingy buildings. Market Street cut me off from the financial district as dramatically as the Berlin wall. There were no sculptures here, no flower vendors, no cute espresso carts. From here, the city was a gray and charmless hive.

I had expected Perry Verhoeven to float me back uptown on a river of cash. Now what?

My secretary, Gayle, buzzed me. "You have a visitor, Laura. Maryanne More." Her voice was husky with excitement; she knew who More was. Everyone who read the papers knew. Everyone who watched unctuous news reports about "San Francisco's latest lawyer slaying" knew.

"Send her in."

I quickly checked my suit for lint, my stockings for runs. There was nothing I could do about the office, though. There was no last-minute art lying around to brighten it. My ingenuity, or maybe my enthusiasm, hadn't stretched to disguising its cheapness, its serviceable newness. In fact, the whole place stank of licked wounds and lukewarm commitment.

I'd been nursing my grievances too long. I either had to do something about them, come to terms with where I was, or move on. But where?

I opened the door to Maryanne More, motioning her in and speaking the appropriate welcome. I would let her bring up last night. I would volunteer nothing, confirm nothing. That would be simplest, maybe safest.

"I hope you don't mind my dropping in." Her tone was reluctant, as if circumstance had forced her into a conversation she'd rather skip.

If so, that made two of us. "Please have a chair. There's a break in my schedule."

She wore a deep green suit over a steel-gray blouse with a high collar. It made her look every bit as pale as she was. Her eyelids were still swollen. The skin beneath her nose was chapped.

She sank into the vinyl chair beside my desk. She made a visible effort to sit straight, her handbag primly in her lap.

"I wanted to talk to you about last night," she said. Her fingers, long and delicate, seemed to play a slow piano tune on the purse. "I've thought about it all morning, and I can't see any reason not to talk to you about it."

"Please go on." I kept my tone neutral, friendly, as if I waited without prior knowledge.

My response surprised her, I think. She pushed hard against the chair back. "Mr. Arkelett was following me. I think you were with him."

I pasted on a frown. "Following you where?"

"Inquiries are being made of some of my clients," she said quietly. Light from the window caught glimmers of copper in her brown hair. "Clients I couldn't help. It's gotten back to me."

I waited. "You're accusing Sandy?"

She nodded. "He's selected certain cases, certain clients to research. He followed me yesterday to meet a client whose situation somewhat matches the others." Her eyes, as gray as her shirt, held mine steadily. I had to give her credit: she'd discovered Sandy's research quickly—and he wasn't one to leave broken twigs on the trail. "I've tried to help you; I think you know that, I think Mr. Arkelett knows that. But I don't understand this. He's making some kind of assumption, and"—she shook her head in apparent puzzlement—"I don't even understand his premise. Your premise."

"*My* premise?" My tone implied disclaimer, somewhat accurately. "Sandy does what he thinks best. He doesn't need my permission. If anything, he has a tendency to bully me into going along with his agenda."

"But you do know what I'm talking about."

"I assume he's gotten bulldoggish about investigating you and anyone or anything else that might bear on the shooting. But in terms of my involvement, his . . . intensity has pretty much spared me from having to think about it or deal with it."

"That may be true." She smiled slightly. "As far as it goes. But he takes you along with him. He brought you to my office."

"Because he needed me there. He needed information from me."

"You've spoken to him today?"

I hesitated. "You say he followed you yesterday? To a client meeting? Are you sure he wasn't approaching the client to ask about Ms. Kinsley? That it wasn't coincidence you happened to be there then?"

Coincidence. Judging by the look on her face, More had about as much faith in it as Sandy.

"The client made a special trip to Santa Cruz from San Jose to meet me." It was her turn to be less than forthcoming—Santa Cruz was hardly a halfway point. I waited, but she didn't mention Lovitz's connection to the Boardwalk.

"Maybe Sandy knew your client would be there." The evasiveness was wearing on me. It's always tricky, always tiring, always part of being a lawyer.

More sighed audibly, staring at the now-still fingers on her handbag. "It's been a very confusing few days," she observed. "Capped by Mr. Arkelett's perplexing interest in my failures."

Yes, she'd see her "lack of remedy" cases as failures—if she wasn't offering extralegal options.

"Including last night's client," she continued quietly. "But one thing I'd like Mr. Arkelett to know? If you would?"

"Yes?"

"The man I saw last night first approached me as a client. In that regard, I wasn't much help." She colored suddenly. "But he's a very attractive and intelligent person, Ms. Di Palma."

So she'd gone on a date with him? She'd driven all the way to Santa Cruz for a romantic dinner—days after her partner was slain?

"He's justifiably proud of his work, and he wanted to show it off. And I wanted to let him." She sounded a little defiant. "Mr. Arkelett will do what he thinks necessary, I'm sure." Her voice was steady, her eyes met mine. Only the remaining heat in her cheeks betrayed her embarrassment. "And I don't have anything to hide, although I'm made uncomfortable by his digging into my professional life. I guess if you'd tell him he's entering my *private* life? I don't know him well enough to assume that will make a difference, but I'd like to hope so."

I wondered why she wasn't angrier. I knew from experience how it felt to live in the fishbowl of police and media scrutiny. Now Sandy had added the strain of a private investigation.

"I'll convey everything you've said," I promised. "But I don't pretend to have much influence over Sandy, not when he thinks he's doing what he's got to do."

"I'm a little disappointed." She blinked at me, pale brows raised. "I hoped you'd be more forthcoming. This is difficult for me. Two days ago you asked for my help. I hoped for your honesty in return."

"As far as I'm concerned, this is between you and Sandy." More important, between Sandy and me. "You may be right: he may well owe you an explanation. Have you tried to reach him today?"

She nodded. "He hasn't returned my call yet."

"Then you don't know that he can't explain this to your satisfaction."

"I suppose," she said wryly, "I was hoping you could do that. Or would do that."

She was laying it on so thick. Didn't she get it? I wouldn't speak for Sandy. "I'm sorry you're disappointed. I'm sorry about everything you've been through. I can't even pretend to know how it feels to have your partner killed that way. And then to have your privacy invaded. But I don't know what to offer you except my sympathy. And you seem to expect more.''

She rose, nodding. She looked down at me, nodding again. She seemed on the verge of saying something else, but a quick wrinkle of the nose suggested she thought it unnecessary or unworthy. She left without further comment.

Not two minutes later, Gayle buzzed me. ''Mr. Arkelett on the phone.''

''Sandy—she was just here,'' I told him. ''Maryanne More.''

''Don't I know it.'' His voice brimmed with excitement. ''Listen.''

There was a clicking on his end of the phone, the scouring sound of a tape starting. And then my voice: *Sandy does what he thinks best. He doesn't need my permission. If anything, he has a tendency to bully me into going along with his agenda.*

''Oh, my God.'' I spoke over my taped words. ''I don't believe it. She brought a bug in here with her.''

''She sure did.'' Sandy sounded jubilant. ''Talk about chutzpah. Man oh man.''

''You picked up our whole conversation?'' I quickly reviewed it. It was a little disconcerting knowing he'd listened to me talk about him.

''Yes, ma'am. We accessed it the exact same way— through More's computer system. Knew she was heading over because the paralegal, Hester Donne, popped into her office and they talked about it. More must have had the bug in her briefcase.''

''Handbag. She wasn't carrying a briefcase.''

''Except here's the kicker: either More had a much bigger, more powerful bug—we're talking walkie-talkie-sized—or someone followed her. Somebody stuck fairly close outside your door with a receiver-transmitter. Some kind of relay link between the bug in the handbag and the receiver in the computer.''

"I don't remember More's bag." I recalled her fingers lightly tapping its surface. "But it must have been big enough to hold a walkie-talkie. She had both hands on it."

"Damn, I wish I'd headed her off when I heard she was coming over. Followed her."

"You guys eavesdropped on everything that happened in her office today?"

"Well, yuh, I guess you could put it that way—not that it amounted to much." He laughed. "But hot damn, huh? She came over there and bugged your office."

"She took it away with her, right? I'm not bugged now?" No way I'd let two overgrown boys use their new toys to listen to my every sneeze and phone call.

"Yeah, she took it. We could hear her walk up the block outside your window. Then she either switched it off or she got too far from the relay." Sandy had a side-of-the-mouth conference with Osmil. I heard the latter say, "Yes, Captain."

"I'm glad you found out she brought a bug here. But Sandy, you know what? You can't keep listening in on her forever."

A brief silence. I could hear keyboard clatter in his office. "True."

"Isn't there some way to tell Krisbaum and Edwards about it?" The homicide detectives assigned to the Kinsley case.

"Not without getting in a world of trouble."

"Could you do it anonymously?" Whether or not bugging your own offices was illegal—and we couldn't prove anyone had been taped without consent, anyone but us—it would certainly interest the police.

"Let me put it to you this way. What good would it do the cops to know this unless they knew the rest? About Kinsley's memo that got erased."

"You could send them a copy of the memo, also anonymously." This should be Homicide's responsibility, not ours.

"I shouldn't have called you," he said tentatively. "You're stressing out."

"I might be, yes."

"You did a good job of covering for me," he offered. "Made me sound like a big dumb dog that knocks over the vases and you can't do a thing with him."

"If the shoe fits."

He laughed. He was happy. His electronic chase was more interesting and unexpected than he'd envisioned.

"Do you want to go out for a drink, Sandy? Early dinner?"

"Can't. Data to process, reports to read. It's going to be a late night."

"More told me—"

"I heard. She's made it to her office. I'll call you later." And with that I was dismissed.

Most people would be glad to be through with work by afternoon. But I envied Sandy his data and reports.

CHAPTER

Thirteen

I PARKED MY RENTAL CAR, A JAPANESE SEDAN THAT smelled like cigarettes, in front of the Victorian. It was a tall house with plenty of gingerbread, not as spectacular as the four-color with the small dome across the street, but freshly painted and well maintained, flanked by stately houses with tree-sized rhododendrons.

My father's cousin, my "Uncle" Henry, paid the gardener well, but you could tell he didn't personally care about the plants. They were austerely pruned, not heavy with wet flowers like the neighbors'. This would be his last year as mayor of Hillsdale. I tried to imagine him developing some quiet hobby like gardening, but he didn't seem the type. For thirty-two years, his life had been full of conflict and bonhomie, QT handshakes and meetings roaring with strife.

I slid out of the car. At loose ends, I'd grabbed the one evening flight here. I didn't have anything to do in San Francisco, and I needed to get going on Brad Rommel's case.

Seeing the light in the parlor window, I was glad I'd come. Uncle Henry and I had sorted through my father's things, taken care of his wishes and his savings (spending it on this house, which the two men had lately shared); the hard part was over. Now we could sit comfortably together and grieve. And I could count on Uncle Henry to have some Stoli in the freezer for me. I could count on him for companionship without hassle.

Leaving my Aunt Diana and renting this house with my father had been the smartest thing he'd ever done. He'd relaxed into a state of sloppy comfort unlike the appearances-first formality of his previous household. He'd turned out to be a much nicer, more perceptive person than I'd ever imagined, seeing him beside his frosty, tight-lipped wife.

I stood in the thick drizzle for a minute, listening to distant sirens, inhaling the pungent spice of wood fires. At nine o'clock, only a few porch lights were on. It was freezing, wet; people weren't expecting drop-ins. I could feel gooseflesh rise on my legs under wet hose. My suit would need pressing, and I'd be sniffling with damp hair all evening (the wall heater kept the hall and entry toasty without adding the least warmth to any room). But I liked the way it felt, the chill on my face, the way it coated my lashes, softening the lamplight.

I climbed the steps to the porch, digging the key out of my handbag.

When I let myself in, a voice called from the parlor. "Laura? That you?"

I felt a small rush, like a first sip of liqueur. It was nice to have someone waiting. "Yes. Hi."

My uncle came out to greet me, unlike his former self in sweat clothes and a shawl-collared robe. He carried a drink, almost certainly Johnnie Walker Red; some things never change.

As usual, I was surprised to see white where my mind's

eye stubbornly recalled dark brown hair. His olive cheeks, firm in the way of prosperous Italian men, were desiccating like crepe.

I embraced him. He smelled of drink and shampoo. His hair was damp. "To whose blood do I owe the pleasure?" he demanded.

The last time I arrived suddenly, the police had just analyzed the contents of the trailside bucket.

He held me at arm's length, almost splashing me with whiskey. "Or are you hiding out?" I knew he meant from the person who'd shot Kinsley.

"Partly." I could hopscotch topics with him in a way that often left Sandy behind.

That hadn't been true of Hal, Uncle Henry's son, with whom I'd lived for almost four years. But during those years, family tensions made visits "home" rare. My uncle and Sandy and I were by far the more congenial threesome.

"I didn't have enough to do in the city to bother staying through the weekend. And I've been fretting about Brad Rommel."

Uncle Henry shook his head. He wasn't convinced Brad was innocent. He wasn't convinced his pal, the sheriff, could be wrong. But justice be damned, he wanted me to win.

"I've got news you'll like." He beamed, eyes gleaming. "Come and look."

I followed him into a parlor furnished with a few showy antiques and some comfortable recliners, one of them scattered with newspapers. He bent creakily to retrieve a section. He flapped it, bowing slightly as he handed it to me.

When I saw the headline, I smiled. LOCAL DA MOVIE SUBJECT OF BAR PROBE.

I took the paper, skimming the article. Like others preceding it, it laid out my argument that Connie Gold had shaped her case for TV-movie salability. The newspaper's tone was skeptical and loyal to Gold. But people would remember she'd been accused of something sleazy; she was

Hillsdale's resident celebrity. With luck—and agitation by me—she wouldn't live it down before the Rommel trial.

"You can bet she's on the warpath, Laura." A lifetime of city politics made him smile at the thought.

The door buzzer sounded, interrupting our shared glee. In answer to my querying look, Uncle Henry shrugged. Of course he wasn't expecting anyone, not dressed like this. A few years ago, he wouldn't have worn a bathrobe even in private.

I backtracked to the front door, allowing him to retreat toward the kitchen. The metallic grating of buzzer filled the entryway. I flung the door open, anxious to stop the damn noise.

I was surprised to see Jay Bartoli, a high school friend who was now a plainclothes sheriff's investigator. I'd run into him last year, during my hermitage with Hal. More recently, I'd talked to him about the Rommel investigation, though it wasn't his case. But on the whole, I tried to avoid him. He was forever asking me to dinner to talk about old times. I didn't care about old times. It was hard enough to deal with the present.

He was a dapper man, a former jock who'd stayed in shape, trading youthful bulk for streamlined muscles that looked better in a suit. His hair, wavy and long in high school, was clipped short and mostly gray over a healthy, craggy face. He looked easy in his body and comfortable in his clothes. But I didn't find him attractive. And though he was married, I kept feeling he needed that from me.

I tried to put some warmth into our social embrace. A sheriff's investigator is a good friend to have, and cops as a rule don't like me. More accurately, they don't like the lawyer who defended Wallace Bean, assassin of two U.S. senators.

I stepped back quickly, talking myself out of believing what I'd felt below Bartoli's belt.

"How'd you know I was in town?" I tried to sound

happy he did. "I just walked in the door." Should I say I was tired or should I allow a few minutes before blunt hints? "I was just talking to my uncle."

Bartoli wore his smile like he'd pinned it on in front of a mirror. He looked miserable behind it. I wondered if something was up.

"We haff our ways," he said with a *Hogan's Heroes* accent. "Actually, I watched you pull up. I was across the street."

I hadn't noticed anyone in the few parked cars on Clarke. I took a backward step.

"Why were you there?" I'd had sex with him once while my marriage was breaking up, just before my twentieth birthday. He always let me know he remembered it. I could live with that. I couldn't live with him lying in wait for me.

"I was listening to my radio, getting updates. I came to bring your uncle the news, if he hasn't heard it already." He ran a hand over his Ted Turner hair. "We couldn't raise him on the phone."

"I know." I'd tried to call him from the airport to warn him I was coming. But he had the message tape on, probably the ringer off; he did that when he drank. I sometimes did that, too. It's either too hard or too easy to talk with a third glassful in your hand.

"But he's home tonight?"

"Yes. I'll go get him." It was clearly important. And God knew, Uncle Henry had learned to rise above intoxication.

"So he doesn't know."

"He hasn't said anything. Know what?"

"I'm off duty—that's why I came. Keep them from having to send someone they need." Again he ran his hand over his hair. "Someone blew up the Southshore Mall."

My uncle's baby, Hillsdale's only real mall. The only place within three hundred miles to buy serviceable underwear, sheets and towels, sets of dishes. What was left of downtown had gone specialty—futons and candle art and souvenirs. Old Town was just galleries and empty pubs. And Hillsdale's one premall theater had closed years ago.

"Blew up?" No wonder Jay looked ashen. "The whole thing?"

"I hope not. It's on fire, chemical fire. Or possibly gas-fed—the lines might be broken. Right now it's way out of control. Fire fighters can't get in to determine the cause."

"How did it happen?" I checked my watch: 9:10. There were probably people at the movie theater. But the stores would be closed. And I knew from frustrating experience that the mall restaurants locked tight at 7:00.

"We have reports of a small plane flying over. We think right now it might have dropped some kind of contact oil explosive, maybe something like napalm. We don't know if it dropped bombs or sprayed; we don't know the mechanics of doing something like this. We've got experts coming up from San Francisco."

"The mall." Everyone in Hillsdale—with the notable exception of downtown businesses—loved their "ticket to modern times," as tacky and cookie-cutter as it was. And who could blame them? Department stores and first-run movies were a recent luxury here. Without them, Hillsdale was a consumer wasteland, a sleepover on the highway to real cities.

"Jesus, Uncle Henry'll die." He'd endured five years of meetings and hearings and collapsing deals to get the mall built. He'd steamrollered over the objections of environ-mentalists and the Coastal Commission, sweetening the pot for builder friends and investment corporations. He'd roused the unemployed—thousands of them cast off by lumber mills now sawing boards in Mexico—by promising them jobs. He'd rammed the project through years of tight money and soaring interest rates. And it had paid off: the mall got him reelected in spite of debacles like the abandoned hous-ing project across the bridge.

I glanced toward the kitchen.

"Who did it? Whose plane was it?" I felt a stab of fear, surely unwarranted. Brad Rommel had expressed bitterness toward the mall. Brad Rommel owned a plane.

"Nothing from out at the airport—the small-craft airport. Too foggy up there tonight. Everything's grounded."

The town's commercial airport, where I'd flown in, was little more than a few acres of tarmac and a building resembling a large camp bathroom with a ticket counter and a car-rental company. Ironically, the noncommercial airport was at least as big, atop a fog-socked hill with a tiny weather station. It had hangars for a couple of dozen planes and a mom-and-pop restaurant open five to five. We used to breakfast up there when I was in high school, our other choice being an on-the-highway franchise with tea-weak coffee.

"So the plane came from somewhere else?" I tried not to sound relieved. After all, Brad wouldn't firebomb a mall.

"Too early to tell. Although"—he shook his head wonderingly—"you know what? No one picked it up on radar. Wherever it came from, it stayed very damn low. Too low to show up."

"Have you checked the air traffic around here? Maybe someone dipped under the radar on his way overhead; someone who landed north or south at about the right time."

"We'll be doing a lot more checking, obviously." He straightened, inhaled, seemed suddenly larger and more confident. "I just thought someone better tell Henry."

"You don't know how bad the damage—"

Uncle Henry entered the hall, dressed now in slacks, a polo shirt, and a cardigan. He'd gone upstairs and changed.

He skipped the usual hearty greeting. He must have checked his phone messages. "One of you give me a lift out there?" Emotion deepened the timbre of his voice, reddened his olive skin.

"Glad to." Bartoli seemed relieved not to have to explain. "Are you ready?"

My uncle nodded, patting his pants pockets and pulling a 49ers jacket off a rack by the door.

I grabbed my purse and walked out with them. The stink of fire was stronger now, too strong to ascribe to neighbors' chimneys. Sirens swelled like distant screams.

Bartoli's car was across the street and a quarter of a block down from mine—rather far considering there were spaces in front of my uncle's door. I climbed into the backseat, knowing it would never occur to my uncle to offer a woman the front. The car, big and American with panels of Dad-control buttons, smelled of fast food. I wondered where Bartoli would buy his burgers now. The places along the highway looked worse than ever.

Jay turned in his seat after starting the engine, turned and stared at me a few seconds. His face, never expressive and now trained to a sheriff's deadpan, didn't reveal why.

He pulled away from the curb before clicking on his lights. He sped past neighboring Victorians, fiddling his seat belt into its clasp. He shifted, tugging wrinkles from his jacket and trousers. Even speeding to a disaster, he showed clothes sense; my Aunt Diana would have approved.

Without asking, my uncle clicked on the car radio, a multibutton citizen-band affair. It seemed to be on a police frequency. We heard a female voice say, "Two more fire trucks en route, one from Dungeness, one from state college. What we really need is some manpower out here to help us keep bystanders back. We've had five more explosions in there—we think the fire's hitting combustibles, fuel in the restaurants, chemicals in the gardening and hardware stores. Seems like we got a hundred onlookers at least—we could sure use more help keeping them back. For one thing, the smoke's real nasty."

By the time we rounded the next corner, we could see the glow from the fire, still nearly a mile away. I heard my uncle gasp. The whole horizon was a muted orange, as if bay fog had sponged in the glare, graying and diffusing it.

A man's voice crackled from Jay's radio. "We've got a call in to off-duty uniforms—should have a few more bodies out there pretty quick. What's the status of the fire?"

"They say they've got it contained, but it looks like hell-all—stuff exploding all over the place." There were lots of background voices, shouted commands, a shriek. "I hope we get those off-duties out here soon." Her voice quavered. "You wouldn't believe this, Phil."

"Hang in, Molly."

Jay fiddled with the knob, muttering, "Get on the fire band."

For the next five minutes, racing along the highway through downtown, then past a strip of feed stores and cowboy bars, we listened to the fire captain's urgent conversations with out-of-town rigs racing to help. There seemed to be a shortage of a chemical the captain needed in huge quantity; he was nearly in tears about it.

As we approached a roadblock, Jay clicked back to the police band. He pulled a cherry light out of his glove compartment and popped it out the window onto the roof. Seeing its swirls of red, two blocks of stopped cars inched over to let him zipper between the lanes. We stopped near two police cars straddling Broadway, nose to nose. On the radio a man with a backwoods accent barked: "Get all them cars out of here. Turn 'em around starting at the back. Just get them the hell out. I want Broadway empty by the time the engines get here, you hear me?"

Jay Bartoli and Uncle Henry jumped out of the car, striding to the line of cops between the bystanders and the fire.

I emerged more slowly. Black smoke roiled under the orange-gray canopy of fog. My lungs contracted against the stench of chemicals exploding and plastics melting. Up ahead, men in silhouette struggled with hoses and trucks while the red and blue lights of police cars and fire trucks and ambulances flashed and ricocheted off wet concrete. An area the size of a city block burned like a two-story candle, flames so richly red and yellow they hid all but the bare-bones infrastructure of what they consumed. Even from two thousand yards back, heat poured from it, carrying swarms of sparks.

Behind me, a slow row of cop cars wove through traffic, halting behind Jay's car. Men in police uniforms or jeans and football jackets spilled out and trotted past. Fearing hassle, I crouched back into Jay's car with its still-circling cherry.

The new arrivals huddled with a man I took to be a fire chief. My uncle and Jay were there, too. But I didn't want to join them. I'd never seen a fire so huge. I just wanted to watch it, not hear it discussed as an enemy, nor consider the hardship and grief it would cause. For now, I wanted to watch it as I'd watch Niagara Falls. I wanted to appreciate its grandeur.

When I next looked for my uncle, he was gone. The silhouettes had shifted three quarters of a block south, toward the ENTERING HILLSDALE sign. Probably my uncle was there now. He would be wherever field command had been established.

A low juggernaut of smoke made my eyes water, my sinuses burn. I backed away.

Finally, with the fire no smaller or larger than it seemed when we arrived, I walked away, cutting uphill into a neighborhood of ranch-style houses flanked by fields with occasional donkeys and ponies. I covered long stretches with gully on one side and tract housing on the other. People stood outside looking downhill at the tips of flames and the glow of fire. No one asked me what I'd seen, no one asked me what was burning. They stood in the foggy light of street lamps, watching mass culture's local outlet vanish. Arms folded against the cold, huddled in their wool jackets, neighbors stood side by side saying absolutely nothing.

I called a cab from the first pay phone I encountered. All the driver could talk about was how much more he'd have to pay for his daughter's insulin if the cheapest drugstore in town burned down. "But acourse to her, that's nothing. Not compared to what she's been doing for fun. All the kids hang out over to the mall."

When we pulled onto Clarke Street, he said, "It's like President Kennedy being shot. That's exactly what it feels like."

CHAPTER

Fourteen

I STOPPED WITH MY HAND ON THE DOORKNOB. I COULD SEE the taxi's brake lights like red eyes in the distance. At the end of the block, bundled-up pedestrians stood talking, pointing south toward the fire. Flashlight beams lit widow's walks and rooftops. People were finding high ground from which to view the fire.

I was sure it hadn't been Brad Rommel's plane; it was just coincidence he had one.

But he did resent the mall; he did blame it in part for Piatti's decision to leave.

A hot filament of worry snaked through my confidence in him. I checked my purse for the rental-car keys. I walked back down the porch steps and got into the two-door. It was just a drive, after all. I'd go for a little drive up to Brad's house, reassure myself that he was there and his plane was tucked into its hangar miles away. I wouldn't charge him for my time, and I had nothing better to do, so who could complain?

I sped north, away from the fire, toward both airports and

toward Brad's cabin. Nearly all the traffic was southbound, families braving the slick, wind-whipped highway to check out the excitement. About five miles north of town, two fire trucks flashed and howled past.

I took a sharp turn onto a potholed road. I crossed dairy flats and started up an increasingly steep hill. I couldn't identify the roadside vegetation in the dark, but I'd lived close by here last year. I knew there were ferns taller than me, cow parsnips with stalks thicker than my legs, skunk cabbages, cattails—wet-weather plants, thirsty ancient greenery that couldn't take the frost of colder, drier climates. Soon the road wound beside fir and pine and redwoods. My headlights danced in sparkling particles of fog, painted highlights on the tangled vegetation. Ten minutes later, the road straightened to a messy, tamped melange of dirt and gravel and broken clam shells.

A quarter mile ahead was Brad Rommel's cabin, lights out, no smoke rising from the wood-stove vent, no sign of his truck out front.

Between my car and the cabin, smothered in cold fog, was an airplane not much bigger than my rental car.

I stared at it for a few minutes, searching for a reason Brad would keep it here rather than at the airport. Maybe he didn't recall it had been impounded as a condition of his bail; maybe the airport had lost the paperwork. Maybe he was repairing the engine. Maybe the airport had run out of hangars.

Leaving my headlights on, I climbed out of the car. It was colder up here than down in town, or maybe the dripping redwoods created that illusion. The creak of timber and the crunch of gravel underfoot took on ominous loudness. My headlights cast double shadows of objects in their path.

Standing beside the plane, I tried to peer inside, but the car lights offered only a dim, undetailed picture. I tried the door—surprisingly smaller than my car door—and found it locked.

I went back to the sedan, searching its side pockets and glove compartment for a flashlight. Finding none, I moved the car as close as I could to the plane, and I hit the high beams, creating a sudden wall of the fog.

When I returned to the plane, I could see the interior more clearly, well enough to make out some kind of metal box beneath a pair of headphones on the front seat. Chrome buttons, rows of them under the windshield, caught the light like mirrors. It seemed barely big enough for two inside, with control panels instead of leg room. Stacked behind the seats were standard tool kits and a tackle box with a red cross on it. Two bundles, probably parachutes, also crowded the baggage well. Propped behind the passenger seat was a long wood handle topped with a curved, serrated blade. It looked more like a gardening tool than something you'd find in an airplane.

I walked the plane's circumference, not knowing what to look for, and seeing nothing apparently amiss. No steam rose from the nose, no fans whirred to cool a just-flown engine. Back beside the pilot's door, I crouched, trying to peer underneath. My headlights were aimed too high: I couldn't make out anything.

Growing frightened of the rustle of branches and whistle of wind, I did a quick trot back to the car, flicking the lights to their lowest fog setting. My world shrank to knee- and ground-level, tinged an eerie yellow.

Crouching again, I could see beneath the plane. From its belly dangled leather straps with twists of metal wire attached. I stared at them, reaching under to touch them, my hand a sick yellow in the fog lights. I pulled a strap toward me. It had been badly chopped, with shallow slashes around the severed edge. The attached wire was frayed for inches above the cut end.

Feeling the slimy cold of the plane's belly, I withdrew my hand. My fingers were black with oil or dirt.

I stood abruptly, keeping my hand well away from my

clothes. I'd had enough. I was chilled through and more than a little freaked out.

I looked over my shoulder at the dark shape of the cabin. I considered angling the car to cast some light on it, to check the porch or peer into a window. But what was the point?

Brad's truck would be here if he was.

And what would I say to him, anyway?

I climbed back into the rental, wiping my hand on the back of the passenger seat. I carefully turned the car around and headed home.

I'd come seeking reassurance and I'd found greater worry. I'd found Brad's plane, apparently set to drop objects from beneath, its jerry-rigged straps and wires severed. I'd come to hear Brad's impassioned denial and instead found evidence of his guilt.

But I didn't understand why he'd done it. I wasn't even sure why it had seemed essential to check.

It was almost too hard to think about.

I'd driven to the end of the long gravel road, nearly to the greenery-flanked incline, when I heard the explosion. It bucked my car, skittering it over the remainder of muddy grit onto the pocked pavement of the mountain road. I screeched to a stop, fishtailing with panic, and looked over my shoulder. Several hundred feet back, Brad Rommel's plane roared with leaping flames.

I ground my gears, my first instinct to get farther away. But I made myself wait and watch a little longer. I watched the plane burn red and hot, bathing the cabin and woods in flickering golden light. I watched it, remembering that I'd crouched there not ten minutes earlier.

My fears had centered on the gloom and the fog and the creaking of the woods. I'd been ten minutes from disaster, and I hadn't felt it, hadn't found room for it in my foreboding.

I slumped in the driver's seat, watching in my rearview mirror as the fire consumed the plane.

It was like a Roman torch, localized and sputtering. The fire made no move to leap to wet trees or travel damp ground to the cabin. The plane was parked well away from either, in fact—purposely, I now suspected. Even if the fire was spotted from some other remote cabin, it would look like a big bonfire, staying put, igniting nothing but its own fuel. Not likely anyone would phone for a fire truck—even if one were available tonight. No, the fire would burn itself out, leaving only scorched gravel and melted parts. And I supposed Brad Rommel would get rid of those somehow. With luck, no one would know the plane had been here.

If I said nothing. If I told no one.

If I opted to keep my client free of other accusations so that I could win his murder trial.

Guilty or not.

CHAPTER

Fifteen

MY PREDOMINANT EMOTION, AS I DROVE BACK INTO TOWN, was anger. Why the hell had I gone out there? Why did I always have to push things? When had it ever done me any good to barge in and demand—of all things!—reassurance. Now what was I supposed to do? Get my client rearrested after exploiting every loophole to get him out on bond? Confront him and urge him to turn himself in though he'd never get bail again?

I'd climbed my high horse, challenging Connie Gold's ethics. And now, if I did nothing, if I withheld evidence of a crime, what did that say about my ethics?

I saw a mental image of my uncle, crushed by the destruction of his hardest-won project. I thought about the cab driver paying more for his child's insulin, his daughter having nothing to do after school—a feeling I recalled too well.

I was three or four minutes up the highway from the courthouse/police/sheriff/coroner/DA complex, a cement four-story whose top floor was the county jail.

Uncertain whether to go there, I pulled into the parking

lot of a small bar on the northern edge of town. Usually at
this time of night, traffic on the highway was light, mostly
rigs driving the long road to Portland. Tonight there was
plenty of southbound traffic, but no other hint of disaster,
not a scent or glimpse of the fire five miles up the road. Only
the glow of the bar's neon in the fog, the hiss of truck
wheels on wet highway, the stench of beer and exhaust and
nearby mud flats.

I climbed out of the car. Judging from the number of
pickup trucks around me, the bar was full of Friday-night
cowboys, men with leathery faces and Oklahoma accents
maintained for generations in rural pockets with names like
Elkhorn and Eel. Men to whom the destruction of a mall
wouldn't mean much, men who didn't know they were fast
becoming living history.

Luckily, I didn't have to go inside. The pay phone was by
the door. I dropped in some quarters.

It was after eleven. I found Sandy at home.

I interrupted his immediate enthusiastic recounting of
what he and Osmil had done that night. All that, so huge in
my consciousness six hours ago, seemed like nothing much,
nothing important, nothing about me.

"The Southshore Mall, the big ugly one when you first
drive into town—"

"You've got but one mall," he pointed out. "What about
it?"

"It's on fire. They think someone dumped firebombs or
napalm or something like that from a small plane. It ignited
gas and chemicals—it's burning like a son-of-a-bitch." I
could hear an old Johnny Cash song on the jukebox inside.
"My uncle's out there now."

"Anybody inside when it happened?"

"I don't know. Maybe in the theaters. The stores close at
six or seven." Hillsdale hadn't made it into ten-to-ten culture yet. "Sandy?"

When I didn't speak for a moment, he said, "Are you okay? Laura?"

"I had this paranoia. You know Brad Rommel's got a plane?"

"Yuh, I remember from the bail hearing." The prosecution had argued he might fly off into the sunset to avoid prosecution.

"I drove up to his place to see if he was around. I guess reassure myself his plane was miles away at the airport."

"You drove there this time of night? What happened? What did he say? Nothing happened to you?"

"No, no. I'm fine. I'm back in town."

"So tell me." Sandy's voice had dropped in timbre, as it always did when he got protective of me. "You didn't have a problem with him? You're all right?"

"He wasn't there, just the plane."

"Jee-sus! The plane was there? I thought it got impounded."

"It did. I guess he violated the court order and flew it home." So much for airport security. "But here's the weird part: I checked it out. It was rigged to hold something on the bottom."

"What are you thinking? Bombs?" Concern made his voice tight.

"As I drove away, the plane blew up. It just burst into flames, Sandy, just blew up right there."

I listened to him breathe.

"Sandy?"

"I want you to go someplace nobody knows you—a motel or something—and wait for me. I can be on the road in—"

"No, that's silly. My uncle will be home in a while; the house has good locks; and, really, this can't have anything to do with me. Nobody knew I'd be going to Brad's—nobody even knows I'm in town."

"I could be there in five, six hours."

"Take the morning flight in. You won't be much later and—"

"Did you see the bomb before it blew?"

"I have no idea. I don't know what plane parts look like, much less bombs."

"Got a paper and pencil handy?"

"Why?"

"While it's fresh in your memory, draw some pictures, draw in everything you remember."

"What does it matter where the bomb was, Sandy? I mean, it was certainly there someplace. Planes don't just explode."

"No, no, listen to me. If it was a bomb with a timer, then the plane was supposed to be gotten rid of as evidence, you follow me? He flies it home, rigs the timer so he's long gone, and leaves it to blow up."

"Yeah?" That was the only possibility I'd considered. I felt a stirring of hope. Maybe there was a less inculpating explanation.

"But on the other hand, it could have been set up with some kind of sensor. Triggered when people started handling it, but set to go off X minutes after the motion stopped."

"They have bombs like that?"

He snorted. "They got bombs that do just about anything. But you see the point? If someone stole Rommel's plane then left it on his doorstep, the person would want it found there."

"Why blow it up afterward?"

"Something about the bomb setup? Something pointing to the person who really did it? Did you see anything to tell you how the bombs were rigged?"

"There were leather straps and wires on the bottom. They'd been cut probably with a long-handled gardening tool that was inside the plane—"

"No way!"

"No, really, I saw it."

"No damn way, Laura. I'm sorry, but there's no way you could open an airplane door while you're flying and cut some strap. You'd never be able to gauge where you were going to drop your load."

"The mall's a block square. He'd have some room to maneuver."

"Not enough." A pause. "Well, that says a hell of a lot right there. Say the cops go up there and they check out the plane and they see the straps and all. Their first thought's going to be, Nah, you couldn't release a bundle this way. But then they back off to talk or whatever and blam, the plane blows up. They can extrapolate from the fact it was booby-trapped. But they can't prove Rommel didn't have the greatest damn luck ever and cut the strap at just the perfect moment. Rommel, I take it, is not a mechanically-inclined person?"

"I don't know."

"We'll find out. Maybe his plane blew up to keep anyone from seeing how complex the mechanism was."

As unlikely as it sounded—Rommel framed by some brilliant mad bomber—I found myself desperate to believe it.

"You haven't been to the cops with this yet, have you?" Sandy was asking, not accusing.

"No."

"You're wondering whether to."

"Yes." Maybe I should. If Sandy was right, maybe this would tend to exonerate Rommel.

"It complicates things, you being his lawyer. If the cops had found the plane, it might occur to them it was a frame. But you finding it? They won't be sure you're telling the whole, exact truth. Especially if they think you waited awhile to talk to them about it."

"I'm only ten minutes off schedule, Sandy. I stopped at a pay phone on my way back to town. I'm only a couple of miles up from the county building."

"Do you want to talk to the cops?"

"I'm supposed to." I'd found evidence of a crime. I was an officer of the court, wasn't I? A law-enforcement official just like Connie Gold. One who prided herself on using the rules, not breaking them.

"Of course you're supposed to." It was clear from his tone he knew that didn't settle the matter. "It's not your life, it's Rommel's," he pointed out. "You're supposed to be square with the police, and if it does hang Rommel, well, Rommel's Rommel and you're you."

"No lawyer is an island."

Just then a big-bellied man in a shearling jacket stomped out of the bar, guffawing at the joke of a bleached blonde at least a decade his senior. He drowned out Sandy's comment.

"I don't know what I want to do," I said unnecessarily. He'd surely gathered that.

"You don't have any idea where Rommel is? We could find him, talk to him first. See if we can get him to go to the cops with you."

"How would I explain the delay? Especially if we don't find him for a while?"

"Best you can."

"And Brad's pissed at the cops big time. I can't see him going with me."

"Why don't you sit tight and wait for me? I should be there by sunrise."

A cloud of cigarette smoke and the reek of old beer followed the ample couple. They didn't climb into a truck. They staggered cheerfully along the sidewalk, ignoring the highway traffic, probably heading to one of the dozen motels down the road. Be there by sunrise: exactly what that cowboy would have said, I'll bet.

"No, really, don't be gallant—get some sleep. The morning flight will get you here early enough. I wouldn't drive all night."

"For me? Hell you wouldn't." He sounded sure.

"Take the first flight in." There were only two flights a day, so he knew which I meant. "I'd rather see you a few hours later and not have you be groggy."

Another silence.

"I'm going to bed, Sandy; I wouldn't be awake when you got here anyway. And you'll freak my uncle out, coming to the door in the middle of the night. Come in the morning. I'll pick you up at the gate."

"You're sure nobody knows you're in town?"

"Uncle Henry and Jay Bartoli. That's it."

"And you're okay at your uncle's?"

"Definitely."

"Are you going back there now? Or stopping off at the sheriff's?"

"Going home to bed."

He made a sharp, closed-lip sound.

"What does that mean, Sandy?"

"I didn't say anything."

"Like hell."

"You won't get hassled for waiting a while, an hour or two, maybe even till the fire's under control and the cops stop being so busy. But I would give it a very serious think before you go on home. In fact, I wouldn't go home unless you're sure you're not telling."

He was right. Going home would deprive me of any excuse for waiting. "I could play dumb. Say I went up there to visit my client, saw his plane but didn't think anything of it."

"Silly little you."

"I can't go to the police yet. The least question and they'll revoke his bail. I don't want to screw Brad over."

"You could be doing that by not going."

"I need to think things through."

A pause, into which I read a decision to be loyal rather than right. "Anything special I should bring tomorrow?"

"The usual. Dress for hot weather."

I heard him chuckle as I replaced the receiver.

Of course Sandy hadn't offered a miracle answer; I hadn't expected one. But calling him had broken my connection with irrational hope. I felt worse than ever.

I climbed back into my car, remembering a ride I'd taken with Brad once. We were seniors in high school and my romance with Gary Gleason was off again. I wasn't supposed to date at all—Aunt Diana had persuaded my father I was too wild to be trusted. So I cried out when a police car tried to pull us over, probably for speeding. Knowing my situation—that the cops would recognize the mayor's niece and mention this to him—Brad floored it, outrunning the cruiser. They'd gotten his license number, of course, catching up with him later. He'd paid a fine, maybe even had his driving privileges suspended; I didn't remember.

When I next saw him in Hillsdale High's corridor, his eye was swollen shut. A passing jock had shouted, "Your old man finally sober up enough to hit straight?" Brad rushed away when he saw me coming. I don't think he realized that my family, my aunt—though seemingly top drawer—was as ferocious an embarrassment to me as his father was to him.

When I finally caught up to him, he denied he'd done anything to keep me out of trouble. He rejected my gratitude gruffly and utterly, and he never asked me out again.

I tried to tell myself I still owed him. It would have been nice to bathe my reluctance in the soft sepia of an old favor. When I reached Clarke Street, I'd almost persuaded myself that was part of the reason. But most of it, I knew, was moral sloth. I might talk a fine game, but responsibility was so exhausting.

My uncle hadn't returned yet. I expected he'd stay with the fire until weariness and Johnnie Walker cut the legs out from under him. I left him a short note saying I was back home and in bed. Then I hurried upstairs to make that so.

But I didn't sleep through the night. The extension phone on my night table woke me at about four in the morning. With all that had happened, I didn't leave it for the answering machine. I picked up.

It was Jay Bartoli. "Sorry to wake you." His tone was all business, as if coworkers listened. "I'm phoning in my official capacity to ask if you know the whereabouts of your client, Bradley Rommel."

"No." By now police had checked the airport's roster of local pilots. But were they waking everyone on the list? Or had they found the charred plane beside Brad's cabin? "I haven't spoken to Brad since after Tuesday's hearing. What's up?" I tried to sound more curious than worried.

"We're unable to locate him. We're about to execute a warrant to search his house. Our deputies went up there earlier and found the remains of a small aircraft." He paused for my reaction.

I couldn't think of one.

"The aircraft burned up or blew up last night or this morning in front of his house."

"That's not where he kept it. He kept it at the airport."

Bartoli was silent.

"I'd like to be there when you search my client's house." Though it was customary for the DA to be present during a search, it was a courtesy rarely afforded defense counsel. "Could you swing it for me, Jay?"

"I guess." He sounded pleased I knew it was a favor. "You'll have to park at the end of the paved road and let us escort you the rest of the way up. We're still sifting debris from the plane."

"No sign of Brad?"

"No."

"How bad's the plane?"

"It's a shell."

"Did it crash?"

"We don't wish to speculate." His voice was pure deputy: opaque, formal, slightly impatient.

"You're assuming it was used to bomb the mall."

"I can't comment on an investigation in progress."

"But you don't have any proof of that, do you?"

"I can't comment."

I rubbed my eyes, trying to decide whether to press for answers or show my gratitude by shutting up. "Thanks a lot, Jay. I appreciate the call."

"No problem." He sounded a little relieved.

"Is the mall fire under control?"

"Pretty close."

"Anybody dead?"

"Everybody in the theater got out fine. Fire started at the other end, and the theater's got good sprinklers. Probably not going to have much damage there. A few laggers got wet; that's about the worst of it from that end."

"So no casualties?" His "from that end" suggested otherwise.

"I'm afraid we've got one body on the south side. The mall was closed, but . . . We're worried about finding other bodies—teenagers hang around there. But we haven't had any reports of missing persons. Not yet."

"Whose body? Do you know?"

"We can't tell much from what's left. We'll have to check dental records."

I didn't want that to sink in, not until I was fully awake. "Is the mall going to be a total loss?"

"I never saw a fire so big, but I'm no expert. Your uncle's probably the one to ask about that."

I assumed Uncle Henry was home in bed by now. I didn't ask Bartoli. I'd already spent too much time on the phone. The deputies wouldn't wait for me to begin searching Brad's cabin. "I'll be up there as soon as I'm dressed, Jay. Thanks again."

I hurried. Freezing dampness had seeped through the

walls, making everything—towels, clothes, shoes—clammy and cold. I didn't relish a shivering drive through dense fog. But I was even less happy about seeing Connie Gold—and lying by omission to her and to the deputies.

I tried to collect my wits. Where was Brad Rommel?

For the first time, it sank in: the reticent kid who'd outrun the police and endured a black eye for me might have grown up to become a killer and a bomber.

Jay Bartoli used to wrestle with Brad, play ball with him, go camping with his brother. Maybe that's why Jay had been willing to discuss the case with me until now; he hadn't believed it of an old friend, either. Maybe today he too felt the hackles of uncertainty rise.

I found Uncle Henry slumped at the dining-room table, papers spread over its oiled wood. His face was ashen. Dark circles made slits of his eyes. Even at his drunkest, he didn't look this sick, this old. I stepped beside him, putting my hand on his shoulder.

"I think they're going to accuse Brad Rommel of bombing the mall." Looking down, I could see how much his gray hair had thinned. I could feel how sharp his bones were under his cardigan. The divorce had aged him. His son was gone, his cousin (my father) was dead. Now this.

His head drooped forward. The mall had been his jewel, the one improvement he'd made in a community of dying industries. "Did he do it, Laura?"

"I don't know."

He turned with the suddenness of a striking mongoose, knocking my hand from his shoulder. "Screw the son-of-a-bitch!" His eyes were bright, his lips pulled away from his teeth. "How can you defend a bastard like that?"

I took a shocked step back. "I can't drop him as a client. Everyone would assume I knew he was guilty. That I dropped him because of you."

"Damn it!" He leaped from the chair. "He bombed the

best thing—practically the only good thing—about this county! You're *not* going to get him off scot free!''

The best thing about a county with miles of abandoned beach, first-growth redwoods, plants so lush and ancient it seemed a historic miracle to walk among them? The best thing was its mall?

"I know how you feel.'' To my uncle, trees were goods to harvest, plants were nuisances to clear. Progress and prosperity mattered. "But listen. All they have on Brad is that his plane burned up last night. Someone could be trying to frame him.''

"Oh, don't give me your lawyer bullshit! I get enough of lawyers all day long!'' He sank heavily back into his chair.

I scanned the table for his usual bottle of Johnnie Walker, seeing instead only lists of bankers and developers.

My uncle was sober. His anger was unmitigated. I bent to give him a quick hug. He reeked of smoke from the mall fire.

He shouted something at me as I walked out. Whatever it was, it would wait. The search warrant wouldn't.

CHAPTER

Sixteen

IT SHOCKED ME HOW LITTLE OF THE PLANE REMAINED. IT was a mere skeleton of itself, most of its guts smothered under thick foam. No fire truck could be spared, but available county fire extinguishers had been rushed to the scene in sheriff's cars. They'd been enough to quell what was left of the blaze, which had been close to burning itself out when the deputies came to question Rommel.

The area around it was bright with police spotlights and deputies on hands and knees systematically searching the area. A single fire marshal stood talking to a plainclothes investigator, shaking his head. As I walked past with Jay Bartoli, I heard him say, "No way in the world your people go near that plane for another four hours at least. Make sure everything's cold, good and cold, 'cause you just can't tell sometimes. All it takes is one ember and a few drops of fuel still in the tank, and you've got burned deputies."

The air stank of scorched rubber and smoke and fire-fighting chemicals. We kept our distance going uphill toward the house. I stopped for a moment to gawk.

"All that foam, Jay," I observed. "Are you sure it's Rommel's plane?"

"Whether it is or not," Bartoli stopped walking, "I don't have to tell you there's a difference between enough evidence to get a search warrant and enough to get an arrest warrant."

"If it's his plane, you're going to arrest him for arson?" I infused my tone with shock I didn't feel.

"We've got a dead body on our hands, so we're looking at manslaughter in addition to arson."

"This"—I gestured toward the plane—"could be a frame."

"It doesn't matter if it's his plane. He's got a pilot's license. A witness saw a plane circling the mall before the fire. And here's a goddamn plane. Rommel needs to come forward and explain this." He gestured toward the froth-soaked shell. "We informed the court that we're unable to locate him, by the way."

"You've only been looking for him, what, two hours? Three? A three-hour absence is hardly bail jumping."

"But remaining available is a condition of his bond." One side of his face was white from the harsh searchlights around the plane. The other was golden with light spilling from the cabin windows and porch. "If Rommel's not back soon to explain this, we'll get his bail revoked. We'll go after him."

He seemed braced for protest. But deputies were already searching Brad's cabin. I'd argue later, when it might make a difference.

I started toward the porch. Before I got there, Connie Gold appeared in the door, dramatically narrow in slacks and a square-shouldered jacket. In silhouette, she looked like a stretched claymation figure, in danger of disappearing if she turned sideways.

"Counselor," she said irritably. She glowered at Bartoli. "On whose authority did you bring Ms. Di Palma?"

"She's Rommel's attorney." He stated the obvious.

"But on whose— Oh, never mind." She turned and went back inside. "Let's get on with it."

The source of her testiness (beyond nature and nurture) became clear within the hour. Rommel's house had been searched a number of times already. Everything of possible legal detriment had been long since tagged and removed.

We remained at opposite ends of each room as it was searched, careful not to discuss Rommel or our case or the mall bombing. As we had nothing else in common, we stood in frosty silence, watching beefy sheriff's investigators sort through papers and teaspoons and bed linen and toiletries, finding nothing of particular interest, but evidence-bagging everything not immediately identifiable. Brad Rommel would again return home to find his colognes and after-shaves gone to the lab for analysis, this time to determine if they'd been used to make firebombs.

Eventually, the cabin brightened with the dawn. Even ransacked, it retained a mountain hominess enhanced by a wood stove, a rag rug, and afghan-covered couches. The one thing it lacked was framed photographs. Brad had several scattered over walls and dressers the last time I was here. But most of them had been of himself and Cathy Piatti—at parties, skiing, kayaking on vacation. I guessed he couldn't bear to have her smiling at him from happier times.

I made a list of everything the deputies bagged. I doubted any of it would help the cops, but it might help Brad to have the list, if only to shop for replacements.

The things I'd dreaded seeing—leather straps, buckles, wire—they didn't find in Brad's house.

I was relieved to step out into the cold morning. Nothing obviously damaging to Brad had been discovered in the cabin.

As Bartoli and I walked the margin of the driveway, one of the men sifting gravel for clues looked up. "They know yet whose plane it is?" he wondered.

I stopped, turning to Jay. Connie Gold was just a few yards behind us, returning to her car.

"That's not Rommel's plane?" I accused him.

He hesitated, glowering at the big-mouthed deputy.

"Is that Brad Rommel's plane?" I repeated.

From behind me, Gold said, "His plane was impounded by order of the court." Her tone was sarcastic. "As you should know."

"Orders can be violated." It was an effort not to add "you sneaky bitch."

"Mr. Rommel's plane remains booted at the Dungeness Airfield."

"Then whose plane is this? Where did it come from?"

Bartoli said, "We won't know till the fire marshal says it's okay to pick through it."

The sun had risen behind a wall of white cloud. Above the torn-paper silhouette of trees, the sky glowed like a yellow pearl. In the pale light, the skeleton of the plane dripped foam in spots, steamed in others.

"When we find out where Rommel got the plane," Gold said sourly, "we'll be sure to let you know."

I didn't turn. "You and your Hollywood agent?"

I continued walking with Bartoli.

"Someone's out to frame him, Jay," I said. "Leaving this plane here and blowing it up so you couldn't get prints off it. Someone's after Brad Rommel. You've got to protect him." I stopped, putting my hand on his sleeve. "Maybe you believe he's innocent, maybe you don't. But the possibility exists. You've got to protect him."

"If we can find him," Jay said simply. "Though I doubt he'd want our protection."

Until this moment, I'd have insisted the police keep away from my client, allow him his privacy despite the fact that he was under indictment and legitimately their concern. "This plane changes everything. What if he'd come home and seen it parked there? He could have been blown up with it."

If the bomb had in fact been rigged with a motion sensor, it might easily have been intended as a trap for Brad.

"If you'd found Brad's body in the plane or near it, you'd have assumed he'd flown it, wouldn't you? You'd have closed the books on the Piatti case and on the mall bombing both, wouldn't you?"

Jay looked down at me with his best poker face. "I really couldn't speculate."

"I wish you'd told me it wasn't Rommel's plane," I fretted.

As if I could have done something useful. I looked at my watch. Five hours until Sandy arrived. I wished I'd let him be chivalrous, after all.

CHAPTER

Seventeen

By the time Sandy arrived, we knew the worst. The body at the south end of the mall wasn't a loitering teenager, as Jay had feared. But I almost wished it had been. I wished it had been some stranger, some random tragedy, not part of my case.

Burnt beyond recognition was the woman Brad Rommel was accused of murdering. Cathy Piatti's body had finally turned up.

It proved Brad hadn't tossed Piatti off his boat. But it eliminated the hope of finding her alive. And the corpse was too badly burnt to establish date or cause of death. The DA would probably attempt to prove Rommel had stashed Piatti somewhere, bleeding her to keep her quiet.

Connie Gold, pointing to the charred plane in Brad's driveway, would probably accuse him not only of murder but of bombing the mall.

I sat in the municipal-airport waiting room—two rows of connected orange plastic seats—staring at gray-and-blue-flecked linoleum and listening to the clatter of an ancient pinball machine. Sandy's flight would be filled with free-lance reporters. The ones from UPI and AP and *Newsweek* had arrived in leased planes already. Those from the Bay Area had driven up in camera-intensive vans. They all wanted to talk to Brad Rommel today. Unfortunately, they'd settle for me.

I recalled a thousand instances of people rapping at the door for my Uncle Henry, his eyes lighting as conviviality (real or assumed) hit him like a shot of whiskey. And after the shouting roomful had cleared, it took several shots to wind him back down. Just like me and my vodka.

Except that my uncle seemed to enjoy it. And I was tired of publicity. I was tired of limelight and reproach, of framing cautious responses that were sardonically accepted but never believed. I was in the business of speaking for the record. But sooner or later, I always seemed to succumb to the desire to really say something. It had cost me my last job. I'd have to be careful to keep myself in check this time. The prospect made me weary.

Right on cue, a reporter from *Time* magazine pushed through the door. Sandy's plane had landed without my noticing.

The reporter walked swiftly by, hitching the straps of his camera and carry-on. Bill something—I'd met him several times, unfortunately—glanced at me, walked on, stopped. Then he turned back, a smile of wondering good fortune stretching his lean face.

"Di Palma!" He spoke the name with a collegiality he had no right to feel. "You're not gonna diddy?" Diddy-mau-mau: decades-old slang for "leave." Like Bill's pony-tail and denim workshirt, it was supposed to tell the world he was a hippie at heart. A hippie who wrote for *Time* magazine, organ of the dull, long-winded middle.

"I'm meeting someone." It was no use being rude, just

as it was no use being friendly. Neither would change his behavior.

He sat on the plastic seat next to me, letting his bags slide to the floor. "Have you talked to Brad Rommel today?"

"No." I watched the door to the airport's only gate. An older man and woman, as plump and colorfully dressed as Care Bears, entered together.

"When was the last time you talked to him?" Bill kept his tone casual, as if that would lull me into relaxed chat.

I ignored the question. "I'm going to go look for my party." I stood and walked away, certain he'd follow. But I'd rather have him trailing behind than sitting beside me.

I hadn't taken five steps before Sandy entered, duffel slung carelessly over his shoulder, laptop case in his hand. His glance over my head told me Bill was indeed close behind. His greeting was a public "Hello. Which way to the car?" His free arm went around me, turning me. We marched almost into and hastily past Bill. But our problems came from behind.

A hand on my shoulder nearly pulled me off balance. By the time I recovered equilibrium, a half-dozen people had surged past to stand in front of me. Sandy positioned himself as a shield.

I remembered other times he'd blocked me from cameras, offering me the option of shuffling behind his bulldozing body. He'd be expecting my hand on his back now, motioning him to move aside. It didn't pay to run from reporters. Might as well refuse to comment, or make some vacant, unincriminating statement. To push past was to invite misinterpretation. Whereas in these investigatively moribund days, the press was likely to quote even obvious bullshit without comment.

I could feel Sandy's surprise at my hesitation. He glanced over his shoulder, his brows high with inquiry.

"Let's go," I said. "Let's just diddy."

"Oh, come on, Ms. Palma," one of the reporters protested. "Give us a minute."

A photographer added, "Quick pose, okay? Get this guy out of the way, okay?"

Sandy began to walk in the wide, step-aside manner of the cop he'd been. I followed as if sewn to his jacket.

"Ms. Di Palma, where is Bradley Rommel?"

"How did Catherine Piatti end up at the mall? Was she alive or dead?"

"Are you just arriving from San Francisco, Ms. Di Palma? Did your client call you?"

I heard the whir of a video camera behind me and made the mistake of turning. On some station tonight there would be footage of me looking foolish and startled and underdressed.

Sandy kept walking, preceded by backward-trotting reporters.

"Ms. Di Palma, can you tell us about the airplane?" "Can you tell us where your client is?" "Is Bradley Rommel in custody?" "Was Catherine Piatti already dead?" "Can you comment?" "A few quick photographs—get your best side." "Come on, Laura, give us a smile." "Give us a break." "Give us your take on this."

They surrounded the car when we finally got there, video cameras hoisted and microphones outstretched. I drove through them carefully, conscious of my desire to plow over them, give them my "take" for real. I watched their gestures of anger and disappointment in my rearview mirror. They might not get another crack at me before their sound bites were due at the station.

Leaving the airport parking lot, I suppressed the desire to turn north instead of south. My cousin Hal was in Alaska, indulging his antisocial nature. It sounded like a fine idea to me.

"Getting a little harder to believe it wasn't supposed to be you," Sandy commented.

"What wasn't supposed to be me?"

"Kinsley."

I'd almost forgotten about Kinsley. "Why?"

"Because trouble's following you everywhere you go."

Just what I wanted to hear.

CHAPTER

Eighteen

Sandy and I noticed the commotion before we rounded the corner onto Clarke. We glimpsed the yellow plastic of police-line tape in the ravine. The heavy sky muted reds and blues from swirling police lights.

"Uncle Henry." Fear strangled me.

I nearly slammed into two uniformed officers standing in the middle of the road. I braked to a whiplash stop.

"No ambulance. Wrong vehicles," Sandy pointed out. A city cruiser and a sheriff's car blocked the street. More surprising, a hazardous-waste car with a nuclear symbol was parked directly in front of my house.

Sandy was right; the scene didn't suggest injury. A crime was being investigated.

"Brad showed up." I replaced one foreboding with another. "Maybe they arrested him for arson." I hoped I'd arrived in time to keep him from saying anything.

"They blocked off the gully," Sandy contradicted. No need to throw up a police line if Rommel was in custody. Unless he'd led a chase. Unless, perhaps, he was hiding there. "Reporters five minutes behind us," he reminded me.

I'd have to do some fast thinking after some even faster inquiry. I jumped out of the car, not bothering to pull it over.

The sheriff's deputy and city cop I'd almost hit were in my face before I took two steps.

"You'll have to leave the area." The cop waved me away without really looking at me.

"My uncle lives there." I pointed to the Victorian, wondering if Uncle Henry was inside. I needed to know he was safe. Since my father's death, my uncle seemed a fragile and transitory blessing. "Henry Di Palma." I guessed they knew it was the mayor's house. "Is he all right?"

"Yeah." The deputy seemed surprised by the question. The city cop trotted over to his cruiser, speaking into the radio. "But you'll have to move your car. We don't want it getting hit."

Sandy, whom I hadn't noticed behind me, muttered, "I'll take care of it."

"What's going on?" I demanded. If Brad Rommel was in the ravine, I wanted to know now, before anyone began to question him.

There was shouting and commotion to our left, coming from the Victorian's backyard. I gave the deputy a second to say something. When he didn't, I slid by to see for myself.

At least two men tried to stop me as I walked through the side yard past the dripping rhododendrons and rosebushes. "I live here," I informed them, and walked on.

In the backyard, where the lawn rolled down to a deep tangle of gully, Jay Bartoli squatted beside something. Whatever it was, there were tarps on the lawn around it. Men with Ziploc evidence bags walked from the site. Two photographers stood chatting, cameras dangling from their hands. A half-empty sack of plaster littered a flower bed.

Apparently casts of footprints had been taken, evidence had been gathered and bagged, photographs had been snapped. In the two hours since I'd left the house.

I approached Bartoli and the tarps with trepidation. This couldn't be about Rommel; the scene was wrong for a capture and an arrest. Clearly, they'd found a thing, not a person. Even from across the yard, I could see that Bartoli stared at something no bigger than a small dog.

Within two paces, I knew it was a bucket. Another rusty old fisherman's bucket.

I stopped, conscious of my feet sinking slightly into the damp lawn. Bartoli, as if sensing me behind him, looked over his shoulder. The men who'd tried to stop me walked past, conferring with Bartoli as he stood.

I approached more slowly now that I knew what they'd found. Jay maintained eye contact with me as he spoke to the men, saying, "Call in that I'm questioning her."

Sandy caught up to me, grabbing my elbow and murmuring in my ear, "You'll get more out of Bartoli alone. I'm going to go chat up the help." He was gone so suddenly I wasn't sure the conversation had happened at all.

Jay met me at the edge of a blue tarp. He gestured behind him. "I was having a last look before the HazMat people take it to the lab."

Hazardous material—blood was among the scariest since identification of the AIDS virus.

"We've been over the yard area. We're out there now"—he gestured at the gully—"expanding the scope. Seeing if we can get a lead."

I stepped past him, but he thrust his arm in front of me to bar my way.

"I'm not going to touch it, Jay. I just want to see how much is in the bucket."

"More," he said simply.

The other bucket had contained one and a half liters, not a fatal blood loss, but close to it. If this one contained more, all from the same person, then that person was dead for sure.

"It's Brad's blood," I worried. "I thought I'd find you

out here arresting him. But I'll bet it's his blood. I'll bet that's why I haven't heard from him.''

"If he did all this—the mall, this bucket—he's long gone; that's what I think. We'll be meeting with Connie Gold as soon as we're done here." Jay's face was pinched, creped with tiny lines like an old cowboy's. "See about revoking bail."

"You're talking about Brad Rommel." We'd smoked joints with him, hung out (in my case, sneaked out) with him. "Not just somebody."

"It's been a long time since we knew him, Laura. Nice kids harden up over the years. The best stuff gets layered over." He gripped my arm. "Everybody in prison has child-hood friends that remember good things about them." But his eyes were bright with the plea that I contradict him.

It struck a sour note, somehow. Brad was my client; I'd renewed the connection. But Brad and Jay had been out of touch for over twenty years. What made Jay so sure? So maudlin?

He let go of my arm, blinking at whatever he saw in my face.

I repeated, "I want to look at the bucket."

He didn't stop me this time.

I took a few cautious paces forward. The air smelled strongly of pine and skunk cabbage and mud, as if the tramping of men had broken some settled membrane and released the essence of the gully. The wind rustled through its broad-leafed plants, whistling the anthem of cold foliage. In the center of the tarps on a tiny patch of uncovered lawn was the bucket, dented and rough with rust. Inside, filling it to the two-thirds mark, blood had congealed to a purplish pulp almost as thick as liver. A few small oak leaves were trapped on its surface, a few pine needles, what might be bits of lichen or ash. In spots, the surface was depressed as if pocked by water drops. The whole bucket, including contents, was glazed with condensed fog. I guessed it had been outside awhile, at least overnight.

I stood still, willing the bucket to tell me on some cellular level that it contained Brad Rommel. But it spoke to me only as an anomalous horror in my own backyard. I felt nothing more than that.

I wasn't sure why I thought I should, why it came as such a surprise that I didn't.

I turned back to Jay. "What do you know so far?"

"We got a call telling us Rommel was in your backyard." His face flushed. He tugged at the collar of his shirt. "The officer who checked the tip found the blood. The call came in at eight fifty-six this morning."

Right after I left the house. "Rommel didn't put this here." I watched Jay carefully. Maybe he knew different. "Why would he? I'm his lawyer. Whatever kind of statement this makes, I'm not the person to make it to."

"Maybe the statement has to do with you." Bartoli cocked his head. "It's got to have crossed your mind."

"What?"

"That Rommel's got a thing about you."

"No way." My surprise couldn't have been more genuine. "It's all business, believe me."

"He had a thing about you in high school." Bartoli talked over my attempt to interrupt. "Your breeding and your brains and how confident you were, how you were like Queen Elizabeth or somebody. Somebody imperious."

"Every teenager's imperious," I protested. "It's practically the definition of adolescence. Look, I don't know or care how he felt twenty years ago. There's nothing but business to our relationship now." I'd let him rattle me. "Whoever called you wanted you to find this. Whoever called you put it here. But it wasn't Brad. Brad didn't do any of this." I almost added, I can feel it.

Bartoli scowled at me. I couldn't think why. And why seemed important.

"Did you find footprints?" I tried to get things back on track.

"A few partials, we think."

"You think?"

"When the ground's this wet a big dog stepping on a leaf can make a mark that'll pass for a partial." He took two steps closer. "I'm not kidding about Rommel," he said, with an urgency disproportionate to the situation. "He was really gone on you. He had a thing about your power."

"My power?" I'd felt enslaved to my family, to my Aunt Diana's "appearances."

"Whatever you'd call it." His eyes were red-rimmed, his cheeks aflame. He looked almost ill. But then he'd had very little sleep.

His voice grew husky. "He really loved you, Laura."

I felt the hairs on my neck rise. I'd slept with Jay once when I was nineteen. I'd gone to him when my husband was unfaithful because I'd known he'd say yes. What if Jay was projecting his then feelings about me onto Rommel? What would that do to his investigation? To my case?

"Brad doesn't have a 'thing' about me. I'd have picked up on it if he did," I insisted.

"You would?" His tone made me wonder if I'd missed noticing something, not about Rommel but about him.

"Don't revoke his bond, Jay."

"You know it's a condition of bail that he remain available."

"That doesn't mean he can't go camping in the land above his cabin for half a day."

"Are you saying that's where he is?"

"That's where he might be; you don't have any reason to think otherwise. It hasn't even been twelve hours." But I was unsure of both my facts and my law. I'd never had a client on bail drop out of sight.

"Don't kid yourself." Bartoli's lips curled. "We have

enough evidence right now to arrest him for this.'' He nodded toward the bucket.

"You don't even know what that is. It could be cow blood.'' I wanted to smack Bartoli for playing sudden hardball.

"We're going to get more aggressive, Laura. You can count on it. If you hear from your client, better bring him in fast or he'll be sitting in a cell till his trial.''

No more calling Jay Bartoli for inside information, I was afraid.

Nineteen

From my bedroom window, I could see the last of the city cops straggle out of the gully to chat with sheriff's deputies rolling up tarps. Broken twigs of rhododendron, mashed berry vines and skunk cabbage leaves littered the yard. It had just begun to rain, dull and steady, hard enough to be inconvenient but not hard enough to be picturesque.

Behind me, Sandy said, "Maybe the rain'll get rid of the reporters."

They were out front, barred from the yard by adamant deputies. But once the cops pulled up stakes, the reporters weren't likely to respect my property rights. They weren't worth their wages if they did.

"God, I wish they weren't here." I turned to Sandy. "It gets so tiring."

I thought back on hundreds of interviews, some at my request and some unwilling. I was not only sick of reporters, I was sick of myself, of my usual responses, whether guarded or goaded. I was sick of my "spin," of my own manipulations. It struck me—horror struck me—that bouts with the press had made me good at Aunt Diana's appearances game. And that I was as unhappy playing it today as I'd been at sixteen.

"Designer crimes." Sandy lounged against the door, looking somber. "I don't like what's been happening to you since you heard Kinsley say that."

"Designer crimes?" I couldn't make the mental leap, not after a night of worrying about Brad Rommel. "Designer crimes is down there." San Francisco seemed a thousand miles away. "This is up here."

"And yet, no matter where you go, you've got trouble. Literally in your backyard." His shoulder unstuck from the door. He stood straight, but kept his distance. "I say let's find out if it's related. Let's move faster, do the obvious thing. Let's try to set More up."

"You've already eavesdropped on her and followed her," I pointed out.

"She knows we followed her—that's what has me worried. I want to try to turn that around, use it to help reel her in."

"Reel her in for what? We don't know she did anything but have dinner with her boyfriend." I felt almost lightheaded, trying to make the transition from Brad Rommel to Maryanne More. "Can't we talk about this later? We need to find Brad Rommel."

"Agreed. But when we get home, I want to approach More. Tell her we've been checking her out, trying to decide if she could help you get a little plain vanilla vengeance. We're already halfway there: she knows you hate Sayres, but that you can't prove anything or do much about him. You're in a perfect spot to tell her you want revenge— not a lawsuit, but revenge."

"I can't do that. She could go to the State Bar. They're not going to believe I was kidding." Days like this I almost wished I would be disbarred. I'd follow my cousin Hal to Alaska. I was glad we'd broken up, almost ready to be friends, certainly ready to visit him. More than ready to embrace hermitry.

"You could convince the State Bar you didn't mean it—if it came to that. It might take a little talking, is all. But you might not have to: you might find out exactly what Kinsley meant by designer crimes."

"Not if More has any sense. She won't do anything illegal—assuming she ever does—while they're investigating Kinsley's murder."

"No?" A quick scowl. "Last I heard it was illegal to eavesdrop electronically without a person's consent." He shook his head, taking two strides toward me. "Look, I've had my best talent working on this and I still can't get a clear set of tracks. We need to learn a hell of a lot more about it before something else happens."

"By having me pretend to order my own designer crime?" It was a silly notion. With only one thing to recommend it: "I wonder if they could get Sayres, really get him."

Sandy grinned. Then his attention shifted to the window behind me. "Reporters," he told me. "Want me to try to muscle them? Get them out of the yard?"

I had to laugh. "I admire your versatility. But no, better leave them. My uncle's not into gardening anyway. Let them stomp over stuff; what's it matter?"

"They're aiming their telephoto lenses at this here window."

"Parasites!" I stepped back. "Okay, go muscle them."

CHAPTER

Twenty

I WAS STARTING TO FEEL LIKE A YO-YO, FLUNG TO HILLS-
dale, yanked back to San Francisco. I'd meant to remain
north for a while this time. I assumed I'd be conferring with
Brad Rommel, consoling my uncle, investigating the new
developments. But Brad didn't get in touch with me. My
uncle was away at constant ad hoc meetings. And the sheriff's department most definitely didn't want me interview-
ing Cathy Piatti's friends and neighbors, not while they
were doing the same. They threatened to arrest Sandy if he
didn't stay away from Rommel's cabin and what remained
of the mall.

Sandy left Hillsdale Sunday evening; he had to testify in
a civil trial the next morning. I couldn't go with him. I
needed to remain long enough to defend Brad Rommel's
bail. I also hoped for word on the new bucket.

First thing Monday morning, I learned the blood belonged
to a human, but not one whose DNA was on file anyplace
the sheriff had thought to look. It wasn't Cathy Piatti's
blood; that much was certain.

The bucket—and, of course, the charred plane—outweighed my arguments. Brad's bail was revoked that morning. I went straight from the courthouse to the airport.

By afternoon I was back in San Francisco, back in my south-of-Market office. I sat at my desk trying to find things to do for the two minor-matter clients still in my Rolodex. My secretary had instructions not to put through, or even message-log, calls from reporters. Sandy was out of court, but not in his office; I didn't know where.

I was surprised when Maryanne More phoned, asking if I could spare her half an hour. I'd been contemplating, out of desperate frustration, making an appointment to see her. Sandy was right: at least it would be forward motion.

I sat in More's office in the gloom of a gray-sky day, again admiring her sullen chiaroscuros, her dark wood furniture. She was as well dressed as usual and as carefully groomed, but she looked awful. The puffiness around her eyes had settled into small pouches, pale blue and occasionally throbbing. Her skin was sallow under a sprinkling of freckles. Instead of attending to business, I blurted out, "Are you all right? Are you holding up?"

She nodded, then scowled. Finally shook her head. "When I heard the shots," her voice was a confiding hush, "I hid under my desk. I was on the phone and I pulled the receiver down under with me, and my only thought was that the person shooting would notice the phone was off the hook and know I was down there. I didn't do anything—do you understand? Not anything to help. I feel like it's partly my fault."

"What could you have done? Gone out and flung briefs at him?" But I could see her pain was beyond the consolation of reason. "Survivors always feel guilty." Unfortunately, I knew this from experience. "Feel they could have or should have done something. But I was here, too. I know how quickly it all happened. There's nothing you could have done."

"I could have hung up, called building security or nine one one. Or maybe just screamed or said something to him. I mean"—she leaned imploringly forward—"who knows what might have made a difference?"

"Hiding was smart. Maybe she"—I couldn't bring myself to speak the dead woman's name—"would have done the same if she hadn't been with a client." God, why did I have to think of that? "And nothing you could have done would have stopped him. It was over too fast." Her wince of pain made me wonder: "You don't keep a gun here?"

The color drained from her cheeks. She did keep a gun, I was certain.

"It doesn't matter," I said quickly, "even if you had a gun. You couldn't very well whip it out and shoot him. You didn't know if he was aiming at anyone, if he was just making noise, what was going on. And maybe he'd have shot you because you had a gun. Just like that, before you felt confident enough to fire."

Her face was slack with desolation.

I knew I was right. I also knew nothing would have consoled me in an analogous situation. I sat back, trying not to let Maryanne More's emotions trip my own domino chain.

Finally, all I could think to do was change the subject. "The reason I came to see her that day?" I searched More's face to make sure she knew we'd changed direction. "The reason for my appointment? All of that is still unresolved."

She blinked as if I'd shone a sudden light in her eyes. "Your problems with Mr. Sayres?" Her tone hid none of her incredulity.

"Yes." I didn't recall having mentioned Sayres to her. Perhaps she'd overheard me tell the police the reason for my interview, or read Kinsley's jottings. Or maybe she'd been on the listening end of the bug in her partner's office.

"Sometimes," I hesitated, knowing Sandy would approach this with more stage presence, "I don't think a legal remedy will work. I know enough labor law to worry that my business will go bankrupt before my case gets to court. I keep thinking the only thing that'll help . . . I don't know.'' And I don't want to express a criminal intention if you're taping this conversation.

I'd paved Sandy's way. Perhaps I could leave it at that.

"It is unfortunate," she said. Her voice was low and full. "You might not be able to save your business. From what I know of White, Sayres and Speck—they've represented management in a few of my cases—I'd guess they'll fight you, no settlement, to the end. But if and when you do win, you might be looking at a very nice package.''

"What do I do in the meantime?'' I felt the stirring of an unreasonable wish: maybe she really could tell me what to do. "I need to shut Sayres up now. I need a plan now. Not the hope of a good outcome in several years. I need to fix this right now, because I just don't have a parachute.''

A parachute. I flashed back to the plane in Rommel's driveway, the explosion, the mess of black smoke and chemical foam.

More leaned back in her office chair. Her eyes widened, moved slightly as if she'd entered a REM state.

For a long moment, we were silent.

"My practice is not lucrative,'' she said quietly. For a moment, she just watched me.

I braced myself. It was coming now, a description of her designer-crimes service.

"Neither Jocelyn nor I ever managed to take home a six-figure salary and draw, not even close. We end up doing so much pro bono work, you see. The hard-luck stories we hear. It's all so unfair, what's left of the labor laws, the working conditions, the take-backs, the plant closures. It's all so hard on the working person. And because it's a relatively uncomplicated area of the law, we have a lot of competition. My high-technology specialty was supposed to be our hedge against that, but high-tech is the hardest hit segment of today's market; it's collapsing all around us."

I waited. Then I said, "But you've found a way to stay in business?"

"Jocelyn was frugal. Our overhead is low. I have a private source of income."

I felt myself stop breathing: here it came.

"Jocelyn's gone." A tic afflicted the corner of her eye. "Her office is just sitting there empty. She has clients who need attention. And I'm too upset to deal with my own clients." She leaned forward, forearms extending across the desktop. "Why don't you join me? I know how good you are; I've followed more than one of your cases. I know you have integrity; I admired the way you spoke up for Dan Crosetti in spite of everything. You'd have to get up to speed on labor issues on your own time—we couldn't bill Jocelyn's clients for it. But it wouldn't take long, not if you were committed to it. And you'd retain the absolute right to expand her practice, your practice, in any direction you wish. Except management labor, of course."

I was speechless. A job offer: the last thing in the world I'd expected. Not an invitation to break the law, but a job offer. "I'm sorry, I'm— I thought you were going to— I don't—"

"It's sudden. Maybe presumptuous—you do corporate work, not . . . I know this isn't anything you'd thought of." She shook her head as if shaking off water. "We hardly know each other. We don't know each other's methods or business practices. I guess I just—" Her lip trembled. "I need someone in Jocelyn's office. It feels haunted. It's horrible. I feel like I could accommodate anyone rather than be alone. But I shouldn't have presented this now. This way."

I didn't know what to say.

More & Kinsley was a more cheerful address than mine in spite of the tragedy, no doubt about it. And it was a full caseload; it was work. It was better politics than anything

I'd done in a long while. And I could make some interesting additions to More's client list.

I almost laughed at the irony of it. I was considering joining forces with a firm I suspected of criminal activity. Get my stuff all moved over here, get my name linked to More's, and then what? Discover she'd been masterminding antiemployer scams? That she'd ordered a hit on her previous law partner? That she was about to be arrested by federal marshals?

"I've been thinking about this all weekend, wondering if it would be appropriate to bring it up." More looked like an eighth grader who'd been rudely turned down for the prom. "I didn't want to shock you or offend you."

"I'm just surprised." I seemed to see her at greater magnification, as someone who might possibly enter my life. "I wasn't expecting . . ."

A line dance of suspicions left me speechless. Was this offer designed to throw me off track, keep me from digging into her background, force me to call off Sandy? Was she trying to neutralize me? Hide something from me? Maybe even arrange to have something happen to me in Kinsley's office?

"Please let me think about it," I said. I couldn't afford to dismiss such an offer. Ready-made work. Something new, something that would take me out of Steve Sayres's orbit. "If you could keep the offer open awhile, I'd like to consider it."

"Yes, of course I'll keep the offer open." She sounded reluctant, looked a little panicked.

The room took on the sparkle of unreality. We'd been strangers. Now we were discussing partnership. It scared me so badly I stood abruptly and walked out.

I walked past Hester, the office manager. She looked flustered and startled as I passed her computer terminal. She said something about another appointment. I didn't stop to clarify or respond.

On the street, I wondered if Sandy had returned to his office in time to tap into More's bug, if he'd eavesdropped on the conversation.

I stood staring at the twelfth floor of the building across the street, at the windows of my old office. I'd worked so hard there and done so little good.

I shivered in the cold wind, looking up at the gray building against gray sky.

Sandy would be suspicious, even more than I was. He'd remind me of all the worrisome facts I hadn't forgotten. But it wouldn't change the nature of the carrot More dangled before me: I might feel okay about myself again, practicing labor law. I could throw off a load of career insecurity. I could put away the thought of moving. Even put away some of my hatred for Steven Sayres: he couldn't touch me in a labor practice; his friends were all management, the enemy. No one who hired me would heed their slanders; no one who hired me would respect Sayres enough to care what he said.

Living well is the best revenge, they always say. Maybe I finally had a chance to test the adage.

Or maybe I was being set up.

CHAPTER

Twenty-one

HAVING TENTATIVELY CONSIDERED A MORE MATURE RE-sponse to Sayres—finding an arena in which his slanders meant nothing—I was shocked by Sandy's news.

Sandy looked plenty shocked himself, hovering over my desk as only a very long man can.

"It's somebody's handiwork, Laura," he insisted. "This didn't just happen, timed just right for you, out of the blue."

I was still reeling on the brink of delirious cheer, afraid to believe and celebrate. For the very reason he cited. "Tell me again, Sandy."

"Steve gave advice that caused two different clients to maybe violate RICO." The Racketeer Influenced and Corrupt Organizations Act. "That's the news hitting Montgomery Street today."

I wanted to laugh. It was probably untrue, certainly unfair: the racketeering laws, written to nail organized crime, were now being used against businesses and political groups. They added a heavy federal component to allegations that the law had been broken more than once. If a pattern of lawbreaking could be shown, conspiracy repeatedly to break the law could be charged. By calling this "conspiracy" racketeering, the feds upped the ante, slapping on penalties far exceeding the total for individual violations.

Corporations dreaded RICO because minor violations of the law—almost unavoidable if one did complex banking—could be patchworked into a charge of conspiracy. Businesses were then wide open to civil suits as well—suits entitling plaintiffs to three times their actual money damages. And the word "racketeering" made investors nervous, bringing to mind wiseguys and sleazy practices.

That's why corporations insisted their lawyers provide protection from RICO. Rules might be interpreted to a client's benefit, others might be cautiously ignored, but the lawyer was there to make sure this didn't appear conspiratorial, didn't trigger RICO.

Because, once alleged, a racketeering charge was going to be expensive, whether it stuck or not. At best, investors would bail, and lawyers by the battalion would arrive to comb business records, requiring an expensive army of one's own. At worst, it meant treble damages and other stiff penalties on top of years of legal fees.

Leaving a client vulnerable to RICO was major egg on a lawyer's face.

But before I rejoiced, I needed to be fair. "Steve's a jerk, but I can't imagine him letting two RICO patterns develop." Some rule bending was normal practice for any client, but a vigilant lawyer put a lid on it before it got noticeable.

"The banks will beat the charges, if that's what you mean." Sandy had worked for White, Sayres & Speck long enough to know who was doing what. "Hell, I doubt if they'll even be indicted. Just investigated."

"Then why the RICO rap?"

"Somebody's gone and done a bunch of legwork, that's what I think. Presented the feds with a good strong brief, something they can't ignore and feel like they have to at least check out."

"Someone set the banks up?"

"Looked through their business records with an eye toward RICO, yeah. The feds wouldn't have put these cases together. The violations are too small, no red flags. This was someone fine-toothing to see what they could find." Sandy's scowl deepened.

"How long have the feds been investigating?"

"They haven't really started. Notified the banks this afternoon they'll be wanting documents. Probably just received the information themselves. Like I said, chickenshit stuff. Get dropped eventually."

"But in the meantime, it's an expensive hassle. And it looks bad. Especially for Sayres." It was impossible not to smile.

"That's the most interesting part: that it's on the street already. Sayres had calls from other clients."

"I'll bet. Two of his banks facing RICO charges." His current clients might hang in there with him; they'd been together a long time. But they'd worry about advice he'd given; worry that he'd left them vulnerable. And strangers would think twice before hiring Sayres over others in the howling pack.

"Someone went to a lot of trouble to make Steve Sayres look bad. And to get word out fast. He's bound to think it was you." Sandy put his hands on my desktop, leaning closer. "I'd think it was you if I didn't know better."

The hell with fairness. I laughed outright.

"Stupid bastard has been maligning me all over town. Now he's got this big old cloud over his reputation, and I don't care if he deserves it or not, Sandy. His stock has dropped, and it doesn't matter anymore what he says about me." I leaned back, grinning. "Sayres can think what he wants. He can come here and have a major hissy fit in my face. He can choke on his own damn medicine."

"Before you get too euphoric—"

"Too late."

"Better consider this—"

"This won't hurt you, Sandy. Sayres will need you more than ever to get information to clear the clients, help restore his rep."

"I know that. But you're not thinking this through. Why would someone go to this kind of trouble? It'll cost the banks, but put that aside for a minute. The one person who really gets hurt by it is Steve. Someone went after him big time, and probably he thinks it's you. We know it's not. But what are the odds of anyone else hating Sayres as much as you do?" He shook his head. "I know the firm, I know the clients, I know a hell of a lot more than I'd like to about Sayres's private life after working for him ten years. And I'm telling you, there's nothing there. Whoever did this did it for you."

He'd leaned closer, only inches from my face. "Somebody shut Sayres up for you. That's a hell of a favor. You better ask yourself who did it, and what they want in return."

"Maryanne More offered me Kinsley's office." I put it out there with no clue where it fit in.

Sandy's jaw dropped. "What do you mean, offered you her office?"

"Offered to make me her partner. Give me Kinsley's clients."

He straightened, waving an arm. "Jesus! Why didn't you tell me?"

"It happened a couple of hours ago. I left you a message to call. I half expected you to say you'd eavesdropped via the office bug."

"I haven't been back to my office. I've been playing catchup. Stopped by to see Sayres about something else and was there when he got the calls." He tilted his head, considering me as he might a strange insect on his screen door.

"If More did this for you, found this way to shut Sayres up and solve your problem, she did it to keep you in business, to keep your office afloat. So why offer you a partnership?"

"After making sure I'd turn it down?"

"Just to seem friendly? Get you in her corner? Keep you from getting all antagonistic and bothering her clients?" He shook his head. "Either way, why ask you? I can't get a fix on her."

"At the time, I worried she was trying to neutralize me in some way," I confessed. I skipped the reasons the offer appealed to me. "If she knew I wasn't going to accept, if she knew this was coming around the pike for Sayres—" I had to laugh again. "My God. Verhoeven. I wonder if Perry Verhoeven will come back to me. How soon can I call him without seeming like a vulture?"

"You are a vulture." Sandy's tone was not unkind. "Jesus, what a profession."

My hand had unconsciously strayed to the telephone. I pulled it back to my lap. For a few minutes this morning, I'd considered doing a different kind of work, being a different kind of lawyer.

"I don't like this, Laura. Every alarm in my head is ringing. I'd bet a year's salary this has to do with you getting shot at, that it's part of the same thing. I think this is the worst news you've had in a long while, no matter if it's gift-wrapped and sweet-smelling."

"Maybe Sayres did it." The thought chilled my flesh. "Maybe he saw this coming, knew the feds were investigating. Maybe he blamed me. Maybe he . . ." It was hard to say the words. I hated Sayres's guts, but he was someone I'd spent years with. It was painful to believe. "Maybe he hired someone to kill me."

Sandy looked grim. "If so, he did a hell of a job looking surprised about the RICO shit today."

"Coincidence you were there to see him look surprised."

He nodded. "The thought crossed my mind."

"But you'd know on some level if it was Steve, wouldn't you?" Wouldn't I?

He came around to my side of the desk, dropping to a crouch. "I don't always trust my instincts." He was at eye level now. "Because it's damn hard to tell how deep a person's feelings run."

I was startled. Did he mean Steve's feelings? Or mine? I was off balance, therefore off key, "Is there a punch line?"

His face changed. "Why did you leave me, Laura? We really had something. More than what you gave it away for."

I'd wondered when or if this would come out into the open. I'd certainly tried on a few explanations for size, painful though the fit had been. But now none seemed worth defending.

I watched Sandy's face flicker with angry memories and wounded pride.

"I'd hate to be without you again, Sandy." I was afraid to say more. "I was with someone else, but I didn't have anyone."

He stood. "Then why'd you stick with Hal?" He turned away. "Those were four very long years for me. With a hell of a half-life."

"I guess I wanted . . ." To reinvent a past blighted by Hal's mother, my Aunt Diana? To rescue myself through him? I should have guessed his problems would overwhelm us both. But I hated to admit defeat; I'd ended up lotus-eating his denial. "I guess I stuck with it because it was my mistake."

"Which mistakes are you sticking to now, Laura?" His posture was stiff. I'd seen this anger in him plenty of times in the last four years.

I wanted to say something to allay it. But I knew it would have to wear off; it was too deep to simply turn off.

He shook his head as if coming out of a trance. "Unfortunately, I've got another meeting with Steve." He turned back toward me. "I'm already late."

"Come back when you're done? Come to my place?"

"If it's not too late, sure." His glance was sheepish. "Didn't mean to go and get heavy on you. You know you can count on me?"

I nodded.

He stood in the doorway a few seconds before walking out.

CHAPTER

Twenty-two

WHEN THE TELEPHONE RANG, I PRACTICALLY JUMPED on it. I'd set the cordless next to my pillow, hoping Sandy would call. I knew reporters wouldn't phone so late. Anyone else was likely to have something important to tell me.

I'd been dreaming about home, the house I'd lived in as a child. I'd been dreaming about my father. The pain of his death hit me in first consciousness, exploding as if to crack my ribs. But my first real thought was for Uncle Henry: what if he didn't forgive me for representing Brad Rommel?

The phone call put a quick stop to family worries.

"Laura. I've got to talk to you."

"Brad!" His voice was a shot of adrenaline. I sat upright in my bed, skin suddenly hot. "We've got serious trouble. Where are you? Where have you been?"

"The minute I saw the plane in my driveway, saw it on fire there, I knew I was being set up. I knew I better make tracks."

"Wait a minute, back up. Where were you when the mall was bombed?" If he had an alibi, a lot of damage could be undone.

"I got a call to go there." His voice was gruff, suddenly ironic. "The call was such that I couldn't refuse."

"What does that mean?" I didn't do well with cryptic pronouncements at—what?—four in the morning.

"The person who called was, or said she was, Cathy Piatti."

He had my full attention, every cell straining to hear.

"Was it really her?"

"Sure sounded like her. At the time, I was pretty positive."

"Tell me exactly what she said."

Maddeningly, Brad paused.

"What did Piatti say?" I could have shaken the phone, I was so impatient.

"What was that?" His tone bordered on hostile. "Are you taping this?"

I was about to snap out, No, of course not. But after my recent experiences with Sandy and Osmil, I couldn't guarantee no one was.

"It's a cordless phone," I waffled. "There are ways to eavesdrop. But I'm not—"

"I'm close to your house. Meet me."

"We need to get you to a police station as soon as possible. You're wanted for questioning—they've already searched your house. They revoked your bail this morning. Yesterday morning, I should say."

"For what? I'm trying to save my goddamn life!" He sounded incensed. "Considering they arrested me for murdering a woman that certainly didn't sound dead when she called me—when she tried to get me inside the mall before it blew up. Then somebody lands a damn plane in my driveway and sets it on fire. I might be a plain humble fisherman, but I'm not stupid. I'm not going to stay put and wait for the next thing."

"You need to tell your story. You can't hide. That's not doing you a bit of good. They'll end up arresting you for arson, too." I was amped nearly to the point of palpitations. "We need to do some quick damage control."

"Damage control? Grow up!" His anger was a slap in the face. "Someone's trying to kill me and frame me. I've got bigger problems than damage control!"

"Talk to me, Brad. The odds of someone listening in to this call . . ." But if the eavesdropper was private, not a cop, his tape or testimony would be admissible in court. It would be a disaster if Brad lied to me, contradicted himself, incriminated himself. The stakes were too high to justify even a small risk. "No, you're right. Why don't you come over?"

"Reporters. I was going to come earlier, but you had a couple parked across the street."

"Are you sure?"

"They were typing on laptops."

"There's nobody at this hour." But it might be morning before we finished our discussion. It wouldn't do to encounter camera crews on our way out. "Hold on. Let me think."

I hopped out of bed. One thing for sure: I wasn't going out alone at night to meet anyone, for any reason. That was B-movie bullshit. I'd gotten burned that way myself.

"My friend and detective, Sandy Arkelett, has an office down near Pier Seven, do you know where that is?"

"I have a map. But I don't want to talk to a detective."

"You won't." No way I'd break the lawyer-client privilege by having a third party present. "He'll be in the next room because I'll need him right after we get through. Don't worry, he won't call the cops." Because I'm going to take you to the Hall of Justice after we talk.

"I don't know."

"You've got to trust me, Brad. And I've got to hear this. Find Pier Seven on the map." I gave him a street name and address. "I'll get hold of Sandy and meet you there as soon as possible."

I gripped the handset so tightly it hurt. This was a call I didn't want to let go of. I wanted to know right now what Cathy Piatti had said, what Rommel had done.

But I hung up to remove my temptation and help ensure Brad's compliance.

CHAPTER

Twenty-three

THE STREETS AROUND SANDY'S OFFICE ARE ALWAYS gloomy. In the morning, the light hits the stark flat-front buildings and is absorbed by dull stone and concrete. By afternoon, the sun stops reaching over the high-rises of the financial district, and a thin wind whips litter down the shadowed street. But at night, with restless Bay mist stirring the unornamented stillness, the neighborhood could be a movie set, fog-machined and ready for Jack the Ripper.

I parked my car, checked my locks, and settled in to wait for Sandy. I hoped he'd hurry. He lived a little farther from downtown than I did, and in the opposite direction. He'd wanted to pick me up, but that would have doubled our ETA, and I didn't want Brad getting nervous and leaving.

I was beginning to regret my decision. I hoped Sandy arrived before Brad. I believed what Brad had told me, but I'd been wrong before. And middle-of-the-night rendezvous had gone wrong for me before.

There was no one on the street. Homeless men and women had melted into the minuscule parks behind new townhouses near the piers. Beside the bay, a few bars might still be cleaning floors and rattling garbage cans, a few restaurants might be readying breakfast. But this was a district of California-cuisine lunches, its infrequent eateries closed by evening.

I heard the car before I saw its lights. It rounded the corner slowly, heading toward me. I sank low in the bucket seat, waiting for it to pass under a street lamp, waiting to see if it was Sandy or Brad.

A knock on the passenger window startled a cry from me. As the car passed, flooding the interior of mine with light, I saw Brad Rommel crouched beside my passenger door. Before he turned his face away, the headlights made a frightening mask of his scowl. He tapped at the window again, his hair glinting red from the car's brake lights.

I clicked the door lock, watching Brad climb into the two-seater with large-man awkwardness. Then I realized the other car had turned the corner, hadn't parked, must not have been Sandy. Distracted, I hadn't even noticed its make. For reasons I didn't have time to analyze, that upset me.

But right now Brad took priority.

"Brad! I didn't see your car. How did you get here?"

He pressed back into the seat as if soothing aches. "It's a couple of blocks away. Was that your detective friend who just drove by?"

"I don't think so. He'd have parked." Instantly when he saw Brad.

"Jesus! Then move, would you?"

"Move?"

"The car. Take off with your lights out and go around some corners or something. Just let's make sure that car's not here looking for me." He tapped the keys dangling from my ignition. "Come on. Hurry."

I hurried. He was right. If a reporter had followed me (after eavesdropping on my cordless call?) he could be dialing the police now. I didn't want Brad to get arrested before I could persuade him to surrender.

I pulled out of the parking space, lights still off.

"Hit it!" Brad insisted. "I hear a car."

Most likely Sandy. But I could smell Brad's fear, acrid and animal, and I knew it was justified. I kept the lights off and took my first right. I drove just slowly enough to see by street lamp. I pulled beside the curb a block and a half behind Sandy's office, a space from which I'd be able to see his office light through breaks in intervening buildings. Sandy had shown me this spot, happy as a boy to have discovered the oddity, halfway hoping he'd need to use it soon. There was no sparkle of light in his window yet.

We were closer to the bay now, close enough to hear wharf boards groan and chains clank, close enough to smell ship oil and salt water. Moisture beaded my windshields, cocooning us in a car made tiny by Brad's bulk.

"What happened, Brad?" My tone was sharper than I intended; I might have been blown up by the plane in his driveway. "What do you know about all this?"

"Somebody's trying to mess my whole life up." His voice was an explosion of anger. But a distant street lamp caught tears brimming his eyes, deep lines in his face, the slump of fatigue in his posture. "I ask myself over and over why. Why me? I don't get it. I'm scared shitless."

"You say you got a call to go to the Southshore Mall?"

"Cathy. I know her voice." His head lolled against the seat back; he seemed too tired to support it. "It was Cathy. She said she'd been up in the Yukon, hadn't told anyone but I don't remember why, I don't remember if she explained that. I was so emotional, you know?"

"Did you try calling the police? Or me?"

"I tried calling you, but your machine picked up. I was kind of overwhelmed. It just seemed like I didn't know where to begin on an answering machine. And I didn't want to call the cops until I knew it was for real."

"Did you tell her to call the police?" I tried to imagine what I'd do, hearing the voice of someone I was charged with murdering.

"I don't even remember. Only that she insisted I meet her at the mall—not at my house, not anyplace that made any sense to me. But she was set on it, and I was afraid she'd up and disappear again. So I popped into my car and went."

I watched him, willing the rest of the story out of him.

"But my goddamn bad luck. At least, I thought so then." He closed his eyes, then covered them with a rough hand. "I get to the bottoms"—the flat dairyland before the woody rises leading to his cabin—"and here's this lady waving me down, crying. I actually tried to drive around her. I didn't give a shit what kind of trouble she was in; I mean, compared to a call from Cathy. But she was like right in front of me. I had to stop. She was all freaked out because her car had broken down and she wasn't from around here and was scared to death out in the middle of nowhere at night and et cetera."

"What did she look like?"

"Big lady, tall, almost looked like a guy." He uncovered his eyes, watching me with intense focus. "Sound like anybody you know? Because I've wondered. It was a hell of a coincidence getting stopped right then. I mean it saved my life. If I'd got there on time, they'd have found my body with Cathy's."

"Do you remember her well enough to describe her to a police artist?"

"Yeah. No. I don't know, I think so. I'm so wiped, I hardly know my own name anymore."

I reached out, squeezed his arm. "We'll try to get this straightened out." I wasn't ready yet to tell him that meant a trip to the police station. "Where did you take this woman?"

"Back to her car. Where we wasted a shitload of time with her looking for her keys, which she never found. And trying to get in with a coat hanger and looking under her hood. All of this with me basically saying, Hell with it, I'll drop you off in town so you can do this tomorrow, and her saying, Please please please, just give it another minute because otherwise her husband's going to be so pissed he'll go berserk." He shifted in the seat to face me. "Have you ever felt like you'd go nuts, just completely lose your mind right there on the spot? Because it just all got too damn weird for me. I got so crazy listening to her whining and her trying to keep me there a little longer when I couldn't see bless-all wrong with her engine. I just flipped out, screamed at her; finally took off in my car and left her standing there."

He grew quiet. I waited. Power lines above my convertible dripped water, tattooing on the vinyl top.

"I was about a block from the mall when the sucker went up in this ball of fire, just bammo, big fireball at one end and then a bunch of little explosions and fire and smoke all over the place."

"Did you see a plane overhead?"

"No. I wasn't looking up. I was close to the mall, way close, no perspective. My truck got this layer of black over the front. That close."

"What did you do?"

"Freaked the hell out." He leaned nearer, his face taut with recalled shock. "I thought about driving around to see if Cathy was there someplace, and then I thought, Man, I need to get out of here. I need to think."

"Did you go straight home?"

"I got home maybe an hour and a half later, or close to home. I got close enough to see a plane burning up in my driveway, and I thought, Screw this, I'm gone till someone figures out what the hell happened."

"You saw the plane burning?" I tried to calculate the time: the mall was already aflame when I reached town; I'd been at Brad's when the plane exploded.

"What did you do for an hour and a half? Or was it longer?"

"I sat up on top of the hill and watched the fire, the firemen, the cops. Waited to see if they were bringing out any bodies."

I nodded. I might have done that. It made sense to me.

"When did you leave town?"

"After I saw the plane. Went all the way up to Klamath to fill my tank in case they were after me." Seventy-some miles north. "Then backtracked south off the highway, came down here. The only plan I could think of was drive here and talk to you and ask you what to do next. You weren't around, so I got lost and waited for you to come back."

"I've been back all day. Did you try calling earlier?"

"I saw you were home, but I thought I'd better wait a little longer—in case they were watching you or whatever." He looked away, making me wonder if there wasn't more to it. "But then I just couldn't take any more waiting. I haven't been sleeping much, and tonight I thought, If I don't do it right now, I'll go crazy." His eyes locked on mine. This, at least, rang true. He seemed on the brink.

I swallowed my frustration. No use chastising him for keeping me waiting an extra day. My anxiety wasn't the issue.

"There's only one thing you can do, Brad. The court revoked your bail—the police'll arrest you as soon as they spot your truck. We've got to go surrender before they find you. Tell them everything you've told me, give them a chance to clear you. No one else has the resources and the pooled information to make sense of your story." I felt almost traitorous saying so. Why should he entrust his freedom to anyone after so many inexplicable and horrific events? "We'll try to get the charges dropped as soon as—"

"I knew you'd say that." His voice was petulant, almost childish. "I won't go."

I glanced out my window, hoping to see Sandy's office light. Why hadn't he reached his office? Had he discovered it was being watched? Encountered some other problem?

"You've got no other option, Brad, not really. You can't keep hiding. Plus the police need to know Piatti called you. They need to know she was alive. You withhold a piece of information like that and you could screw up the whole investigation, get them off on the wrong foot entirely." I wondered if the coroner could tell from her charred remains that she hadn't been dead when the fireball hit.

"I've been thinking about all this." His voice was unusually deep, almost a whisper. "You can't imagine how hard I've been thinking." He hunched forward. In the close car, his sweat and fear became a pungent presence. "I try to step outside the situation, pretend like it's happening to someone else. Because it really doesn't have anything to do with me—I'm just a regular workingman. It has to do with other people's strange trips that I got sucked into."

"What exactly did Cathy Piatti say to you on the phone?"

"Strange trips that have to do with other people," he repeated, his tone suddenly hostile. "Like you. I was thinking how this started when you came back to Hillsdale."

They'd executed the warrant to search Brad's boat the day of my father's death. An obituary in the local paper alerted Brad to the fact that I was in town. My Aunt Diana had called me a "hard little number" for taking a case "at such a time." She chose not to understand that aiding an old friend helped me deal with the loss. The opportunity to assist Brad had been a tiny sluice, relieving the pressure.

But after a weekend of tormented fretting, Brad was imagining a more sinister relationship between my presence then and his problems now.

"This started weeks earlier," I pointed out gently, "when Cathy Piatti bled into that bucket."

"Maybe," he said. "But your dad was already sick then. You were in town off and on all month."

I pushed away memories of that month, still too painful to contemplate. And I braced myself, knowing what he was going to say next. Knowing it because I kept hearing it from Sandy.

"I think this is about you, Laura. I think somebody talked Cathy into giving blood, maybe over days to get the volume where it needed to be. Or maybe giving her a transfusion to get her blood level back up." His voice had a singsong quality, as if he repeated something he'd memorized. Had he spent the weekend litanizing his denial? "I think someone talked Cathy into it so I'd get arrested. So you'd be my lawyer. I mean, you were in town; we were friends. I'd go to you, right? This whole thing could be about you."

"I didn't even know Cathy Piatti. She has nothing to do with me." The suggestion made me angrier than it should have.

"And everybody knows the Southshore Mall was your uncle's Frankenstein." His eyes burned with a furious light. He'd been dragged into something he might not ever get out of, and he was choosing to believe it had to do with me, not him. Scared and sleepless, he was determined to find an out, a scapegoat.

"No one would have any reason to go to that much trouble on my account, Brad. I have no idea what all this is really about. But what you're thinking doesn't make sense."

A low rumble started in his chest and climbed to his lips. At such close quarters, my car windows obscured with claustrophobic moisture, Brad Rommel was frightening me.

He was in a fury of panic and bad choices with no outlet except me. His mouth opened to a silent roar, eyes pressed beneath a thousand-pound brow.

I erupted from the driver's door, driven by pure instinct. He was like a bomb of seething emotion, and right then I wanted to put some distance between us.

I took several paces out into the street, the driver's door still open. Shaking with the chill of my flight, I tried to see what Brad was doing, tried to hear something besides the pounding of my own heart. I backed toward modest warehouses and studios, all closed, all unlighted.

Maybe I missed some tip-off sound, a motor engaging, wheels spinning on damp concrete. But I saw the approaching car at the same moment I heard the engine. It was large and dark; that's all that registered. Its headlights were off.

That scared me. That and the car's speed. And the fact that it was bearing down on me.

I ran, not back toward my car, not back inside it. I ran across the street. I ran to the curb, that traditional haven of pedestrian safety.

Maybe I still feared Brad. Maybe I thought I'd get clipped against the open car door.

I didn't think. I just ran to the sidewalk.

Evidently that wasn't what the driver of the dark car expected. In the second it took to reach where I'd been standing, it had already begun its swerve into the wrong lane.

I heard the crunch of my car door being ripped from its hinges, then flying off the hood of the other car to bounce along the concrete in a scraping, rolling little light show of sparks.

The black car continued on, zipping around a corner.

For a moment, all I could do was stare at my car door, lying up the street like discarded junk.

The next thing I knew, Brad Rommel had bolted from the passenger side, running in the opposite direction the car had taken.

He was gone around a corner before I had a chance to shout his name.

And I knew I'd better get the hell out of there myself. I did a staggering reel, looking between buildings toward Sandy's office. Still no light.

I considered dashing there anyway, if only because it was a destination, a place I'd always felt confident and secure.

But the no-headlights car might be close by. And I couldn't let Brad slip away. However furious and confused he might be, it was surely transitory; he'd managed to contain it until now. And my obligation toward him was as firm as ever. I needed to get him to the police before explanation became hopeless.

I ran back across the street to my car. The keys were still in the ignition. As far as I knew, only the door and body were damaged.

I twisted the key, pumped the gas. The engine whined. I turned it again. Again it whined.

But the third try got me going. This time I decided I needed the headlights. I needed to be able to find Brad and see the dark car coming, see who was inside.

Though the engine sounded wrong to me (maybe just my imagination), I covered every inch of the neighborhood, searching. Searching, worrying, freezing to death with the damp bay air buffeting me through the hole where my door should have been.

My arms and hands began to shake. It was five in the morning, the darkest, coldest hour of the day, and I'd been wakened and frightened and almost hit by a car. And now I couldn't find my client, Sandy hadn't shown up (my God, why not?), and I knew danger could strike with force enough to rip a metal door from its hinges and bounce it down the concrete.

There wasn't a drop of adrenaline left in my system. Frazzled nerves jerked me like a puppet.

I pulled up in front of Sandy's office just long enough to be sure he wasn't inside. Long enough to burst into tired, frustrated tears.

Then I went home, feeling frozen and exposed without the car door I'd left lying in the street.

CHAPTER

Twenty-four

I FOUND SANDY WAITING IN MY APARTMENT. A PHONE message at his office, supposedly from me—and apparently sounding enough like me—had sent him there.

It took me awhile to soothe him, and it took him awhile to soothe me. But now I was nearly recovered from my fright and he'd managed to master his thwarted protectiveness.

"The whole thing's as phony as a three-dollar bill," he repeated. "And that includes your client's story. You didn't get eavesdropped on or followed—or at least chances are slim compared to the most obvious solution. Which is, Rommel called you, set up the meeting, got an accomplice to get me out of the way, and then had her—or him, if a guy could imitate your voice—try to run you over. That's why you didn't find Rommel again. Damn black car picked him up and drove his butt out of there."

"All I know is, when he was talking to me, I believed him." I was sprawled on my couch, too tired to be sure what made sense. "His anger at me and all that, I can see it. He can't understand why this is happening to him; he's looking for an explanation, and he's blaming me. If he was guilty, he wouldn't have to do that. I don't know how else to say it.''

"Try this way: crock of shit.'' He was pacing my living room, running one hand over his hair, jerking the other elbow. A mass of tired mannerisms and up-too-early crankiness, he'd jettisoned his usual explore-all-alternatives approach. "Brad Rommel is a psycho, that's what I think. I think he's behind this whole thing, and furthermore I think that's the only way this makes sense.''

The dull light of morning brought scant cheer to my seen-better-days furniture and wall paint.

I tried to stay calm. "We can check parts of Brad's story: whether Piatti was alive when the mall blew up, whether he got gas in Klamath.'' For the tenth time, I cursed myself for not bringing up the bucket of blood in my uncle's yard. Did Brad know anything about it? "Who the hell's in the new bucket, Sandy? Who can we call this early?''

His hand was already on my cordless phone. "Bartoli. You've got to tell him about Rommel.''

"Not yet. I'm too exhausted.'' I'd have to do it soon, within the hour. But not now. Not this very minute.

Sandy paced with the cordless to the window, looking out on the drab neighborhood that became my home after I lost my White, Sayres salary and the Presidio Heights apartment it supported.

I listened to him ask for Bartoli. His pause made me sit up straight: apparently he'd gotten through, was being connected. He glanced uncertainly over his shoulder at me.

I reached out for the phone. Tired or not, here I come.

By the time the phone was against my ear, Bartoli was saying, "Hello,'' impatiently, as if for a second or third time.

"It's Laura,'' I said. "Calling from San Francisco. What do you have on the contents of that bucket, Jay? Anything yet?''

"Laura! I was just going to call and ask you—"

Hastily, "I've been worried about Uncle Henry, all the reporters hanging around there. With everything else he's got to cope with. And I know they'll dog him until they've got the information. Do you know yet whose blood it is?"

"We flew some down to one of your labs in the city. There's a test'll tell us if it's all fresh blood or if some was frozen. Have you heard from—"

"Frozen! Someone bleeding themselves or getting bled gradually and freezing it? So it looks like they lost enough to kill them." I hoped my way of briefing Sandy sounded conversational. "What makes you think that's true?"

"Just that it couldn't be ruled out—something about how it looked under the microscope—and we need to rule it out. But listen, have you—?"

I jumped off the couch and ran into the bathroom, listening to the connection get overwhelmed with static. I could almost say in good conscience that I hadn't heard him ask about my client.

"Jay?" I said loudly. "Jay? Damn cordless! Let me try another channel."

I turned to find Sandy framed in the bathroom door.

Phone at arm's length, I told him quietly, "They've sent the blood down here to check if some of it was frozen."

His brows went up. Then, "Better tell Bartoli."

I pressed the phone to my ear, passing Sandy as I walked closer to the base unit. I had no energy left; I'd lost it to fear and shock watching my car door get ripped off.

I said, "I just saw Brad Rommel."

CHAPTER

Twenty-five

I SPENT THE MORNING AT SAN FRANCISCO'S HALL OF JUS-
tice, talking to homicide inspectors, and, via phone, every
cop in Hillsdale. A small army of men were fired up and
ready to capture Brad Rommel should he show himself
again. And despite my insistence that someone might be
after him—I offered the gaping hole where my door should
be as proof—all they seemed to care about was his capture.

I reached my office in the early afternoon, feeling scoured
by their questions. I was lucky to leave so soon. They could
have made more of the fact that I'd delayed calling until after
meeting Brad. Either they believed I'd meant to lead him in
for surrender, or they hoped to tap my phone and follow me
to him next time.

I paced and worried, wondering whether to remain in San
Francisco on the theory that Brad would contact me here
again, or go up to Hillsdale and check on my uncle, check
in with Jay Bartoli. Irresolute, I shuffled papers on my desk,
looked out the window at traffic creeping past warehouses
toward the freeway, considered calling Perry Verhoeven.

I was underoccupied, with a crackling charge of nervous energy. I tried to find or make work for myself. Never before in my entire career had I needed to do that.

For fun, I imagined what kind of day Steve Sayres was having. Sandy was tied up with him again, continuing investigations that would clear his clients. That meant I would no longer get news from him about Sayres; it would be unprofessional of him to discuss it.

Finally, driven by a restlessness to do something business-related, I phoned Perry Verhoeven.

His tone was guarded. "Laura. Is there some loose end you'd like to discuss?"

"Actually, Perry, I was hoping we could set up a meeting. I feel that perhaps I contributed to a false impression on your part, and I'd appreciate the opportunity to mention a few things I neglected to bring up earlier." I'd said it all and we both knew it. But it might be a foot in the door if he was having second thoughts about having hired Sayres.

"My schedule's tight, Laura. Maybe we could have lunch next week or early the week after." Don't call me; I'll call you.

"I have some information that would interest you, Perry." If he took the bait, I'd think of something. He had to be a little nervous about Sayres after yesterday's rumors. He had to have a few qualms about having acted on Sayres's slanders. If he'd meet with me, I could at least stress my relative cheapness: I knew his business better than Sayres did, I billed at a lower rate. And I'd never been accused of malpractice.

There was a chill silence. "What information?"

"Something I've learned." I'd bring up the RICO stuff, as if perhaps he didn't know yet. Sayres didn't have a lock on disingenuous insinuations.

"All right," he said. "Let's take a few minutes now." Not on the phone. "Have you had lunch?"

"Yes. What's on your mind?"

"Let's talk face to face." I needed time to think, to devise a strategy to charm him. "Why don't I drop by? I could be there in an hour." I'd rather sound underemployed, even desperate, than allow his window of availability to slam. He was big-ticket; worth the loss of face.

And meeting him was something to do, something besides worry.

He'd barely finished saying, "All right," before he hung up.

I replaced the receiver, feeling deflated. I'd talked him into a meeting he didn't want, to discuss nothing he didn't already know. I'd have to say it awfully persuasively.

Again Maryanne More's offer crossed my mind. If it should turn out there was no ulterior motive (as far as Sandy was concerned, a very big if), maybe I should do it. Even if I could sweet-talk Verhoeven back onto my client list, all I had was Verhoeven's work, the usual corporate protection, stock offerings, litigation. It paid well, it was complicated enough to be interesting, it had a certain status in a town with more corporate counsel than corporations. But it was hardly what anyone would consider "meaningful." It was just commerce.

Labor law would take me places I hadn't been. It would put my skills at the service of people facing losses as dramatic as livelihood and reputation. And I could continue doing criminal defense without disdainful corporate clients jumping ship.

I rose with a sigh. All of that was beside the point right now. More's offer might be window dressing; she might be a felon, even a murderer. But assuming she was sincere, I couldn't "choose" unless I had an alternative. I had to try to get Verhoeven back.

I drove to his plant, a two-story cement-and-glass building in the middle of a huge parking lot east of San Francisco. Bracketing Walnut Creek's Stepford-yuppie neighborhoods were endless drives of new concrete plants and corporate offices. Twice I mistakenly pulled into places that looked just like Perry's. Finally, I saw his logo: Ver-Techs. (His employees, I heard, called it VerTigo.)

I went into a lobby heavy on beige and teal, and told the man at the security desk I had an appointment with Verhoeven. Barely glancing up at me, he told me to have a seat.

I retreated to a vinyl couch, idly picking up a *Wall Street Journal* from the end table. The name Super Prime leaped out at me from below the fold.

The machine parts it shipped on Friday had begun to rust before arrival. A chemical analysis revealed that water had been "mistakenly or maliciously" added to its primer, causing accelerated oxidation. The analysis also revealed a fifty-five percent decrease in the expensive antioxidant that was Super Prime's hallmark.

The security person looked up in alarm at my exclamation.

Jocelyn Kinsley had feared Super Prime's spraying would be disrupted. That would have cost the company the price of a delay. Instead, its primer had been contaminated, leading to exposure of its cost-cutting shoddiness.

It was ten minutes before security got a call instructing that I be allowed in. I had plenty of time to admire the elegance of the sabotage. Super Prime had fired quality-control workers over minutes of tardiness and inappropriate jewelry. Now those excuses would be seen as the sham they were. And what the company saved by cheapening its product it would lose in future business.

I wondered if the contamination happened while Sandy and I kept vigil. Why hadn't we seen anyone run out of the plant?

I also had time to consider the RICO problems plaguing Steve Sayres. Did the two things share common authorship?

Finally, security accompanied me upstairs to Perry's office. He tapped twice at the door. He had to tap twice more before Perry finally said, "Come in."

I entered alone, crossing to him and extending my hand. His office looked just like the lobby: teal and beige industrial carpet, plain wood desk, cloth furniture. Perry obviously didn't need to express himself through his decor.

Behind him, a glass wall overlooked slow conveyor belts moving flat green and gray objects, each stopping under a series of metal arms that etched tiny pathways and embedded semiconductors to guide the robots used in other kinds of factories. Down below were the brains of machines to replace thousands of skilled workers. Machines to build machines to build more machines; it was a vision out of an Asimov novel. A robotic tomorrow, for better or worse.

"Thank you for seeing me, Perry."

His broad face, squared by imposing jowls and gray hair thicker on the sides than on top, looked rigidly composed. But a flush of cheek and a hostile squint suggested much stronger emotion.

"I only have a moment," he said. His tone was arctic.

For the first time, I realized there might be more to this than Sayres's slanders. For the first time I wondered if Perry disliked me. Independent of what he might have heard, disliked me personally.

"Then let me get to the point." I sat down. I hadn't prepared a rap. I'd thought it important to get a sense of Perry's mood first. I was glad. "Reviewing our last meeting, I've become concerned that some sort of misunderstanding led you to feel animosity toward me, that something undercut your confidence in me despite what I think was excellent work. Am I right?"

He sat slowly, eyes steadily on me while his face remained impassive. "I don't feel it's necessary to explain further."

"I've been under the impression that Steve Sayres influenced you. I'd like to know if that's the reason." Seeing anger flood his face with color, I hurried on. "Also, as your former counsel, I feel obligated to continue serving your interests. You probably know two of Steve's clients are being investigated for RICO violations." It was a tacky damn approach. I just couldn't think of another. "You expressed concern that I'd be spending too much time with other cases. Now Steve's going to have his hands full with these RICO allegations. I thought that might be important to you."

Perry's face continued to redden. "The qualifications and workload of my present lawyer are none of your damn business."

"In the interest of a smooth transition, and because I worked with you long enough to feel loyalty—"

He smacked his hand onto his desktop. "Loyalty! That's a laugh! I'm surprised you don't choke on the word."

His sudden vehemence knocked my point right out of my head.

"What do you mean?"

"Get out of here." He stood. "You don't work for me anymore, and you never will again, and that has nothing to do with Steven Sayres and it never did."

I remained in my chair, stunned. "Perry—"

"I said get out." He picked up the handset of a sleek black phone. "Or I'll have security haul you out. You're here under false pretenses; you said you'd learned something. You lying—" He crimped his lips, shaking his head.

"I just wanted to tell you about the RICO . . ." I stared up at him. For a moment he'd looked scared as well as angry. What had he thought I'd learned? "And I wanted to tell you one other thing."

I was stalling, also fishing. What in the world made him doubt my loyalty?

Perry replaced the receiver. "Go on."

I continued staring, saying nothing. Nothing, in fact, was occurring to me. I'd have to leave if that didn't change immediately.

"What?" he demanded. His hand clenched into a fist.

I rose hastily. Perry's anger seemed huge even in partial suppression.

"What? What do you have to say to me? Say it. Go ahead and say it." He was practically bellowing.

There was no way our lawyer-client relationship could be salvaged; that much was finally clear. And a sudden instinct told me to leave. Right now.

I decided to heed it. Whatever more I might learn scarcely mattered: the Verhoeven file was definitely closed.

A twinge of regret slowed me: why did Perry feel this way? Would he tell me if I waited? If I goaded him?

I backed slowly toward the door.

"You're trying to break my balls here today, is that it?" He stepped around his desk. "A trick you learned working for criminals?"

Information be damned. I didn't want to be here anymore.

I dashed out, clattering back downstairs and through the lobby. Only when I reached my car did I pause to let my heartbeats slow, to take the deep breaths I needed.

I got stuck in traffic on the way back into the city. I sat sweltering in the claustrophobic heat of stalled bridge traffic, with plenty of time to worry. What in the world had Perry meant? What did he think I'd done to him?

Whatever it was, it had nothing to do with Steve Sayres; I finally believed that. In a way, that was the hardest thing to accept.

CHAPTER

Twenty-six

"Loyalty." I stared at Sandy. "I have no idea what he meant."

Sandy looked troubled. "What in the hell is making you so unpopular?"

I leaned back in my office chair. I'd been unpopular for a long time, but always because of some case.

"The only thing Perry could possibly be angry about is me taking the Rommel case." Which, in fact, had been his stated reason for leaving. "He told me that's why he was dumping me, but I didn't believe him because it made no sense. I mean, so what? So I had another case. For him to think it was disloyal"—I shook my head—"there's got to be some kind of personal hot button."

I supposed I was beyond assuming men were sensible just because they ran corporations.

Sandy was flopped in the chair opposite my desk, sitting on his spine, long legs crossed at the ankle. His skin looked almost ashen in the gray light of a fading afternoon.

"Then there's this." He tapped the *Wall Street Journal*

on his knee. "I wish I knew how they pulled it off, how they contaminated the primer."

"Maybe it was someone still employed at Super Prime—some kind of solidarity thing."

"That would explain why we didn't see anyone run out. But the not-so-false alarm's got to figure into it."

"Maybe it was someone who works in another part of the plant, someone unfamiliar with security in the spraying area."

"And we just happened to be parked out back? No. More likely the alarm went off for our benefit." He sat straighter, the newspaper sliding off his lap. "I'd guess the primer was ruined earlier, that the alarm was set off to get us caught. If you'd been two minutes slower, the cops would have pulled you over for questioning."

"What would that have accomplished?"

"Mess with us, make us look stupid, hopefully get us out of their hair." He pinched the bridge of his nose as if trying to relieve a headache. "Maryanne More knew we were in town. I was breathing wine fumes at her half an hour before."

"I don't know, Sandy. The times I've met More, she hasn't seemed like a vigilante, she's seemed like, well, like a lawyer."

"Speaking of which . . ." He checked his watch. "I wish I didn't have to get back to work. It surely is dull, sifting through bank documents trying to disprove RICO. But Sayres is frantic." A slight grin. "Do you good to see it."

"How long do you think it's going to take?"

"Rest of the week, at least. I'll be in D.C. tomorrow, at Graystone Federal's corporate office; back on Thursday." His expression changed. "Why? You're not thinking of going up north?"

"I have to." I spoke quickly, hoping to forestall his objections. "I think Brad will go back to Hillsdale, hide out where he knows the countryside, maybe try to clear himself." I hurried on: "And Jay Bartoli should have a lot more information about the plane and the mall and all that by now. Maybe if I work with Jay, I can help Brad. Whoever did all this has to have left some traces."

He sat forward, elbows on his knees. "Don't go, Laura. I can't abandon Sayres right now."

"I can't sit down here while they're building a case against Brad. I've got to go try to do something for him."

Sandy stared across my desk at me.

He knew I was right. I had to go where my case required me to be. And he had to stay where his work was. But I could see he found it difficult.

I did, too. Danger aside, I didn't want to leave Sandy.

"Cathy Piatti." Sandy's voice strained with concession. "That's the place to start—assuming the sheriff stops being so territorial." He sat back with a sigh. "Say Piatti did phone Rommel. Where's she been? And don't say the Yukon. Even if she told him that, there's no reason to think it's true. You've still got the addresses?"

I'd stopped by the houses of her coworkers and friends weeks ago when DNA tests revealed it was her blood in Brad's bucket.

"Yes."

"Just don't go alone. When I get back from D.C. I'll ask around, get you the name of somebody up there. Either a private or a security guy. Okay?"

I hesitated, unsure of the necessity. "Call me with a name." I'd see how I felt when I got there. "I'll try to get the story on this new bucket. And generally, I'll see what I can get out of Bartoli."

"You'll watch your back?"

"Nobody's tried to hurt me up there. You should be glad I'm leaving San Francisco."

"I just wish I wasn't tied to Sayres's apron strings right now. I wish I was going with you."

I had a brief flash of paranoia: maybe someone had discredited Steve Sayres just to keep Sandy occupied, just to keep him from traveling with me. "I can't expect you to drop everything to be with me, Sandy."

"Can't you? We could change that."

He squinted at his watch again; he was late.

This wasn't the moment to say yes.

CHAPTER

Twenty-seven

I WAS ANNOYED WITH JAY BARTOLI, TO PUT IT MILDLY. HE was supposed to be part of this meeting, the human neutral zone between me and Connie Gold. I'd spent ten long minutes in her office waiting for him. Gold and I were beginning to snipe at each other, our professionalism showing dangerous cracks.

It was my turn to display ill-temper. "Why don't you tell me what you know? You've been briefed already. What's the point of waiting for Jay?" I'd said much the same thing two minutes ago, five minutes ago, and when I first walked in.

She wore an expression of superior disdain as if it were part of her purple wool, black-velvet-lapel suit. She obviously aimed to present a picture of calm elegance. To me, she looked like a skinny, rat-faced woman in lounge-singer drag.

She said, "Mr. Bartoli asked to be present. I think we can do him the courtesy."

As far as I knew, Jay had no ego stake in briefing me

himself. Moreover, we'd get more done today if I was up to speed. But I'd said so more than once already. Gold was just being difficult: withholding information because she could, because she wanted to, because I'd made valid objections to her defendants-as-movie-rights approach to the law.

"You're being very stupid about this." The words popped out of my mouth; I'd been biting them back too long. "We could have covered a lot of ground by now. I could have described my meeting with Rommel."

"I have the police reports." She tapped a stack of papers with a witchy fingernail.

I sat back, sighing elaborately. Once again, I looked around her office. Corny redwood-country art, framed diplomas from schools named after robber barons, framed photos of her with the stars of her TV movie about Connie the Great, Defender of Raped Women.

"Why don't I go see what's keeping Jay?" I suggested.

We'd phoned his office five minutes ago and were told he was away from his desk. We'd assumed he was on his way. But even a man with a walker could have taken an elevator up one floor by now.

"I'll walk out with you." Her tone was clipped, mistrustful, as if I might corner Bartoli in the hall and coax confidences from him.

What could I say besides "Fine."

We stepped out of her shrine to herself and Hollywood, and into a bustling outer office of overdressed clericals in stilt-high heels. A glass wall with round vents like a prison visiting room separated it from a tiny waiting area. We went through a door locked from the outside, passing two sad-looking men in vinyl chairs. When we stepped into the corridor, I let Gold take the lead.

She walked unnecessarily fast, her shoulders bouncing. I watched her, trying to get some perspective before I boiled into a childish tantrum. From her point of view, she was a get-results professional, a DA with a nearly perfect record.

And I was her Steven Sayres, bad-mouthing her, undermining her hard-won reputation. She had reason to be testy, and so did I. But this was supposed to be about Brad Rommel, not me and Connie Gold.

She stopped at the elevator, punching the button. The door opened immediately; the elevator had been sitting there waiting for somebody somewhere to summon it. That never happened in San Francisco; there was always a wait. I was trying to decide how big a minus that was when I heard a sound behind me.

Gold was just about to step into the elevator. I was several paces behind, about to be preceded in.

A sound captured my attention, a small click different in pitch and type from the drone of air conditioning. It was a nondescript noise, not loud, not startling; it obviously didn't catch Gold's ear.

But I suppose I recognized it. I suppose some part of me was hyper-alert, heedful of Sandy's warning, worried about two close brushes in eight days.

Unlike Connie Gold, I wheeled around. I saw a figure at the end of a corridor, not the hall we'd just come down, but one that elled into it.

The figure wore an unbelted trenchcoat, had both arms extended, appeared to be holding something, pointing something.

My veins flooded with fear. I couldn't see a face, no face, just a continuation of the dark shape. That's what scared me, I think. I squinted and saw darkness where I expected to see skin. I saw something my brain had learned to register: I saw a ski mask. And something pointed at me.

I ducked. I folded at the waist and bent my knees. It was the quickest way to change my location, and I did it without thinking, without waiting to hear a shot, without strategy or regard for how it might appear. I almost felt, later, as if Sandy's instruction to watch my back had taken on a life of its own. As if his worry had staked out part of my awareness and forced me to turn, pushed me into a crouch.

Almost immediately I heard a blast. I smelled gun smoke. I rode my crouch to the floor, letting myself collapse to my knees, covering my ears with my forearms.

Behind me, I heard a thump as something or someone hit the floor.

Then I heard shouts, footfalls.

I looked down the hall and saw the dark figure running. I looked behind me and saw Connie Gold sprawled face down on the elevator floor, trying to crawl toward the control panel. Her blood soaked the carpet in a widening circle beneath her.

I was too shaken to move quickly; I reached her only seconds before office workers who'd heard the shot and rushed into the hall.

Gold was flat on her belly, still wriggling toward the elevator controls. She said nothing, made no noise I could hear. She shuddered when I touched her. The people who'd materialized behind me began asking if she was all right, what had happened.

"I don't know. I think she was shot."

I heard someone say they were calling 911. I heard someone run part way down the hall, then stop when someone else cried, "No! He's armed!"

"Call the sheriff," I said, looking over my shoulder into the face of a young woman with shiny makeup. "The man's heading downstairs, he's got to be. Call the sheriff."

It would be too ironic to learn the ski-masked man had run past the sheriff's office on his way out of the building.

My hands were still on Gold's back. I could feel her short, labored breaths. It was like touching a heaving bird. I recoiled, scooting backward into the woman with the makeup.

I felt strong fingers on my shoulders, thought for a wishful instant Sandy had come to protect me.

It was Jay Bartoli. He helped me to my feet, looking at Connie Gold. With an intense glance at me, he shouldered me aside to take my place over her.

The spot where I'd knelt was completely soaked with blood. The smell of burnt powder was stronger than earlier.

Bartoli seemed to be reaching beneath Gold, speaking quietly into her ear. I heard her murmur something, but I couldn't make out the words.

Gently Bartoli rolled her backward so she was on her side facing the back of the elevator. He hunched over her, bracing her body against his lap.

He reached back a hand, saying, "Give me your jacket."

"Anything." I slipped my jacket off and handed it to him. He pressed it to Gold's chest or shoulder.

He leaned close to her ear and spoke in soothing tones.

I stood frozen among strangers, willing Gold to pull through. I watched her, knowing it could have been me; he was aiming at me.

It was true. Someone was trying to kill me. Someone had come very close three times now. Three times in nine days.

I looked around, suddenly panicked. Where was the person with the ski mask?

I edged beside a knot of gawkers who'd bled out of adjoining offices.

I wrapped my arms around myself, cold without my jacket, frozen in my belated acceptance of the truth.

Somebody had killed Jocelyn Kinsley trying to kill me. Somebody had ripped the door from my car trying to run me over. Someone had shot Connie Gold trying to shoot me.

And I had no idea why.

CHAPTER

Twenty-eight

I DON'T KNOW WHY. I'M JUST TELLING YOU WHAT'S been happening." I couldn't keep the whine out of my voice; I felt battered, scared, and aggrieved. The county sheriff, a rotund bald man who didn't say much, and Jay Bartoli, who'd joined us midinterrogation, seemed unduly obtuse. "You can check all of it; it's all on paper somewhere. I'm not inventing it."

"We never said that." Bartoli glanced at his boss uncertainly.

The sheriff remained stock-still, hands folded over his ample belly, his face as serene as the Buddha's.

Bartoli pressed on. "Of course we believe you. We already know about most of it. We just want your side, your thoughts. You know how these investigations are: the more we hear, the more it ups our odds of figuring things out."

"What have you done so far?" It came out sounding like an accusation. "Brad Rommel is too scared to show his face. The mall went up in flames. Somebody with a gun can walk right into the county building—maybe right past your office—and start shooting. What have you figured out?"

Bartoli sighed as if his patience were fraying. He glanced again at his boss.

"Let's stick to this morning," he said evenly.

"That's where we started. We've been over it and over it. Let's talk about the mall and the blood in my uncle's yard."

"This morning," he repeated. "What made you and Connie leave her office?"

"You did." My stomach churned; my eyes were on fire. I couldn't handle this much longer. "You were late and we decided to fetch you."

"How long had you been waiting?"

"Maybe fifteen minutes."

"That's not very long."

"It is if you don't get along." Damn. I'd meant to leave my feelings for Gold out of this.

"Were you quarreling?" He was perched on a corner of his boss's desk. He leaned closer.

"No. We were impatient."

"What did you mean, it's a long time if you don't get along?"

"That Gold didn't want to start without you, and I didn't see why not."

He folded his arms and raised his brows. "You had no idea why she wanted to wait for me?"

"No." I watched his face. Was he saying there was a reason? Something more than Gold's stubbornness? "Are you keeping something from me?"

"Let's stick to the matter at hand."

"Is that it? Did you find out something she didn't want me to know? Was she going to try to limit what you said?" DAs routinely made it laborious for defense counsel to gather information. But in this case we'd had information to swap; it was in her interest to be cooperative. I'd thought.

"Who suggested leaving the office to look for me?"

"I did." As Bartoli and the sheriff already knew. "I've told you that a dozen times. I said I'd go get you, and she jumped up and said she was coming with me. She was acting like she didn't trust me to talk to you alone."

He kept his arms folded, practicing his best poker face. The sheriff stifled a yawn.

"You've known Connie how long now?"

"I met her last year. When she was—or rather wasn't—prosecuting Ted McGuin. When I ran into you again." Before that, I hadn't seen Jay Bartoli since the morning after our quickie tryst at age nineteen. I was beginning to wish I'd stayed away longer, stayed away forever.

"But you've had a number of meetings with her since."

"Yes. Several since I took on Brad Rommel." I knew her, if that's what he was driving at. I knew how territorial and ego driven she was. I might have guessed she'd insist on playing hall monitor rather than allow me a moment alone with Bartoli. "But if you're asking whether I expected her to go with me out into the hall, no. I didn't. In retrospect, I can see where she might. But at the time, I was just trying to speed things up, get the meeting going."

And now, in addition to more immediate concerns, God knew when I'd get the information I needed.

"Is it fair to say you've had your differences with Connie?"

"No, it's not fair. I challenged her practice of selling film rights when she prosecutes. I believe that's unethical. I wanted to make sure she didn't do it in this case."

"Because you felt the portrayal of you would be negative."

I practically snorted. "Every portrayal of me is negative, Jay. I've gotten a lot of press and it's pretty much all been bad. I'm used to it."

He looked suddenly sympathetic. "It must be hard to get used to something like that."

"Not if it's an indication you're doing your job well."

"But you expect an unflattering portrayal from Gold, if she sells the film rights to this case."

"She's not going to sell the film rights. The State Bar's on her butt."

"It's a gray area in terms of legal ethics, isn't it?"

"Yes."

"So you can't really be sure the Bar will stop her. That they *can* stop her if she decides to go ahead."

"It's not that simple, Jay. The State Bar has ways of making its displeasure felt. It's kind of like having the IRS mad at you."

"You've bucked them in the past. Am I wrong? Haven't you challenged the State Bar?"

"Yes, I have." It wasn't common knowledge; I was surprised he knew. "And the result was a state assembly bill backed by the Bar. It made a defense I'd pioneered flat-out illegal." My reputation had been tarnished. My stock at White, Sayres & Speck had gone down. "That's my point. It doesn't make sense to tangle with the State Bar unless your client's life depends on it." My client's had. "Gold's not in that position; she's just after a buck." I remembered her bleeding on the elevator floor. "I don't mean to criticize her. I'm saying, I was trying to do my job."

"Based on your stirring things up, two women are suing her now." The victims of the rapist she'd prosecuted were feeling betrayed by Gold's commercialization. "That sounds like personal animosity on your part."

"No. I want the fairest possible trial for Brad Rommel. I won't get it if Gold tailors her prosecution for a movie script. It's not personal, it's professional."

There was a tapping at the sheriff's door. The sheriff came briefly to life, gesturing for Jay to get it.

We watched each other for the moment it took Jay to open the door. What was he thinking, sitting there in flaccid silence?

Behind me, Jay spoke quietly to the person at the door.

When he returned to his perch on the desk edge, he had a Ziploc plastic bag in his hand. It contained a slip of paper.

He handed the bag to me. "Don't open it, just look at the contents."

It was torn from a larger sheet of paper. It had a phone number scrawled across it. I didn't recognize the number or the handwriting.

"I've never seen this before. I don't know the phone number."

"You're sure?"

"Yes. Absolutely."

"You're aware that you're under oath, and that anything you say can and will be used as evidence against you?"

"Yes." I knew the interrogation was "custodial"—that I couldn't get up and walk out. "I signed your disclaimer to that effect."

Bartoli and the sheriff watched me frown down at the scrap of paper.

"Whose phone number is it, Jay? Did you find this in the hall?"

He reached out a hand for it. "Tell us again what made you turn around and duck."

I told them again. I told them all morning and well into the afternoon.

For all the good it did me.

CHAPTER
Twenty-nine

THE AFTERNOON HAD GROWN DARK, WITH LOW CLOUDS over damp gray streets. The air shivered with mist that soaked through clothing, raising gooseflesh and chilling to the bone.

I parked a block from Uncle Henry's Victorian. There were two vans in front, news vans ready to disgorge men with minicameras on their shoulders, women brandishing tape recorders and microphones. They already had the story of today's shooting; I assumed they'd been quick to interview county office workers. But they didn't have their sound bite from me yet. They'd hover here until they did.

I sat in my rented Toyota watching moisture coat the windshield and run off in snaking rivulets. Hillsdale seemed a cold and gloomy place to me today, a place to stay indoors nursing chip-on-the-shoulder provinciality. It seemed a town of hermits—I'd been one myself—lashing out at one another for frustrated lack of other amusements. It no longer matched my fantasy of blessed freedom from convention; today I longed to be back in San Francisco, warm in my apartment with Sandy beside me.

The last thing I wanted was to be on television. I'd parked in front of a Queen Anne heavy on the gingerbread and rosebushes. There was no sign of movement behind its windows.

I slid to the passenger side of the car and got out. I walked quickly through the Queen Anne's side yard into its backyard. Though I might have to climb a few fences along the way, I should be able to trespass to the back of Uncle Henry's.

Determined to avoid the hassle of reporters, I didn't care who or what I might encounter. I traipsed through four neighboring yards, two of them cyclone fenced. Had someone stepped out a back door, I'd have moved on without explanation. But no one stopped me. A corner of my consciousness noticed flowers and pagodas and covered spas, making note of ways to improve the Victorian.

Our yard looked worse than usual, still strewn with greenery cops had carried from the gully on their pant legs. The wet lawn had borne too much traffic and was pocked with muddy indentations.

I climbed the back steps and twisted the old-fashioned key buzzer beside the backdoor. I wanted to give my uncle some warning before I let myself in. I was just inserting the key in the lock when he flung the door open. He was red-faced, his lips parted as if to read the riot act.

He blinked a couple of times, readjusting his reaction. "Reporters been bothering you?" I guessed.

He nodded, the flame fading from his cheeks. "I've been on the phone with Harrison"—Harrison Turitte, the sheriff—"getting the updates. You've had a hell of a day."

I gave him a quick squeeze on my way in, taking comfort in the familiar mingling of aftershave and Johnnie Walker. "What's his take on this? Why'd they keep me there so long?"

"He's being tight-lipped. I don't like it."

"I don't trust it. They kept me a lot longer than they

needed to. And their questions . . ." I shook my head. "A lot of stuff about how much I dislike Connie Gold. How I must have expected her to come out into the hall with me. They seem to think I lured her out there, had a contract killer waiting." It sounded preposterous, but there it was.

He nodded grimly. There were bags under his eyes, a tired twitch beneath one gray brow. He was dressed for company, in dark slacks and a flecked black cardigan. "I didn't like what I heard. I've been worrying about you."

It did my heart good to hear him say so.

"I guess you know Gold is okay—just nicked, really," he continued. "But I hear she's mad as a hornet; really putting the screws on Harrison. He doesn't seem to know what to think about all this." He reached for a tumbler of whiskey he'd left on a table by the backdoor.

"What's their big secret, Uncle Henry? Do you know? What didn't Gold tell me this morning? Why was she so set on waiting for Bartoli?"

Uncle Henry didn't ask what I meant, seemed up on the chronology. It was a tribute to his status that he'd gotten details from the sheriff.

"The mall." He looked deflated.

I braced myself. The last time we'd discussed it, he'd been furious with me. "What did they find out?"

"It wasn't firebombs or anything like that. The witness who claimed to see a plane, he melted away in the crowd and never came forward again. The police doubt the whole story."

"So it was arson? On-the-ground, garden-variety arson?"

He shook his head. "The latest theory is an earthquake."

"I didn't feel a quake." Maybe it happened before I reached town.

"I didn't either. But there was one, four point something. Epicenter not far south of the mall. Although it was a good hour before the fire started. I guess it can happen like that." He paled, looking away.

The mall's location had been a bone of contention; environmentalists had packed every planning session, complaining of the instability of mudflats. Uncle Henry had taken up cudgels for the consortium of developers, stressing that no more suitable location had been offered.

"Gas mains burst," he said. "That's what they're saying now. Gas-fed fire. I was just"—he gulped, blinking back tears—"writing the council a letter stating I'll retire at the end of the month. Leave before they chase me out of town."

"But it doesn't make sense. How's a smallish earthquake going to cause that kind of explosion? And an hour later, at that? Maybe someone used the quake as a cover, manually tampered with the gas lines."

"I'd like to believe that." He took a long swallow from his glass. "But you know, either way, I'm out. Because it could have happened that way even if it didn't."

"No, that's not fair. You don't know that. If someone smashed the gas lines, it's arson, not a natural flaw, not something you glossed over, not something that's your fault." I dropped into a kitchen chair. "Whoever said he saw an airplane, maybe he's the culprit. He was right there at the scene. He could have known a plane was being flown to Brad Rommel's house either to blow him up or get him arrested."

My uncle turned toward the window, bracing himself against the sink.

"Earthquake my butt," I continued. "We have quakes that size all the time."

But culpability was too heavy a mantle to shed easily. Uncle Henry didn't speak.

"Think about it," I urged. "This whole business of someone spotting a plane, and a plane turning up at Brad's—it means something. It's part of the same thing."

To take advantage of the earthquake as a cover, the person had to recall the brouhaha about building on mudflats. That meant he'd lived here at least eight years. Either that or he'd been lucky enough to have his sabotage coincide with a quake.

"Whoever said he spotted a plane, he's the one who phoned Brad Rommel—or had Cathy Piatti do it. He screwed up the gas pipes. He flew the plane to Brad's."

My uncle turned, his expression heartbreaking. "Who'd go to the trouble, Laura? Listen to yourself. Blow up a mall to frame somebody who's already been arrested for murder. What's the point?"

"I don't know." I shivered in my damp clothes.

Maybe it had to do with Uncle Henry. With him or with me. He and Hal were all the family I had left. He meant the world to me.

"What else did the sheriff say? Anything?" The news about the mall would have made Gold cagey enough. The plane in Rommel's driveway was beside the point if there was no firebomb.

"The blood in our yard." Uncle Henry looked mystified. "They still don't know whose it is. But they do know some of it was frozen and thawed out later."

"Meaning it could have been siphoned over a period of time. That it wasn't necessarily a fatal amount."

He nodded.

"Sandy's right," I said. "This whole thing's as phony as a three-dollar bill. Rommel was charged with murdering Piatti, but according to him, she phoned him. Supposedly he blew up the mall and set the getaway plane on fire, but it wasn't his plane and the mall didn't get bombed anyway. And we end up with a bucketful of blood on our lawn, but it wasn't really enough to kill anybody because it got drawn over a period of time."

I didn't add, And someone tried to shoot me, run me over, and then shoot me again.

"They're going to put the mall thing to bed, Laura. Say the earthquake did it and quit worrying about it. And Rommel's still on the hook for Piatti, no matter if they ever figure out this other bucket or not." He'd put his drink down; he was squinting thoughtfully.

"What was it you used to say to Hal when we were kids? 'It's not supposed to make sense, it's supposed to make a point.'"

A half-smile lit his face.

"It's scattershot," I mused. "Somebody roaming around making as much trouble as possible around Brad. Or around me. I'm not sure which."

We stared at one another.

"It's like someone's out to get me where it hurts most," I said. "My client, my family." My life. "It's like someone bought a complete anti-Di Palma package. Oh my God, I wonder if that's where the circle closes."

"What circle?"

Fear almost froze the words in my throat. "Designer crimes. I wonder if someone went out and bought me all this trouble."

CHAPTER

Thirty

I WAS SURPRISED TO SEE JAY BARTOLI AT THE DOOR. I'D scarcely had time to take my morning shower and make myself some coffee. I'd just left a message on Sandy's machine, asking him to phone me when he got back from D.C. I'd missed his calls the day before, and hadn't had the heart to fill his tape with my woes.

Uncle Henry had gone out an hour earlier to tour the charred remains of the mall. He'd left in a buzz of excitement. Apparently the damage wasn't as extensive as originally feared. The fire had been gas-fed and therefore deceptively huge. But it had burned out before destroying the mall's infrastructure. The damage was mostly cosmetic, probably fixable—if it could be proved the gas lines hadn't burst because of earthquake damage.

I hoped Bartoli had come to tell me that; perhaps to tell my uncle. I hoped he hadn't come to question me again.

"Are you here about the fire, Jay?"

"No." He seemed as faded as the anemic morning. "We've got Brad Rommel."

"Where?"

"Over at the county jail."

"I mean where did you find him? Or did he turn himself in?"

"He turned himself in because he heard Gold was shot; that's what he says. That he heard it on the six-o'clock news. Said he was afraid we'd try to blame him if he didn't come forward."

I was relieved he'd turned himself in, but I wasn't sure I understood his logic.

"He surrendered down in San Francisco. He just got delivered to us."

I felt my jaw clench. "You've known about this since dinnertime last night."

"He didn't ask for you till now."

I wanted to sock Bartoli in the jaw. "I don't care if he asked for me or not. You knew my client had surrendered and you didn't call me."

Bartoli flushed, his blond brows sinking irately.

"Don't give me any cop bullshit," I forestalled him. "I don't care what your excuse is. You went to school with Brad, for Christ's sake. You could have done him the favor of telling his lawyer he was in custody." I turned away, paced a few angry steps into the hall, wheeled back around. "Rommel has never needed anyone's protection more than he needed mine yesterday. Depending on what he said, he could have screwed himself over big time. And it's your damn fault, Jay!"

Bartoli's fist clenched. He moved his arm a menacing fraction as his face grew ruddy with anger. "Your boyfriend didn't ask for you! Blame him if you're going to blame anyone!"

I filed the "boyfriend" remark for later consideration. "Who do you think you are? Who do you and Gold think you are? The Tsar and Tsarina of Hillsdale? This is supposed to be a twentieth-century town, not a damn fiefdom.

By what right do you hide information from defense counsel?" I was trembling. I turned away, searching the hall for my coat. "I'll tell you this much, this would never happen in San Francisco. If they learned my client had surrendered, they'd goddamn tell me. They wouldn't wait for him to ask for me—that's nothing but good-old-boys playing keepaway."

I was losing it, venting frustration after a long night of little sleep; falling prey to fear that Rommel had said too much, said something wrong, damaged his case without me there to shut him up.

I turned back to Bartoli. Behind him the sky was leaden.

Bartoli squinted at me, his lips tight. Finally he said, "Consider this notification that your client is being held on the fourth floor of the County Building in the county jail. He has—just now—asked to see you. You know the procedure if you want to speak to him." He turned, taking the porch steps quickly.

I slammed the door before he made it to his car. Stupid bastard. He knew it compromised Rommel to be in custody without counsel. Why the hell hadn't he told me sooner?

One good thing: Rommel had surrendered in San Francisco. Though technically he'd had time to drive the six hours from Hillsdale, he appeared to have an alibi for Gold's shooting. I wouldn't put it past her to try to implicate him.

I didn't realize she and Bartoli would be getting together this morning to implicate me. I didn't realize they'd be cobbling evidence for an arrest warrant against me.

CHAPTER

Thirty-one

BRAD ROMMEL COULD BARELY KEEP HIS EYES OPEN, barely remain upright in the visiting-room chair. He'd had almost no sleep since running away. Every glimpse of a police car, every set of headlights jangled him awake. Every minute he spent not racking his brain was a minute he felt he'd wasted. And last night, spent getting processed and then bussed north, had offered little rest.

"Probably the biggest reason I turned myself in was to get some sleep," he admitted.

"It was the smart thing to do, Brad. They were bound to try to connect you with Gold's shooting. They're the least imaginative, least professional group of law-enforcement officials I've ever dealt with."

I regretted the words the minute they passed my lips. Brad looked devastated, his ruddy face paling.

"That doesn't matter, Brad. You did the right thing. We needed to get your explanation on record. If Piatti phoned you, then obviously someone's been trying to frame you, and your fear—and flight—make sense. If we can get the court to see that as the starting place, it won't weigh as heavily that you spent a few days in San Francisco.'' It wasn't likely the court would look at it quite that way, not initially. But Brad needed to take the long view. He needed to keep the faith. He was too exhausted to dwell on the depressing interim. ''The main thing now is for you to say nothing, absolutely nothing. I'm going to do all the talking for you, all right?''

He nodded, rubbing his red-rimmed eyes. ''I didn't say anything when I turned myself in except who I was and all that. I figured they'd get it that I couldn't have been up here if I was down there.''

I ignored the drive-time factor. ''Well, we may be dealing with a contract killer. The mask and the level of planning—he was in the hall one minute and then just gone. I've heard that's characteristic of hired guns.''

Brad laughed feebly. ''So they could say I went to San Francisco just to have an alibi. That I hired someone.''

''They can say anything they want. But they're not going to find any evidence.'' I kept it open-ended, inviting him to contradict or elaborate. ''Let's go through it all again, Brad. I know you're tired. But it'll help me get you out of here. Start with Friday night.''

''I told you: I got a call from Cathy. I went to the mall just like I said.''

''You were delayed,'' I prompted.

''Right. Right.'' He massaged his forehead with rough fingers. ''Kind of a big lady with a locked-up car. Maybe we could find her? Do you think that would help me?''

''There's a possibility the mall's gas lines were tampered with. Finding her would prove you were in the wrong place to have done that. But you're not charged with that crime.''

''Yeah,'' he sighed.

''The hour and a half between the beginning of the fire and you going back home—anybody see you then, while you were up the hill watching? Anybody who might identify you?''

He shrugged. ''I doubt it. Everyone was looking down at the fire.''

''Well, the plane in your driveway probably didn't have anything to do with the fire. It was caused by gas igniting. The gas lines might have cracked in an earthquake that night. But they haven't ruled out arson—tampering from on the ground.'' I watched Brad. His reaction was subsumed by exhaustion. ''Someone at the scene claimed he saw a plane. He might have said that to implicate you, to get the police up to your cabin.''

''If I'd gone to the mall on time, I'd have been crisped. They'd have found me dead inside, and a burnt plane next to my house. What's been bugging me—don't those two things cancel out? If I'm dead inside the mall, who's supposed to have flown the plane back?''

''The big woman,'' I said. ''She made sure you didn't get there in time to get caught in the fire. That has to have been part of the plan, to keep you away long enough. Because you're right, it doesn't make sense to try to kill you *and* frame you. One or the other.''

''Guess I should be happy they went for framing me.''

''Except, you know what? Arson investigation is a fairly exact science. Whoever did it must have known they'd eventually figure out it was an on-the-ground operation.''

His eyes were as bright as blue lights. ''Framed for a few days until they figure out it wasn't my plane, and anyway a plane didn't do the damage.''

''I wonder why someone would want you in jail, or at least under suspicion, for a few days.'' If he hadn't run off, screwed up his bail, he'd probably be getting out about now. ''Or maybe out of the way. Maybe Cathy's phone call, the burning plane, all that, maybe it was supposed to spook you into leaving town.''

For the first time since they'd brought him to the visiting room, he looked alert.

"You're saying I did what they wanted me to do? That I played into their hands?"

His sudden flush warned me to shift gears.

"These complications and loose ends are going to help us, Brad. Put aside that we only have your word for Piatti's phone call and the big woman delaying you. Look at the other things: the so-called witness who said he saw a plane, the plane in your driveway when one wasn't used to set the fire, the bucket of frozen blood on my uncle's lawn. It won't be hard to make them look like part of a scheme against you. We'll use them to cast doubt on the rest of the DA's evidence. With luck, this crazy stuff will get you out of here."

Brad nodded, his weariness seeming to ebb as I offered hope.

But I was more tired than ever. It was going to be a long day.

CHAPTER

Thirty-two

IT WAS EVENING BEFORE I REACHED SANDY. I SAT ON A
wooden chair in my uncle's hallway, too dispirited to walk
the cordless phone into the living room.

My uncle was still off conferring with fire marshals, construction consultants, seismologists and the mall's original
developers. I hoped the length of his absence was a good
sign.

Sandy and I had gone through details of the shooting,
most of them twice. More tiring, we'd been at pains not to
exacerbate each other's worries.

"Bartoli's got someone watching you?" Sandy asked
again.

"Yes," I lied. Sandy hadn't had enough sleep to drive
here; he was flying up in the morning. No use perturbing
him from afar. If my uncle didn't get back soon and I got
nervous, I'd go visit Aunt Diana. If someone was after me,
maybe he'd shoot her by mistake.

"I talked to two of Piatti's neighbors this afternoon," I
told him.

"Did you go with the guy whose name I gave you?" He'd left a message with the number of a local security "escort."

This time I answered honestly. "Yes. But he'd have been useless in a pinch. Enough brawn, but completely witless." I'd have asked him to stay the evening if he'd made a better impression.

"I'm sorry. He came recommended."

"We didn't have any problems. It was fine." He'd presented a striking contrast to my usual partner. "Except I missed you."

"Did you?"

I thought his question was rhetorical. By the time I realized it wasn't, I'd waited a second too long.

He continued, "What did you learn?"

"Nothing much. Nothing I didn't hear the first time I interviewed Piatti's neighbors. They still don't buy it that she took off. They're positive she'd have called them."

"That would depend on why she left."

"I brought that up, that she'd been arguing with Brad about it, maybe wanted to leave without a final scene. That she might have gone someplace remote or exotic with bad mail service."

"Yeah? And?" He sounded tired, seemed to be stifling yawns. He'd probably worked through the night, rushing to conclude Steve's business.

"They're positive they'd have heard from her. And they flat-out don't believe she called Brad last Friday and not them. They think he put her dead body in the mall and burned it down." One neighbor, burly in his flannel shirt and surly drunk at three in the afternoon, had grown furious. "Guy across the street got so hostile—about the mall as much as Piatti—that I left. Didn't ask some of the questions I wanted to. I'll let him cool down and then go back."

"No shit?" Sandy sounded pleased. Usually I ignored the warning signs. But the last ten days had taught me caution.

"The situation's gotten so complex, Sandy. I can't get a grip on it. Either it's all part of the same thing—something big and crazy''—I hesitated, not wanting to say, Something about me—"or there are several different convoluted things happening at once with me at the fulcrum."

"Did you get anything else out of Bartoli?"

"No. I was so pissed at him this morning I said some things I shouldn't." I was still angry. But not in the exhilarating way that masks regret. "I guess I'll have to mend my fences. The bastard."

"When I get up there, we'll see if the sheriff has anything new on Piatti," Sandy said. "She's the key. At least to the Rommel part of this. If she's been dead awhile, then Rommel's been lying—and going to a lot of trouble to make this as confused as possible. If Piatti was still alive on Friday, then she was in cahoots with whoever's behind this, maybe including the mall thing."

"I walked by her old store. Tried to look inside."

"Graffiti, anything like that?"

"No, nothing."

"Kind of a shame." He paused. "What happened to the downtown, I mean."

"It wasn't much in its heyday." But he was right: it was depressing to see the boarded-over windows and empty interiors. The artier stores had moved to Old Town. The more commercial ventures had run laughing to the mall. But the places I remembered best—the luncheonettes and five-and-dimes—had folded like Piatti's boutique. "At best, it'll be months before the mall's back together. Maybe downtown'll get a jolt of cash."

"More likely the waterfront area will." Lately Old Town had been dying, too, for all its new brick and polished brass. A few of those windows were soaped over now.

We sat in silence.

I knew it had been hard for Sandy to learn I'd been shot at—again. It was hard for him to remain too distant to keep vigil. The only thing he could do for me tonight—the only thing that would help rather than upset me—was to let me talk about the case. But so far, I'd vented without the reward of insight.

It was his turn. "Okay, Laura, possibility number one: Cathy Piatti was bitter her business was ruined, and wanted to blow up the mall. She was also mad at Brad. She stole a bucket from him, bled into it, went into hiding. He got arrested. She waited till he was out on bail, called him so he'd be at the scene, then torched the mall. Except she didn't get out in time to save herself."

"And possibility number two?"

"Piatti was working with someone. And that person decided last Friday she was expendable."

"Any idea who?"

"Nope." He sighed. "Possibility three: Rommel's lying. He killed Piatti. He set the mall on fire. Rigged a plane to burn up in his driveway. Put that other bucket on your lawn."

"Why?"

"Beats the hell out of me. Maybe he killed Piatti for the usual kind of reasons—jealousy, anger; she was leaving town, leaving him, he didn't want her to go. But after he killed her, he got flippy about it, decided to act on behalf of dying businesses like hers."

"What would the plane accomplish?"

"Since the mall wasn't strafed, it didn't inculpate him. It made him look framed. Probably it'll help him if you go to trial on the murder thing, right? You'll bring up all this stuff that looks like someone's out to get him. Could be that's why your car door got smashed off. Rommel had someone do it—make it look like they were out to get him."

I'd thought of the possibility, but I didn't like it.

"Fourth," he continued, "is designer crimes. Say it is a custom crime operation. Brad was an old friend; you were in town for your dad's funeral. Maybe 'designer crimes' set up a situation where he'd get arrested just so he'd call you. Then you made an appointment at More and Kinsley, and they thought you were on to them—whatever the hell they were trying to do. So they had a guy walk in to shoot you."

"Right in their own nest?" Though I'd entertained the suspicion myself, it struck me as damned silly.

"Yeah, it's unlikely. All right, let's say the Rommel thing boils down to either Piatti doing it, with or without help, or Rommel doing it. The other stuff—the two shootings—let's call that topic number two. Number two is where designer crimes fits in."

"I don't have it in me to worry about that tonight."

He ignored my protest. "Say Kinsley was on to designer crimes—whatever it's about and whoever it is—so they shot her. Maybe they became afraid you were on to them, too. So they tried to shoot you."

"Sandy—"

"Designer crimes could be the reason Gold got winged yesterday. So hear me out." Without pause: "Maryanne More came to your office and asked why we were talking to her clients, her 'failures,' right? Assume she was sounding you out. Assume she did design crimes for them, helped them do what the law couldn't. And when she didn't like your answers—thought you were hiding something, thought you suspected her—she tried to protect herself."

"I'm not sure about this designer crimes thing, Sandy. I can't see Maryanne More hiring a contract killer. I can't see her behind all this."

"We know almost nothing about her, Laura."

"Maybe so." But I'd gotten a feeling for her, somehow. I'd gotten an impression of sadness and vulnerability, not of scheming self-interest. "I suppose you're right." Maybe I wanted to believe her partnership offer was sincere. Maybe I was tired of working alone.

"And somewhere in all this," his voice deepened, "we've got Perry Verhoeven quitting because he's pissed off that you're disloyal—whatever that means. And we've got someone going to a whole lot of trouble to make Steve Sayres look incompetent."

"Every cloud has its silver lining."

"You don't know how bad off Connie Gold is?" he asked.

I repeated what I'd already told him. "I only know the bullet went through her upper arm—I don't even know if it hit the bone. She hasn't exactly phoned with details. In fact, she left instructions at the hospital that no one's supposed to talk to me. If it weren't for Uncle Henry, I wouldn't know anything."

"Well, there's the other possibility: the person could have been aiming for Gold."

I felt as if we'd switched roles. "What are the odds of me being present when two people in two different towns are shot by someone in a ski mask? If the person wasn't after me—"

"Maybe he was after you *and* Gold."

"We have nothing in common!"

"The Rommel case. You've got that in common."

I toyed with a pad of paper my uncle kept near the hall phone. It was plain white paper with a city and county of Hillsdale logo on top. There were a dozen or so sheets folded over, the top page scrawled with phone numbers of construction consultants.

I flipped idly through the folded-over sheets. They read like a log book of the week's disasters: appointments with council members, messages from the sheriff, results of lab tests on the backyard bucket of blood.

One of the pages had the bottom half ripped off. I wasn't sure why that disturbed me. I fingered the ragged edge, feeling scared, focusing my anxieties on it like sun through a magnifying glass.

Another minute and I'd have understood. But just then the door buzzer sounded.

"Hold on, Sandy." I walked to the door.

Plagued by reporters, my uncle had just installed a peep-hole. I squinted through it. Three grim-looking men in suits faded in and out of the fog. One held a badge ID up to the fisheye.

"Cops, Sandy."

"You sure?"

"They've got ID. I'll call back after I hear what they have to say, okay?"

"I'll sit tight and wait."

I hit the disconnect button and set the phone down. I opened the door.

The man who'd displayed his badge said, "Laura Di Palma?"

I nodded, expecting information, at worst expecting further questioning.

The last thing I expected was to be arrested for conspiring to murder Connie Gold.

CHAPTER

Thirty-three

I'D NEVER BEEN ARRESTED BEFORE, THOUGH I'D COME close.

I seemed to fixate on all the shiny surfaces leading to the holding cells. The flecked linoleum gleamed, glass cabinets and one-way mirrors flashed back fluorescence, metal desktops made bright snakes of the long bulbs, chrome chair legs glinted. Other times I'd been here, it had seemed a place of sickly beiges and yellows; tonight it was like being inside a flash cube.

I trotted beside the arresting officer, noticing the enormity of his arm, the roughness of his hand as he fingerprinted me, his foot-to-foot shuffling—as if his bulk were a difficult burden—while I was being photographed.

I gave my full attention to details—the facial hair of the policewoman snapping my picture, the paperwork my arrest was generating, the smell of moist towelette as I wiped away fingerprint ink. I was determined to back-burner my anger; I would show more sense than some of my clients. I wouldn't rail at the cops; they didn't care if I was innocent.

They didn't care if Connie Gold was a scoundrel. They were just doing their jobs.

Instead I forced myself to focus on the patina of waxed linoleum, to follow its sheen toward lockup. I didn't let myself think about Gold. I strained against the floodgate.

It had been years since I'd seen the inside of the jail; I always spoke to Brad in the visiting room. I watched with interest as two separate doors, each several inches thick, were unlocked from inside after papers were slipped through narrow slots.

Finally, I was turned over to a chunky woman in a strangling police uniform. She glanced through my papers, exchanged a few words with the refrigerator of a cop who'd arrested me, and led me off to the farthest of four small cells, the other three unoccupied.

My cell contained a vinyl shelf and a seatless toilet. I wore a gray dress that tied in the back like a hospital gown with overlap. I still wore my street shoes, gray suede flats. I was sorry they matched the dress; they would always remind me.

When I got out, I would challenge this arrest. I would try to make it cost Hillsdale money, not because I wanted to burden its beleaguered coffers, but because the city needed to realize how expensive a bad DA could be.

I sat on the vinyl bench. It was as cold as steel through my cotton dress. At the other end of the room, the seam-straining cop put her feet up on her desk and commenced reading a paperback.

My Uncle Henry would detonate when he heard about this. He would bring me some lawyer he knew from the Elks Club. And that would be fine for now. I'd guide him until I could get someone more experienced.

I expected to be granted bail. I'd be out before this reached arraignment, if it did. That was a big if. Gold and Bartoli had managed to get me arrested, but that didn't mean much. The whole town was in a panic over the mall, over the shooting. The knee-jerk response—grab the first person the DA claimed to have a case against—was typical of backwater justice. But the charges wouldn't hold up. I'd probably be released soon; the DA wouldn't want to go public with an embarrassing nothing of a case.

I was amazed they'd found pretext enough to put me away for a night. It was certainly a tribute to my unpopularity.

I was startled by a buzzer almost as loud as an airhorn. The policewoman yawned and put down her novel. "ID?" she said into the intercom.

"Sheriff's Investigator Jay Bartoli," a voice crackled.

The cop took a folder from the metal pass-through tray. She looked through it, then hit the unlock button.

Bartoli pushed the door open. "Why don't you take a break while I talk to Ms. Di Palma." It wasn't a question.

"Fine." She didn't sound happy about it. "I'll be out there. Buzz for me."

I remained seated, staring down at my shoes. I heard the squeak of leather soles on the shined floor. I didn't look up.

Bartoli cleared his throat, grabbed a bar, his wedding ring clinking against the metal. "Are you comfortable?"

I said nothing, being under no obligation to do so. I wouldn't be here if Jay hadn't cooperated with the DA's office. If he wanted to pretend we were going to chat sociably, that was his problem.

"I shouldn't do this," he said.

I looked up.

Bartoli was pale, gray circles beneath his blue eyes. He wore the same sports jacket and slacks he'd worn this morning. Apparently he hadn't been home.

"I shouldn't tell you this, Laura. But you'll find out soon enough, and at least this way you'll understand why the DA had you brought in."

He waited for me to say something. But I had nothing to say.

"The piece of paper, that's what did it. The piece of paper I showed you yesterday in Turitte's office."

The paper in the Ziploc bag had been similar in size and shape to the missing half-sheet of my uncle's telephone message pad. I'd been on the verge of realizing it when cops appeared at my door to arrest me. "I have nothing to say until my lawyer arrives."

"I'm here as a friend, not a cop." Jay stepped back as if I'd slapped him. "The phone number on the paper is—"

"Shut up, Bartoli." I rose, crossing swiftly to the bars. "Right now I have no idea what the number on that piece of paper is"—I'd kicked myself for not memorizing it while I had the chance—"or why it's so important. That won't be true if you tell me. And since there's nobody here with us, all you'd have to do is deny you mentioned it."

He was less than half a foot away from me. I could have slugged him through the bars.

But it wouldn't have approached the harm he could do me with his inexplicable confidences.

"I just thought you'd like to know." His voice was husky, tinged with wronged nobility.

"No, I don't want to know. Go away, Jay. I don't trust you. Just go away."

"It was the Southbay's number," he continued.

I turned away.

"The Southbay Motel. We've been going through its registrations, checking for false names and addresses, phony driver's license numbers, all that. We've turned up two already. Gold got the warrant after the first one."

So they'd been fishing for hired guns at the Southbay Motel. But even if they got lucky, even if the gunman had stayed there, he'd be long gone by now. And maid service would have wiped away his fingerprints and stray hairs.

I returned to the cot. They found a motel phone number on a slip of paper. They connected it to me—I could think of only one reason why. And as soon as they found a false registration, they arrested me. I wondered how many people didn't give real names; didn't think it was anybody's business; didn't want their adultery discovered.

"Go away," I repeated. "It's improper for you to be here without my lawyer present."

"I'm trying to help you!" His blue eyes glinted. "Friend to friend! I couldn't keep Connie—her pals in the office— from going after you over this. But I wanted you to know how come. I wanted you to know what they had."

"I'd have found out when my uncle brought me an attorney. If you'd wanted to be a friend, you'd have gone to my Uncle Henry." I felt a sudden stab of paranoia. Did they find my uncle's prints on the paper? Could they possibly suspect him, too? "You'd be talking to him now, helping him choose the right lawyer." I submerged the renegade fear. "You're not here to help me, and you're no friend of mine, Jay."

He gripped the bars as if to strangle them. "You were like this in school, too, but not this bad. Why do you always have to be like this?" He tried to shake the bars, his body shaking instead. He was red-faced, his light brown mustache and brows looking blond in contrast. "Why can't you ever let me in?"

It struck me as an ironic metaphor. "Go away."

"Yeah, I've heard that from you before!" He released the bars, giving them a whack with the sides of his fists.

He paced angrily to the desk, rummaging through its drawers. He withdrew a key ring.

I closed my eyes, taking a deep breath. A moment later, I heard the sound of metal against metal, the turn of a lock. I never thought I'd dread the sound.

But I felt cornered. I remained seated, head bowed, eyes closed.

Bartoli grabbed two fistfuls of my dress and hauled me up. The garment's back laces gave. I almost fell out of it, but Bartoli backed me against the wall.

"No, you can't let me in, can you? I was your friend that whole goddamn year, wasn't I? And I knew there was plenty wrong between you and Gleason." Gary Gleason, the boy I'd married out of high school. "You came to me to get laid when you heard about him and Kirsten, but you wouldn't even return my damn calls after that—you didn't even answer the door when I came to your house."

The wall was cold against my back where the dress gaped. Bartoli pressed against me. I could feel his chest heave with twenty-year-old anger. Maybe I had treated him badly. But it was so long ago.

I looked up at him, reminding myself not to fight back, not to hit a cop. The smallest bruise or scratch on him would excuse any punishment he inflicted.

"I can hear what you're thinking." His voice was a harsh whisper, his breath sharp with coffee. "That it's ancient history. Well, maybe it would have stayed that way if you hadn't come back. Broken up my marriage."

I held my breath, feeling my ribs would crack if he didn't back away. I certainly hadn't broken up Jay Bartoli's marriage. I hadn't even known it was in trouble.

"What did you call this town the other day? A pissant little borough?" He backed up just enough that I could breathe. I didn't know if he was giving me air or preparing to slam me against the wall again. "Yeah, sure. You went off and became a big-city lawyer, right? And I'm just a pissant cop. You let me take you to dinner and you play ice queen. It's only when you talk about your scummy murdering client that you come alive. He's the one you've got the hots for! Yeah, well, screw you, Laura! You're too fine to take any help from me? Screw you!"

It took everything I had not to fight back. There was no way I'd prevail, no chance I'd be believed afterward.

Rage rose in me with a ferocity that was much more my enemy than Jay Bartoli. My fists were alive; I could barely control them.

I managed to keep them by my sides. But I couldn't keep my mouth shut.

"You put that slip of paper into my pocket. *You* put it in there, Bartoli. I gave you my jacket so you could stop Gold's bleeding. That's the only place the paper could have been to get me arrested. You ripped it off the pad in my uncle's hallway. You did it when you visited him. You wrote the phone number on the paper and you put it in my pocket when I gave you my jacket."

He maintained a steady pressure, his mustache bristling against my forehead.

"The Southbay's the biggest motel in town, isn't it, Bartoli? So it'll take a while to check on everyone who registered day before yesterday, everyone who checked out yesterday or today, every call to every room. And then it'll turn out to be a dead end. Just a way for you to get me arrested and get me in here and pretend to do me a big favor by telling me what the DA had on me." I could hardly catch my breath, he leaned so heavily against me. "But I won't play. I don't take favors from cops. And I don't believe their bullshit, either."

He backed off. Turned and left the cell, slamming the door behind him.

He hit the buzzer, letting himself out when the policewoman, thumb in her paperback, came back in.

If she was surprised to see me trembling against the wall, dress hanging askew, cheeks scarlet, she didn't show it.

I remained there, heart pounding, for a few minutes. I remained there wondering.

Did Bartoli take the slip of paper for some legitimate reason? Did he tear off a piece to write a note to himself? Did the phone-number scheme suggest itself when I handed him my jacket?

Or did he take it knowing he'd be planting a phone number in my pocket? Did he take it knowing the occasion would arise? Knowing someone would try to kill Connie Gold?

It was bewildering enough to recast Jay Bartoli as a scorned lover. It was nauseating to think of him as something much worse: a cop willing to hire a killer.

I lay down, adjusting my ripped-tie dress as well as I could. I shivered the night away on my bench of cold vinyl. I told myself my uncle had been foiled only by the late hour; in the morning he'd ride to my rescue. And Sandy would arrive shortly afterward.

The phone number would turn out to be a dead end. The magistrate who'd issued the arrest warrant would cringe over the flimsiness of Gold's "evidence." I'd be released at my initial appearance, home by afternoon.

The alternative—that the phone number was correct, that the gunman had stayed at the Southbay—would mean Jay Bartoli was a killer.

That would mean trouble. That would be hard to prove.

I slept fitfully, praying to be released in the morning. If I was, I'd walk straight into the hornet's nest of reporters. For once, I'd be straight with them.

I'd tell them a sheriff's investigator planted evidence on me and roughed me up. I'd tell them the DA was so slipshod and vengeful she arrested first and inquired later.

Bartoli and Gold could go ahead and deny everything. I didn't care. They wouldn't sue me for slander because the accusations were true. They'd have to live with the media's depredation.

Gold was used to thinking of show biz as her golden goose. It was about time she saw its other side.

Bartoli had hoped to put me into his debt tonight. But he'd find me to be a more devoted enemy than I'd ever been a friend.

CHAPTER

Thirty-four

MY INITIAL APPEARANCE AND BAIL HEARING WERE AT four-thirty the next afternoon. I doubted there was enough on Hillsdale's criminal calendar to justify the delay. More likely, the deputy DA had claimed to be shorthanded, trying to stall into—maybe even through—the weekend.

A lawyer friend of Uncle Henry's sat beside me at the defendant's table. I'd guided him through the process step by step. He was a damp-faced business attorney whose hands trembled at the prospect of appearing in criminal court. But he'd been vetted by my uncle as someone who got it done your way. Later, if necessary, I'd find a criminal lawyer in San Francisco, where I knew the players.

"Your honor," he said to the judge, "I know this isn't the time or place for trying the merits of this case, but you must realize that the evidence against Ms. Di Palma is of the flimsiest nature. It's questionable even whether it was sufficient for an arrest warrant."

"You're right," the codgery old judge snapped. "This

isn't the time to discuss the merits. And as for the basis for the arrest, you can make those arguments at the arraignment. We're here now to talk about whether your client is a good bail risk. So you can sit back down, Miss Leiden.''

Leiden, the deputy DA who'd presided over my arrest, had leapt to her feet. She smiled as she sank into her chair.

But my lawyer was well coached. ''I realize that, Your Honor. I'm simply stating that the motivation for the arrest appears to be an irrational vendetta on the part of the District Attorney. There is virtually no evidence connecting—''

''Objection!'' Leiden was back on her feet. She didn't bother stating the basis for the objection; it was identical to the previous unstated one.

''Your Honor''— my poor attorney was sweating profusely now—''although I'm not familiar with criminal practice, this level of evidence—a scrap of paper with a motel phone number—would be considered paltry, even ludicrous, in a civil matter. And the burden of proof in a criminal case—''

''Objection sustained! That's enough in this vein, Mr. Huddleston. You can voice these concerns at the arraignment and the preliminary hearing.''

Huddleston looked relieved. I'd browbeaten him into harping on this until he was forced into silence. Though the judge ruled it irrelevant, the information might still influence his decision, might cause him to err on the side of lower bail, might save me thousands of dollars. If nothing else, the media—and there were a dozen out-of-town reporters in the court pews—would hear my side of the story now.

I tried to relax. I whispered to the lawyer. There was one other thing I wanted him to say.

He didn't look happy about it. ''But, Your Honor,'' he said. ''There's no evidence whatsoever that a false registrant at the Southbay Motel shot at Ms. Di Palma and Ms. Gold. So using that phone number as—''

''Now you look here.'' The judge motioned for Leiden to remain seated. ''I know you don't usually appear in criminal court, Mr. Huddleston, but that doesn't exempt you from following its rules. I'm not going to cite you for contempt— yet! But one more reference to the merits of this case, and I will. Do you understand that?''

My lawyer said yes, glancing at me to make sure I got the point. I'd guessed he could get away with blurting out information that a criminal lawyer, knowing better, could not. He'd agreed to try—but his trepidation had been evident. Luckily, he owed my Uncle Henry many favors.

And the main thing on my agenda was to tell the world I'd been railroaded.

I wanted it on tonight's news. I wanted it in tomorrow's papers.

I heard a faint snicker behind me: Sandy, recognizing that my plan had worked. I didn't turn to look. I didn't want to be ogled by hungry reporters.

''Your Honor,'' my lawyer said, ''Ms. Di Palma was born and raised in this town. Her uncle is its mayor. Together they own a home at thirty-six Clarke Street. She is an important and outstanding member of the bar, and she certainly understands the ramifications of being released under bond. She poses no, um''—a quick glance at the cue-card notes I'd prepared for him—''risk of flight, none whatsoever. We would like to petition the court to release her today on her own recognizance.''

''Miss Leiden?''

The deputy DA rose. ''Your Honor, Ms. Di Palma, for all her family connections and string-pulling ability, is accused of ordering the assassination of a public servant. This is just about as serious a crime as a person in a free society can commit. Obviously our whole system of justice would fall apart if defense lawyers went around hiring assassins to kill district attorneys. The state feels strongly that this court would be sending out a highly inappropriate message if it released this defendant at all. And if Ms. Di Palma is to be released, we would certainly ask, given the gravity of the charges and the potential for further actions of this kind on her part once she's at large, that bail be set at least at two million dollars.''

That caused murmurs in the courtroom. But my lawyer had a response. It was on the cue card beneath the notation, "After she asks for bail in the millions."

"Your Honor?" My lawyer stood. "I know we have to pretend at this point that there is a basis for these charges even though there isn't. I understand that for purposes of setting bail the court must ignore the 'innocent till proven guilty' rule. But''—he spoke quickly to fend off another reprimand—"bail in the millions? For an admired and respected attorney with a sterling reputation? A woman who is a blood relation and periodically resides with the mayor of our city? This is not someone who is going to flee from prosecution, flee the jurisdiction. There is no possible justification for such an absurd bail. Laura Di Palma is not going anywhere, except to the house she coowns with her uncle, the mayor of Hillsdale for the past thirty-two years. If we can't trust her to remain, we can't trust anybody."

I'd asked the lawyer to bring up my uncle constantly—if we happened to appear before this judge. There were others on the bench who might penalize me for the relationship. My uncle had made a lot of enemies as well as a lot of friends.

Leiden restated her overblown and phony fears. My lawyer mentioned Uncle Henry again. In the next ten minutes, nothing new was added to the debate.

When it came time for the judge to rule, I felt a comforting hand on my shoulder. I knew it had to be Uncle Henry.

The bailiff would have intervened had anyone else in the pews tried to touch me.

I covered my uncle's hand with mine. It was so familiar— short-fingered, tough-skinned, with the faintest scent of alcohol. I noticed the judge watching us, his eyes misting over. I held my breath.

"I don't believe we have much reason for concern here, Miss Leiden," the judge said at last. "I think if there was ever a defendant who fit the criteria for minimal bail, we have one here today."

I felt my uncle's hand tighten its grip on my shoulder.

"Let's set bail at a nominal amount. Let's say ten thousand."

"Your Honor—"

"Ten thousand, Miss Leiden." He rapped his gavel.

"That's an insult to Ms. Gold!" Leiden protested. To speak now, after the judge had ruled, was a huge impropriety. Either she truly thought I was guilty or she needed to demonstrate her devotion to her boss.

Since she'd broken with convention, I did, too. "It's no insult. I didn't hire anyone to shoot Connie Gold. That gun was aimed at me, not her!"

The gavel rapped repeatedly. "Bailiff, you will please return Miss Di Palma to her cell until bail is posted! And Miss Leiden, you know better than that!"

I managed a quick turn, hugging my uncle over the railing and making eye contact with Sandy. I wanted to convey some part of my feeling, but there was sudden commotion in the courtroom, reporters rushing out to file stories, others trying to question Leiden, question me, question my lawyer. Again the judge rapped his gavel, calling for order.

The bailiff pulled me out of my uncle's embrace, marching me out of the courtroom as if the disruption were my fault.

It would be only a matter of hours, I told myself, maybe

minutes, until my uncle wrote a check and got me out of here.

But it was all I could do to leave dry-eyed. On the other side of the redwood door, on my way to the prisoners' elevator, stress and weariness got the upper hand. The bailiff gave me his handkerchief and told me I could keep it. I later learned he was a friend of Uncle Henry's, too.

CHAPTER

Thirty-five

I WALKED OUT OF THE COURTHOUSE AND INTO A FIERCE rainstorm. It had been twenty-four hours since I'd glimpsed the outdoors. Yesterday's gloom was locked into my memory; I was shocked to see it had erupted into a tempest.

My uncle and Sandy hovered protectively, trying to run me between them to the waiting car. We'd done our embracing, even cried a little, inside. Now they wanted to hurry me home. But this was the night I'd been waiting for, a night wild enough to match my confusion, overwhelming enough to reduce life to the elemental.

For one thing, it had kept the reporters away. The county building was closed to the public after five-thirty, so they'd been evicted from the lobby. Apparently none had been willing to wait outside in the brutal rain.

I enjoyed the walk to the car far more than my companions, judging by their comments.

As we climbed into Sandy's car—he'd driven up after all, hadn't waited for the morning plane—my uncle remarked, "Good old Huddleston." Then solicitously, "You were happy with him?"

"I thought he did a great job. Especially since he was so nervous about it." I luxuriated in the soft velour of the bucket seat. I hadn't sat on anything accommodating for an entire day. "I'll hold off on hiring another lawyer. I think they'll have to drop the charges—I don't think they've got enough evidence to get them through the arraignment."

"Unless they find the gunman through the motel," Sandy pointed out. He didn't start the car. He shifted in the driver's seat to face me.

He looked as if he had a lot to say. But not with my uncle in the back.

He stuck to business: "Whoever put the paper in your pocket was trying to frame you. That's probably the person who did the hiring. They'd know where their killer had bunked."

"But they wouldn't lead the cops to him—that's too risky; he could roll over on them." I hadn't had a chance to explain about Bartoli. "Jay Bartoli came to my cell right after I got arrested, supposedly to tell me what evidence they had." I held up a hand to silence Sandy. He could express outrage later. "I was pissed off, too. But here's what I think: I gave him my jacket so he could stop Gold's bleeding; and he put the piece of paper in my pocket later— not to frame me, but to connect me with the shooting. Get me into jail long enough to come to my cell and be my hero."

"Why the hell would he want to do that?" Sandy always sounded dangerous when his voice got quiet. Dangerous and maybe jealous.

I hadn't bothered telling him about my long-ago night with Jay. Nor did I want to discuss it in front of my uncle. I kept it simple: "Bartoli's got the hots for me."

In the dark car interior, I couldn't read Sandy's face. I heard my uncle stir in the back seat, probably ill at ease with the conversation's direction.

Sandy started the car, setting the wipers to Fast. Even so,

we could barely see out the windshield. It was all I could do, after a claustrophobic day, not to roll down my window and stick my head out.

At the first stoplight, Sandy grumbled, "It doesn't work for me."

"Bartoli setting me up so he could be my hero?" It sounded foolish, but he hadn't seen Jay. He didn't know our history. "He's obsessed, Sandy." It was embarrassing to say so in front of my uncle. "It was a way to get my attention. Earn my gratitude."

"Obsessed or not." He continued driving. "It's too back-handed. Not something you'd think of if you were in that position."

I wasn't ready to describe what happened in my cell. My fury was too close to the surface. I was too tired to reexperience it.

"I don't know where else the paper could have come from. It wasn't in my pocket when I left the house."

"You're sure?"

"Of course I'm sure." Though I hadn't actually checked my pockets. "As far as I know." I hoped he wasn't suggesting my uncle had put it there.

"What about before you left San Francisco, Laura? You wear the jacket anywhere?"

"To Perry Verhoeven's plant. But if he put something in my pocket he was very damn subtle about it. I sure didn't notice."

He asked my uncle, "You always keep your doors locked?"

"No." Uncle Henry sounded startled. "At night, yes. But during the day? I don't give it a thought."

"Okay," Sandy continued. "So either someone walked in and stuck it in your pocket, or Bartoli did it when you gave him your jacket, or Verhoeven when you visited him, or—"

"Gold during our appointment." It wasn't a promising list. "I think it was Bartoli."

"I wouldn't rule out someone walking into your house."

"How would they know which jacket I'd wear to the courthouse?"

"Doesn't matter—cops could have found the number in your jacket at home."

He was right; Gold could have gotten a warrant to search my house. "Have they been through my things yet?"

"Through everything," my uncle confirmed. "But how can this be? Who would put a paper into Laura's pocket? Who would know this man with a gun would miss her completely? If she was shot," shock muffled his voice, "who would care what was in her pocket?"

"That's true," I agreed. "Unless the gunman was aiming for Gold all along, the phone number was an afterthought. Bartoli—or okay, somebody—put it in my pocket later."

"Not if—" Sandy stopped. Not trusting my uncle?

I turned to face Uncle Henry. His eyes welled, glinting reflections of the dashboard lights. He ran a shaking hand over his sleek hair. He'd been through a lot since my father's death.

"How can you discuss this like it's the grocery list?" His tone was strangled. "People shooting at you and framing you! My God!"

"If we sound cavalier," I reassured him, "it's because we're sure we'll figure it out, bring the sky down on whoever's doing it." I overstated our confidence. "Remember, this is what Sandy does for a living; he's a professional."

"Kids, don't try this at home," Sandy muttered.

He turned onto Clarke Street. There were six news vans in front of the Victorian, some large, some mini, one barely as big as a station wagon. Inside them, reporters must be feeling cold and cramped and tired of listening to the rain.

"No wonder they've got an attitude," Sandy commented.

I recalled my resolution to march straight into their midst

and denounce Jay Bartoli, impugn Connie Gold. But I found I didn't want to.

I told myself it was the rain: I didn't relish standing in a torrent to make my speech. Nor could I invite reporters into my uncle's home, not tonight.

I told myself I was exhausted and hungry and needed a breather. I told myself I needed to think about Brad Rommel, about how my arrest affected him; whether I should counsel him to find a new lawyer or wait for charges against me to be dropped. I needed to prepare a change-of-venue motion; Gold's animosity toward me would certainly taint his trial.

I told myself Brad's business came first. I told myself it was always wise to sleep on major denunciations.

But there was more to it than that. In some recess of my mind, I'd begun to understand what this was truly about.

CHAPTER

Thirty-six

THE PHONE RANG ALMOST AS SOON AS WE WALKED INSIDE. I stood in front of the answering machine, expecting to hear the voice of an ignored reporter. But surprisingly, it was Deputy District Attorney Leiden. I picked up the receiver as she began her message.

"Ms. Di Palma," she said coolly, "you're screening your calls. This is in regard to Bradley Rommel. I'm not certain what arrangement he's made in terms of new counsel?" I let her question hang in the air. "But since you were his attorney of record prior to your arrest . . ."

"It would take an actual conviction to disqualify me, Ms. Leiden. This arrest is irrelevant." I nearly added, "and stupid." "What about Brad Rommel?"

"I've had a message that he's not in his cell."

I motioned for Sandy, shucking his wet jacket, to stand beside me. "What do you mean, Rommel's not in his cell? Where is he?"

"I don't know. I was just notified. I was asked to contact you. We felt that you should be told, of course. And that you might have some information."

Sandy stared at me, hand extended to drape his jacket over the coatrack. "Rommel's gone?" He mouthed the words.

"Of course I don't have any information!" I nodded to Sandy. "I just spent a night in your jail. It's not someplace a person walks out of. What the hell happened?"

"I don't know," she repeated. "He was locked up and under guard. I understand there was a very short lapse during which one guard left his station before the relief officer arrived—"

"Why? Why did he leave?"

"I'm just relaying the contents of the message I received. I gather it was a gastric emergency," she said dryly. "By the time the replacement arrived, Mr. Rommel had vanished."

"From a locked cell?"

"Apparently."

"Someone came and took him away, that's what happened. He didn't escape. Someone with access came and kidnapped him."

The rage I'd tethered in my cell threatened to explode from every pore.

I said to Sandy, "Someone hustled Rommel out of there when he wasn't being guarded." To Leiden I said, "What are you doing to find him?"

"I'm sure the sheriff is following the protocols."

"I don't care about the protocols." And judging from Bartoli's behavior, they didn't mean much anyway. "I want you personally to talk to the sheriff and the city police. There's no way Rommel could have gotten out unless someone opened the door for him. You tell the cops: Don't harm Rommel. Don't shoot at him no matter what it looks like, no matter what he seems to be doing."

"I wouldn't presume to tell the sheriff how to do his job."

"Yes, you would. Because I'm right and you know it—he

didn't just walk out of there. If my client gets hurt as a result of this, I'll sue the sheriff. And I'll sue you personally." It was a sop to my anger, not nearly enough to scare her or to assuage me. I wanted to thrash her. "I presume Rommel's cabin is being staked out?"

"I would imagine so." Something in her voice tripped my alarms; her coldness raised gooseflesh on my rain-soaked skin.

"There is something terribly wrong here, Ms. Leiden. I hope to God you're trying to figure out what it is." I hit the disconnect button.

Sandy shook the rain off his jacket. "Where he is depends on who got him out."

"Bartoli got him out."

"Bartoli again. Why?"

"I have no idea why."

"No. I mean why do you think so? What's the deal with Bartoli?"

I explained what had happened in my jail cell. Sandy listened, scowling.

My uncle came downstairs, threading his arms into the sleeves of a cardigan. "Any calls for me?" He'd run straight up to change clothes.

"I haven't checked." The message light blinked relentlessly; there were doubtless dozens from reporters. "Sandy and I have to go out for a while."

He stopped, looking down at us from midstair. "What's wrong?"

"Brad Rommel's missing."

His face smoothed with relief. "I thought he was in jail again."

"And now he's missing from jail." Why did he look relieved? What had he been afraid I'd say? "I need to go up to his cabin, talk to whoever's in charge of the stakeout. I want to be sure they don't have orders to shoot him." That's what I'd heard in Leiden's voice: tacit agreement with the cops to shoot Rommel on sight. Rommel would be dropped into the middle of a stakeout and he'd get killed. Whoever pulled him out of jail wanted the Piatti case closed. "This town is nothing but a banana republic!"

My uncle, the mayor, looked stung. But he didn't contradict me. "I worry about you." To Sandy, "You'll stick by her."

"Yup." With a sigh, he put his wet jacket back on. His hair dripping and face ruddy, he showed no hesitation.

I wrapped my arms around him. We were much more than friends who worked together. I hoped he agreed.

His embrace didn't leave much doubt. But there wasn't time to extrapolate.

We ran back out to his car, ran quickly enough to befuddle the still-parked reporters. Sandy peeled out before they could hit the curb.

I twisted the rearview mirror, watching their vans' doors swing open, then slam shut. "We'll probably come back later and find they've beaten up my uncle out of pure frustration."

Sandy was frowning, his jaw clamped.

"This doesn't fit your theory that Rommel's lying," I guessed. "Unless you think he escaped without help."

"Course not. He didn't get out of a locked cell without help." He wiped the fogged windshield, hitting the defrost button. The rain beat faster than the wipers could clear. The night was moonless, wild and loud with the battering of water and the whistle of wind. "That's the problem: it just doesn't figure."

Exuding testiness, Sandy drove the slick streets more quickly than I'd have dared. I fiddled with the car radio, checking whether a police bulletin had been issued, whether we could expect every backwoods rifle owner to be on the watch for Brad Rommel. But all we heard was the usual DJ bantering, the same old country songs and mellow rock. The sheriff's embarrassment apparently exceeded his panic. But he'd have to find Rommel fast to avoid admitting that he'd lost him.

"The more the case against Rommel falls apart," I pointed out, "the more they heap on ancillary charges: bail jumping, now escape. I think Brad's right. I think someone in law enforcement"—I didn't bother saying Jay Bartoli; who else could it be?—"is out to get him."

"What's Bartoli got against Rommel? Something from way back? High school?"

"I don't know. He thinks Brad had a thing about me."

"Did he?"

"No. We went out a little. But I had it bad for Gary Gleason. Everyone knew it." I had it bad enough to make the worst choice of my life. Once burned.

I glanced at Sandy's profile, lit by dashboard lights. This was how it was supposed to be: taking comfort in someone's presence, thinking synergistically, speaking in shorthand, having absolute faith and confidence. Gleason had made me too wary too long. I wouldn't let it happen anymore.

I put my hand on Sandy's knee, wondering how to express this. He covered my hand with his.

When we reached the dairy flats beneath Rommel's cabin, I asked, "You think the road up will be okay?" I'd never driven it in this kind of weather.

"Sheriff'll stop us before we get that far. They won't let us blunder in where they've got armed men prowling. We'll spot uniforms before we get up to the dirt section."

I was relieved. For once, I wanted to see uniforms as soon as possible. I wanted to know what their orders were. If necessary, I'd ask Uncle Henry to intercede with Sheriff Turitte.

"Having you in their face will make a difference," Sandy consoled me. "They can't be too stupid with Rommel's lawyer right there."

"Assuming no one panics."

We started up the overgrown rise, tires crushing huge stalks and leaves blown off roadside brush. When the undergrowth gave way to pines and fir and redwoods, Sandy slowed down.

Even with high beams on, it was difficult to look beyond the rain. Timber creaked, the wind howled through trees a hundred years tall.

"We should have seen somebody by now." Sandy sounded worried.

"They wouldn't be too overt. They don't want to scare Rommel off. They'll want him to get at least as far as the cabin before noticing them."

"But we're not Rommel. They've got to be watching the road carefully enough to know that."

"If they can see me in here, they might think I'm meeting him. Maybe they want me to get closer in case Rommel's watching." I was guessing; trying to push away my disquiet. They'd consider Rommel dangerous, that was the other side of it. They wouldn't want anyone bumping into him, even his lawyer. Would they?

"If there's no sign of them by the time we reach the cabin, I'd guess they found him already." He gestured toward the passenger window. "Keep an eye out. See if anything moves in the woods. High beams might catch something if anyone's out there."

I wiped the inside of the window with my sleeve. But all I saw was rain, dismal sheets of it.

We wound farther up the road. Sandy stopped where the concrete ended. "No sense getting stuck in the mud. God damn, I hate to go outside in this."

Up ahead, Brad's cabin was a dark, barely discernible shape. I opened the passenger door, hoping to spot something the windshield had obscured.

"They should have approached us by now," Sandy fretted. "Either it's the most unprofessional damn bunch of sheriff's—"

"It is."

"Or this is a wild goose chase."

"Well, we're already wet." I slid out into a pelting downpour.

Within seconds, I was drenched, my clothes flogging me, the wind trying to batter me back downhill. Sandy appeared beside me, swearing over the roar of forest storm. He clicked on a flashlight and handed me its mate. Then he put his arm around my shoulder, helping me fight the squall as we struggled toward Brad's cabin.

The cabin was unlighted. The ground leading up to it, littered with pine cones and redwood branches, showed no sign of footprints or human scatter, nothing to suggest hiding deputies.

We moved as quickly as we could, seeking the shelter of the porch. Our feet hit the wooden steps, adding rhythm to the thumping of tree limbs against the sides of the cabin.

I blinked rain from my eyes, grateful to be under even so leaky a roof. Drips hit porch planks around me, adding a quick pulse to the drumming. I aimed the light overhead, at the crude outer structure. Sandy, I noticed, shined his light through the cabin windows. After a cursory look, he shined it into the trees.

"Where the hell is everyone? I think they must have grabbed Rommel in town somewhere. I don't see any sign they even made it up here."

But if he was looking for proof we weren't alone, he had it soon enough. A shot exploded somewhere close by, deafeningly loud even against the ambient din of the gale.

Sandy fell against me, pulling me down, almost snapping my leg beneath me. "Cut your light, cut it now!"

I'd dropped my flashlight. I lunged for it. But another blast ricocheted off the boards beside it.

"Leave it!" Sandy ordered. "Get to the other side of the cabin. I'll deal with this."

I couldn't see him in the darkness. But I could feel him

fumble for something under his anorak. He'd brought his .38. At least, I hoped so.

"Run!" He gave me a shove. "Keep low, keep in shadows, don't move. If a light hits you, dive."

"Are you going to—"

He pushed me again. I scraped the heels of my hands, caught my pants leg on a nail, and felt the fabric rip. But I got myself around the corner of the three-sided wrap-around porch. Slipping onto all fours, I ran and stumbled to the woods side of the cabin, away from the driveway, away from where the shot was fired.

I could hear porch boards groan—or maybe it was trees swaying. I imagined Sandy flat against the cabin wall, checking his gun, listening. I heard a series of clunks as of footsteps on the porch stairs. I peeked cautiously around the corner, needing to know what had happened.

My flashlight, still on, was out in the driveway. Sandy had pitched it. Hoping our companion would fire again? Hoping to get a fix on his location?

I almost screamed when Sandy materialized in front of me, almost running straight into me.

He swore quietly. "I thought you were going around to the other side."

"I thought you were still near the door."

"Ran when I threw the flashlight. Didn't want him following the trajectory. God damn. Nasty night."

I looked out into the trees beside the cabin. A wall of water obscured everything but the broadest movements: limbs dropping, plants waving. A glint of headlight from Sandy's car just made it into the foliage, catching a few slick edges.

Another explosion. I don't know what Sandy saw, what made him expect it. But instantly Sandy had me on the ground. Once there, he gave me a shove toward the back of the cabin.

I didn't bother to rise. I moved like some hunched animal, scrabbling in the direction I'd been pushed.

At the back of the cabin, where the porch ended, I jumped down and ran a few feet through the torrent and the mud. I stood panting. I listened with everything I had, but the storm led an orchestra of howling wind, rain on broad leaves and wet duff, limbs pounding the porch roof. I struggled to catch Sandy's footsteps, his voice, his instructions. I waited, the rain tattooing on my cold-numbed skin. I strained to hear him, any sound from him. I fought the sudden worry that he'd been hit, that he'd gone down when the shot blasted. That he'd pushed me away with his dying strength.

I watched and listened, not knowing what else to do. I considered creeping back toward him. But I didn't know where the shots came from, only that Sandy had pushed me in this direction, only that he'd preferred me to be here rather than with him—assuming he was still where I'd left him.

I stood paralyzed in the cacophony of a thousand noises, all of them frenzied and elemental, none of them what I hoped to hear.

I stood until I thought I'd rather be shot than be so wet, so cold, so scared. I hoisted myself back onto the porch. I walked quickly along the side, peering around the corner. This time, there was no sign of Sandy. Rather than skirt the front of the house—put myself in range like a duck in a shooting gallery—I retraced my steps. I jumped off the end of the porch, squelching again through the mud and gravel in back.

When I'd walked the length of the far side, I checked around front. Still no sign of Sandy. My flashlight remained shining on the walkway where he'd thrown it. But I caught no glimmer of Sandy's light; he wouldn't turn it on as long as it would make him a target.

Through the deluge, I saw the car headlights, barely illuminating a six-foot sphere of blowing, racketing rain.

At that moment, when I was busy searching rather than listening, I finally heard something unlike the now-familiar drumming of water and cry of the wind. It was a crackling, sucking sound: footsteps on gravel-covered mud. The same clamor I'd made walking behind the house.

I wheeled around, regretting my brief glance at the car, hoping my eyes were still accustomed to the night.

For an instant, I couldn't decide between flight and confrontation. It might be Sandy approaching. It might be sheriff's deputies, at last. If I ran, I'd only make a target of myself.

I could see a form now, a dark body against the darker backdrop of night. In that instant, I learned a great deal: that it wasn't Sandy, that it wasn't Brad Rommel, that it wasn't a deputy.

But I'd waited too long, trusting to fate. I'd made the wrong choice. If I turned now, I'd be shot in the back, I was sure.

Watching the black shape advance, I wanted to rend my clothing and pull my hair, punish myself for the foolishness that might cost me dearly, might cost me everything.

I'd been stupid. I'd believed what I was told even when it made no sense, when it was scarcely feasible.

The figure stopped fifteen feet from me. It was impossible to see details. But the outline told me enough.

A habit of caution kept me from speaking. Maybe if I mentioned no names, I would be perceived as less of a threat, as someone continuing to embrace false conjectures. Maybe if I remained silent, it wouldn't be apparent that I knew now; it wouldn't be necessary to shoot me. But then again, I'd been brought here to be shot. No more masked men in office corridors. Sometimes you have to bite the bullet and do your own dirty work.

I was near the side of the cabin.

I dove around the corner, hearing the crack of a gunshot and the splinter of wood. Still running, I bent to scoop up anything, anything at all to throw. I was lucky; my fingers closed on a length of broken branch. I hurled it toward the car, heard another bullet blast as the branch landed. I'd bought a few seconds. I made it to the woods side of the cabin. As long as I could keep some corner between us, I was safe. Until my stratagem became apparent, anyway; until I got headed off instead of chased around, I stood a chance. And every shot fired at me told Sandy where to aim. (I couldn't, wouldn't believe he'd been hit, lay dying in the mud. I wouldn't think it; couldn't.)

Behind the cabin, I became lost in dread and indecision. Should I continue around and risk discovery of my transparent scheme, walk right into the outstretched gun? Or should I double back?

Every second I hesitated seemed a year of worry. Every sound seemed too loud, too likely to mask what I needed to hear: the killer's approach.

I dashed away from the house and into the woods. I heard another salvo; couldn't tell if it came from my right or left, whether I should have doubled back or kept circling.

I slipped once. It didn't slow me down. I ran on all fours like a beast until I regained my balance. I ran knowing I wasn't alone, that I was being followed. I knew it because it made sense that I would be. I could hear nothing but the battering rain.

I needed a place to hide. The luck to find a hollow tree or a thick bush—anything to cloak me out here, spare me the need to crash on, making tip-off noises along the way.

But my luck ran out. I didn't find a hiding place. I found a sudden ravine. My foot, expecting spongy ground, slid downward, catching on a root. I fell, slithering down a steep decline, smashing against limbs, ripping my clothing and my skin, inhaling rain and mud, turning in a slosh of duff and vegetation and wet, fungal earth. I fell fast and hard. But unfortunately, not far. Not far enough.

Within seconds of coming to a stop, I saw the dark shape

standing over me. I'd forged an audible path down the hill. One that was easily and quickly followed.

It was no use. I hadn't managed to escape or to hide. I was on the ground with a drop-off in front of me and my worst enemy blocking my way back.

I lay twisted in mud and roots and fallen branches, the rain pelting me to my frozen bones. Running and hiding had vanished as options. There was certainly no weapon at hand to match a gun. I had only one choice besides immediate capitulation.

I seized it: I screamed, long and loud; screamed and screamed, thinking this instant was my last.

The wind carried my cries down the ravine, where they echoed almost louder than the storm. Almost louder, but not quite. I screamed again, opening my lungs, making myself roar against the tempest. Nothing less would make a difference.

CHAPTER

Thirty-seven

I HEARD GUNSHOTS. STRANGELY ENOUGH, TWO OF THEM, one behind me and to my left, the other off to my right someplace. Neither was close enough to have come from Connie Gold.

"They heard me scream," I panted.

She stood just uphill from me, dark and narrow, her arm outstretched, aiming a gun at me.

"They heard me. They'll be here fast. They'll catch you." I assumed one of the blasts came from Sandy's .38. I prayed the other hadn't come from Gold's accomplice, from the masked man who'd tried to shoot me twice already. "Sandy," I screamed. "Sandy—over here."

I watched Gold lower the gun arm, look over her shoulder.

Then she turned away, just plain turned away. Turned and left.

God damn. Was she going to try to walk away from this? Deny she'd shot at me?

"Sandy," I shouted again. "Get her. It's Gold!" I struggled out of the mud and brambles. I clawed my way up the incline until I was back on level ground.

I had to catch up with her. Had to grab her. The sheriff would never accept my identification if I let Gold slip away. He'd scoff: it was dark out here; I'd only seen a silhouette, a form; I had an ax to grind—Gold had had me arrested. No one would believe me.

And though Deputy DA Leiden would confirm (I assumed) that Gold had phoned to tell her Rommel escaped, phoned to ask her to contact me, Gold would claim she'd been disoriented after her hospitalization. Or perhaps she'd claim Leiden had misunderstood. Or something.

Because of course Brad Rommel hadn't escaped from jail. How could he leave a locked cell? Why would he be left unguarded? It didn't make sense; it wasn't possible. And yet I'd believed it.

I'd taken the bait. I'd driven to Rommel's cabin to rein in police I expected to find here. I'd done what any criminal lawyer would do. I'd done what Connie Gold expected.

If I'd arrived alone, I'd have been found dead. Leiden would confirm I'd come based on her false information. Gold would either deny being its source or apologize for having misled Leiden in her wounded haze. Both DAs would issue statements stressing their determination to capture and convict whoever had followed me here to shoot me.

Gold would get away with it. She'd resisted the temptation to say anything to me. She'd made it impossible for me to offer a conclusive ID.

She'd mastered the urge to shoot me. With others close by, she'd never have gotten away. Had Sandy found me dead, he'd have searched instantly and exhaustively for my killer. As it was, by the time I panted out my story, Gold would be gone.

I ran back toward Rommel's cabin, shaking with frustration.

We had to catch her right now, gun still in her hand. If we

didn't, no one would believe us. No one would believe she'd left her bed to lure me out into a rainstorm. No one would believe her hatred was so personal and so strong.

But I knew how I felt about Steve Sayres and his insinuations. Connie Gold must feel that way about me. Insulting articles about her, witnesses suing her, the State Bar investigating—all because of what I'd suggested, what I'd alleged.

I'd brought the cynical, accusatory media machine down on her. I'd undercut her status and her image. I'd left her vulnerable to lawsuits that might bankrupt her. I'd done it just to even the playing field.

It chilled me to think of myself as Gold's Steven Sayres, casually collapsing her security.

No wonder she hated me. She hated me enough to hire someone to shoot me, hire someone to try to run me over. She hated me enough to put a motel phone number in my pocket, probably as soon as she had access to the jacket used to stanch her bleeding. Wounded as she was, she hated me enough to manufacture evidence to arrest me. She hated me enough to concoct a lie to draw me out into the woods, enough to crawl out of her bed, hide her car in some off-road pocket, and hike up here to shoot me herself.

And worst of all, she'd been smart. She'd put her rage aside and walked away while she could.

How would I ever prove any of this?

Anything I said would be discounted by my public feud with her. My accusations would be laughed off as mere bitterness.

She'd failed to kill me. She'd had to cope with an innocent woman's death. She'd been wounded by her own hired gun.

But she hadn't let it make her foolish. She'd been smart when it mattered most.

I reached the cabin, shouting Sandy's name, colliding with him in the darkness.

"Jesus!" he panted. "God damn, where did you come from? I expected you to be way the hell— You okay? What happened?"

"Gold. Tried to kill me. It's Gold. Rommel's not free— that's why there's no sheriff here." I struggled to catch my breath. "She lied to Leiden. To get me out here and shoot me."

"Gold?" Even Sandy sounded skeptical. "She's in the hospital."

"No. She's out. She was standing over me ready to shoot me."

"What happened then?"

"She heard the answering shots when I screamed. She took off. Realized she didn't have a second to waste if she was going to get away."

"Who fired the other shot?" Sandy grabbed my shoulders as if to keep me upright. "That's what I followed, the shot—couldn't tell where your scream came from. Who fired? Do you know?"

"No. No. I think that must be what spooked her—assuming she was alone. She'd seen you already. But there was someone else. Must have panicked her. She just turned around and took off. Just took off. Put her safety above killing me."

Sandy pulled me close. He didn't say anything.

That disturbed me. I pushed back out of his arms, though I could barely see him in the strafing rain. "It was Gold, Sandy. I could tell."

"Positive enough for a police ID?"

"Yes!" I was hot with rage in spite of the storm. "It was Gold, all right."

But I wouldn't be believed. It was too dark, too fierce out here. No one could confirm the identification. Gold would claim to have been in bed recuperating. And my dislike for her was notorious.

"Come on." Sandy began walking me toward his car. "Let's get back before the battery dies."

"We've got to look for her. No one will believe me if I don't catch her!"

"She could be anywhere. We're not going to find her."

"Then let's go to where she's supposed to be. Let's prove she's not home." I couldn't let her get away with this.

"We'll haul down to a phone. Get your uncle to send his cop pals to the hospital, check her bed."

"To her house. She was probably released before we got the call from Leiden. She must have called Leiden from home with this story about Brad. Hospital wouldn't be private enough."

"Let's hurry, then." He hustled me along.

But I got the feeling he wanted to get out of the rain. Get dry. Get safe.

I wasn't sure he believed me about Gold. He knew more than anyone how much I hated her.

CHAPTER

Thirty-eight

I WAS NEVER HAPPIER TO BE DRY, WARM, AT HOME. My uncle had twice refilled my glass of Stoli. Sandy had a fire going.

"Well," I said, "I never thought I'd be so glad to hear my client was in jail. At least that confirms what I've been telling you."

"And Gold being released from the hospital. Lying to Leiden," Sandy added. "That's a match."

We'd spoken several times with the sheriff. Leiden, we learned, had heard of the "escape" via phone message, supposedly from Gold. But Gold had yet to confirm this. Even if she did, the sheriff seemed willing to dismiss it as the confusion of a wounded woman.

Sheriff Turitte wouldn't tell us if he'd spoken to Gold. Initially, of course, she hadn't answered her phone or her door. Whatever the sheriff chose to believe, she hadn't been home asleep; she'd been on her way home after trying to shoot me.

But she'd been back for a while now. She'd had time to deny it all, including, perhaps, the message to Leiden.

"I have to make her furious somehow. Out-of-control, out-of-her-head furious. If she doesn't blow it, completely lose her cool and incriminate herself, no one will believe me." I'd said the same thing with each previous Stoli. Neither Sandy nor my uncle bothered replying.

"Well . . ." Sandy's voice was a slow drawl. "Say Gold really can't handle it that you made her into a public bad guy. Say she did hire someone to take you out. That accounts for Jocelyn Kinsley and maybe the guy in the car and the guy in the hallway who shot Gold—accidentally when you ducked. What about all this other stuff? The buckets of blood? The mall? The airplane?"

"Meaning, let's change the subject before I bore you both to death."

My uncle looked shocked. He slumped in his recliner, much the worse for whiskey. "Somebody trying to kill you is not a boring subject."

But Sandy smiled. "Yeah, enough about you."

"Gold put a motel phone number into my pocket. So presumably that's not the way to find the person who did the shooting. That means he stayed with someone here in Hillsdale or he lives here and took a room when he went to San Francisco." I wasn't ready to leave the subject. "I vote for lives here."

"Would have to be someone Gold trusts beyond anything sensible." Sandy shook his head. "DA would realize more than anybody how easy it is for a trigger to roll over on the person that hired him."

"So someone Gold's very close to or someone who owes her a hell of a favor."

Sandy sat up, taking his weight off his spine. "Or someone she could do a hell of a favor for."

"Oh, no." I watched him. "No. It couldn't be."

"What?" my uncle demanded. "Couldn't be what?"

Sandy scowled down into his drink. He wasn't going to say it.

I glanced at my uncle. "Nothing," I lied. "Just talking around."

I put my glass down. It's a wonder it hadn't occurred to us before.

CHAPTER

Thirty-nine

I SAT IN THE VISITING ROOM OPPOSITE BRAD ROMMEL. HE looked heavy-lidded, shockingly pale given his natural ruddiness. His yellow-blond hair bristled in oily clumps. The gray jail overalls, coarser than the women's wraps, muted his eye color to a sweet powder blue. His hands, palm down on the heavy linoleum table, were chafed and red, fisherman's hands, though he hadn't fished much lately.

"Did you know I'd been arrested?"

His brows lowered. "No. What do you mean arrested? For what?"

"I was arrested night before last. Released yesterday evening. You know Connie Gold and I were shot at in the corridor of the second floor here. That she was nicked." Her wound, which had looked so bloody when Bartoli ministered to it, turned out to be little more than a free-bleeding scratch. "They used my jacket to stop the bleeding. Later they checked my pocket and found a motel phone number in it. They used that as an excuse to arrest me."

"Why?" He was scowling, nostrils flared, hands bunching into fists. "What's a motel got to do with anything?"

"It never would have washed anywhere else. But Hillsdale's got its own rules. Gold had the police check registrations at the motel. Based on a couple of phonies, they claimed the shooter must have stayed there, that the number in my pocket was evidence I hired him."

He shook his head emphatically. "No way—they can't make that stick. Why would you want to shoot the DA? It ain't your ass on the line." His anger, apparently on my behalf, now seemed directed at me. "It's mine."

"The real question is why would the DA be so unprofessional, so nakedly vindictive toward me."

Rommel's lips pinched into a tight line. His eyes narrowed.

"But you know the answer to that," I went on.

"What do you mean?"

"We talked about it at lunch one day, remember? You didn't want me making an issue of Gold selling TV movie rights."

He was silent.

"This poses a difficult problem for me, Brad." It surprised me how much he still looked like the boy who'd outrun a cop car to spare me my family's wrath, the boy who'd endured a beating and never asked for my thanks or sympathy. He looked a little heavier, perhaps, his skin weather-roughened, more lined, his chin stubbled with a blond shadow. But he still looked like my old friend, my one-time date.

"What problem?" he prompted, when I fell silent.

"Knowing what to do about you."

"Won't they let you be my lawyer? Don't they have to prove you did it?"

"Let me talk for a minute. It might be hard for you not to interrupt, but it's better if you don't say anything."

He scraped his chair back a few inches, hands on the table edge, as if he might leap to his feet. But he said nothing.

"Twice, a man wearing a ski mask shot at me. Once, because I fell, he missed and hit the other person in the room. The second time, because I heard him, I ducked and he nicked Connie Gold." I watched him. His eyes glinted in a face crimped with anticipation. "I supposed all along it was a hired job. But I didn't know who'd done the hiring until yesterday. Connie Gold denies it and I can't prove it, but she stood over me last night with a gun. The only reason she didn't kill me is that there were other people close by and they'd have caught her."

"Are you serious?"

"They might have caught her either way, of course. But if she'd shot me, they'd have ended up arresting her. By not shooting, well, even if they'd grabbed her, it's not illegal to be in the woods at night."

His breathing was labored, audible in the small room. Was he wondering what to ask, what to say? Pondering my advice to remain silent?

"She got away," I continued, "so it's my word against hers that she was out there at all. And I'm the outsider here, so her word's being taken over mine. But the bottom line is, last night I realized she was the one who'd hired the man in the ski mask." I held up my hand, forestalling his next question. "And that made me wonder, Who would she trust enough to do a job like that? She's the district attorney here; it would ruin her to have any of this get out. She'd have to be damn sure the person would never turn on her. So it would have to be either a trusted friend or someone who owed, or would owe, her a tremendous debt."

We watched each other across the narrow table.

"Here's my dilemma, Brad. I'm your attorney. I can't do anything to prejudice your case. My obligation to you has to transcend my suspicions regarding your guilt. I'm obligated to champion, if not truly accept, your version of the facts. But that obligation only extends to the Piatti case. If, for instance, I believed you'd committed a new crime or were about to, I'd have to turn you in—the rules of ethical conduct are clear on that. But what if turning you in undermined your defense in the Piatti case? Then I'd have two competing obligations: to protect you in the Piatti matter, and to act as an officer of the court and turn you in for the other crime.''

Brad was leaning closer now, his elbows bent, his shoulders hunched. He looked like a coiled spring, his eyes hard and his mouth pursed.

''If I believed you'd made a deal with Connie Gold to kill me in exchange for her ultimately dropping these charges against you, I'd be in a terrible position. Because if you made a deal like that, it could only mean you were guilty— that you'd killed Cathy Piatti, after all. And since I'm representing you in that matter, I'm not supposed to do anything to undermine your not-guilty plea.''

''Damn you,'' he whispered. ''And damn all this lawyer bullshit.'' He slammed his fist onto the table top. Louder: ''I hate lawyers, you know that? I never met a fish so cold-blooded and slimy as the lawyers I met since I got arrested. You know that?''

''I do know that. I can imagine how you felt when Gold offered you this deal.''

''I'm not saying she did.''

''No, don't. Don't say anything; or, at least, don't admit anything. What we say here this morning is probably covered by the lawyer-client privilege. But there's a gray area when it comes to admission of new crimes, crimes other than the one the lawyer's handling for you. I can't one hundred percent guarantee anything. Especially since— Just take my advice; don't say anything.''

Especially since I would soon be going to the police in San Francisco, the homicide detectives in charge of Kinsley's case. I would tell them who I thought had pulled the trigger. My conclusion wasn't based on Rommel's confidences, so it was outside the scope of the privilege.

But I didn't want to tell him that. We were just down the hall from armed jail guards, but we were alone. And he'd tried more than once to kill me.

"My point is I have a duty to you in the Piatti case in spite of my belief that you killed her—that you got angry and jealous that she was fed up with small-town life and was going to leave you."

"You never used to think I killed her." His eyes searched my face. He sank lower into his shoulders.

"If you weren't guilty, Gold wouldn't have enough of a hold on you. She wouldn't have a real favor to trade. And she wouldn't trust you enough if, number one, she wasn't positive you'd killed before, and number two, she didn't have the leverage that fact provided." I wanted to cry. I'd known him so long. "You must have killed Piatti. Gold couldn't have made this deal with you if you hadn't."

Rommel rose, looming over me like some ruddy, wild-haired Viking.

"You tried to kill me to buy your freedom, Brad. And you accidentally killed a sweet young lawyer with walls full of angel paintings."

I stared up at him, wondering if it still seemed like a good deal to him. I might have gotten him acquitted, guilty or not; I'd done it for other clients. But maybe he'd realized that.

"I'll have to withdraw as your lawyer. I'll say it's because of my arrest; that you wanted someone who didn't have this hanging over her. I won't tell anyone what I suppose about Piatti: that you did kill her; that you buried her somewhere and then dug her up; that you hustled her body to the mall and busted up gas lines so she'd burn; that her remains would eventually give the DA a basis for dropping the charges against you."

I assumed that's how it would work. It would begin to look as if Rommel had been framed: Piatti found dead at the mall, after supposedly phoning him; a plane—not his—obviously rigged to incriminate him; someone trying to run down his lawyer during their meeting. As the case against Rommel became more confused and convoluted, the DA could credibly drop the charges.

"There was a growing list of things suggesting you didn't kill Piatti." The blood on my uncle's lawn was another. "And I was set to get martial on your behalf: present the list to Gold, to the sheriff; demand they drop charges if they couldn't offer an explanation."

Brad continued hovering. "If you were going to get me out, supposedly, why would I want to shoot you? Why would I have to?" He seemed suddenly pleased, as if he'd found a way to deny it.

"Because a deal's a deal. Or maybe you were aiming at Gold, not me, in the corridor."

"But if—"

"Don't say anything, Brad." It was a struggle for me to act as his attorney now. He didn't realize the volcano I suppressed. He hadn't watched Jocelyn Kinsley die. "Let's just leave it at this: I'm withdrawing as your counsel because of my arrest. What happens to you in regard to the Piatti case after this meeting won't be the result of any confidences between us up to this point."

He raised his hands in a slow arc from his sides to his belly, clenching his fists. His eyes were almost closed, his jaw slack. He looked as if he were practicing some meditative art.

I could see him reviewing what I'd said, trying to work out where it left him. I hoped I'd been careful enough that he didn't get it for a while, didn't get it until I was gone.

Because I had every intention of turning him in for shooting Jocelyn Kinsley. I couldn't inculpate him in the Piatti case; couldn't state my belief that he'd lied about her phone call, burning the mall to mask her body's decomposition. But once I accused Connie Gold of making a deal with him, any decent cop would understand the quid pro quo.

"You're saying," his voice was hushed, "that you're

through as my lawyer, but you won't say anything about why.''

''I won't give the real reason, no.'' About why I was withdrawing as counsel. ''I'll blame it on my arrest. I won't break any confidence that would prejudice your chances in the Piatti case. You'll start fresh with new counsel.''

He exhaled loudly, seemingly with relief. I was relieved, too: that he hadn't understood how little I'd promised; how much harm of a different type I intended to do him.

He could dwell on that when I was out of reach.

''I used to think you were like a princess when we were in school.'' Moisture glinted in his eyes. His voice was low with feeling. ''You were perfect—beautiful, smart. But you never got caught up in that rich-man's-daughter kind of clique, never fell so in love with your own clothes and money that you wouldn't spend time talking or going for rides. I thought you were the greatest. I always wondered what you saw in that slick show-off, Gleason.''

A princess. He'd tried to kill me. To hunt me down like some inconvenient possum in the garbage.

As if in reply, he added, ''I had to stay out of jail. You know? I'm a fisher, an outdoor hermit—can't even stand being in a city. You can imagine how I'm standing jail.''

His glance caught what we had in common: a horror of restriction, of squirming under someone's thumb. It had linked us in high school, too.

''I was just in jail. So yes, I can imagine.'' I bit my tongue, willing myself to say no more. I'd have all the time I needed for my anger—more time than I wanted. To vent now, while we were alone, would be merely stupid, certainly not satisfying. But silence was a struggle: Jocelyn Kinsley's last moments were burned into my nightmares. Her law partner's desolation haunted me.

I stood, staring at him.

I refused to empathize, I refused to take pity, I refused to defend. But I would remain adequate counsel to Brad Rommel until my withdrawal.

"I'll be going downstairs now to file a petition to withdraw as your lawyer." I pulled a document from my briefcase. "It'll be granted as a matter of routine, given my arrest. Would you please sign where I've indicated?"

He scowled down at the legal sheet.

My fingers fumbled in my bag, encountering innumerable small objects before finding a pen. I handed it to him.

When he took it, he looked at me, his face creased with confusion.

"I can't continue representing you," I insisted. "You need to sign this."

Still he hesitated.

"The lawyer-client privilege will cease, but it will cover everything we've discussed until now."

But only what we'd discussed, nothing more. None of the incriminating things I'd learned on my own, learned at great cost.

Brad seemed to be replaying my statement in his head. It seemed to assuage him. He bent and signed the paper.

I called for the guard.

He arrived by the time I gathered the petition and pen, closed my briefcase.

I threaded quickly past him and through the open door.

"Laura?" Brad called.

I didn't wait for his parting comment. I couldn't spend another second in his company. I couldn't smother my rage another instant.

For the favor he'd done me in my teens, I'd more than repaid him. For the great harm he'd tried to do me, I had yet to begin settling the score.

CHAPTER

Forty

WITHIN FIFTEEN MINUTES, I WAS PRESENTING MY PETI-
tion for withdrawal. The judge, a twittery woman in her six-
ties, seemed agog to find "the famous Miss Di Palma" in her
courtroom. She told me more than once that perhaps I should
wait and bring this up with the judge assigned to the Rommel
case. But he didn't handle the newly created Saturday-
morning calendar. He wasn't available on weekends, and she
had jurisdiction in his absence, as she well knew. I pointed
out that Rommel needed a new lawyer immediately. I implied that my arrest crippled my ability to represent him. She
finally granted my motion, seeming more confused than persuaded by my argument.

I left the redwood-walled chamber, feeling almost giddy
with relief. This part was over. And luckily the courtroom
had been nearly empty, no spectators except other lawyers
with urgent motions; no reporters, no deputy DAs, no further explanation required.

But even before the heavy wood door swung shut, my
relief gave way to trepidation. So many people to contact

now, with so convoluted and incredible a story. Maryanne More's face floated painfully into my awareness. I hoped she would forgive my accidental role in her partner's death.

I stopped at the ladies' room. Splashing water on my face, I wondered vaguely why Kinsley had spoken the words "designer crimes." She'd been killed accidentally when Brad tried to shoot me as part of his deal with Gold. But she hadn't known that; she'd meant to convey her suspicion. Maybe Sandy and Osmil would figure out who was behind all that—if anyone. I wasn't sure I cared.

I'd left Sandy at home asleep this morning. I'd considered sleeping in myself, but my need to sever ties with Rommel was paramount. I'd wanted my interview with him to be over, my court appearance to be done. I'd wanted to be free of Gold's manipulation and Rommel's hypocrisy.

I tossed my paper towel into the trash, leaving quickly. I needed to get out of the County Building. I was tired of its gray walls and postcard oil paintings. I was tired of its washed carpet and old air-conditioner smell. I was tired of feeling like prey in here, shot at in its corridors, sequestered in its jail, hassled by its cops.

I hit the elevator button obsessively. I felt like a chained rocket, could barely stand still. I hit the button a few more times. How long could it take an elevator in a four-story building, anyway? How much traffic could there be on a Saturday morning?

A couple of grumpy minutes later I abandoned the elevator, heading toward the stairway exit. I wished I'd gone that way first. I'd be outside already, away from this monument to slipshod law enforcement and small-town egos.

I entered the cavernous gray stairwell. I started down the uncarpeted concrete steps when I heard footsteps coming up. A jolt of fear crackled through me. I stopped.

Why hadn't the elevator worked?

I could hear the person climbing, getting closer, but I couldn't see him yet. My disquiet might be nothing but the legacy of being hunted and harassed. But why hadn't the elevator worked?

I wheeled around, starting back up the steps. The footsteps were faster and louder behind me now. When I reached the cement landing, my mind took a snapshot of damp gray aggregate with a dim gleam of fluorescence.

Elevators were quick in underpopulated Hillsdale; stairs were chilly and drab. I couldn't count on incidental foot traffic here. I'd have to reach the corridor to find safety in numbers.

An image seized my memory as I approached the door: a dark car careening out of nowhere to snap the hinges of my Mercedes. Brad had been with me, then. He hadn't been driving the hit-and-run car. And Connie Gold had been up here working. So who had been behind the wheel of that car?

Someone else. Someone working with them. An accomplice, helping them.

Gold was probably at home today, nursing her slight wound—and establishing an alibi? Brad Rommel was still in his jail cell.

My fingers closed on the cold metal handle of the stairway door. There was a third person involved, another person stalking me.

The elevator hadn't worked; I'd been forced to take the stairs. Now someone was here with me, rushing up toward me.

I began to yank the door. Too late.

A hand chopped at the back of my neck. An arm circled my waist, yanking me backward.

I tried to scream, but the sudden jerk to my diaphragm knocked the wind out of me. I staggered against my assailant's body, twirling away from the exit. We did a clumsy backward dance that almost tipped us down the stairs. Struggling not to fall, I backed us into a wall. If I'd had the foresight, I'd have put some muscle into it.

As it was, I used the moment to regain my equilibrium. I stepped forward, hoping to body-slam us back against the concrete wall. But a foot was looped in front of mine, tripping me. I fell heavily onto the concrete landing, knocking my forehead against the edge of the stair, pulling my assailant on top of me.

Face down on the rough cement, I squirmed frantically, beginning to slide down the stairs. I was astonished how easy it was to squirm, how light my load was.

I noticed the thinness of the arm gripping me. I saw that the sleeve was light gray cotton—jail garb. But there was lumpiness beneath it, another outfit. Someone wore prison clothing over street clothes. It had to be a woman: the men's overalls were coarser. It had to be a woman—she was so light, light enough for me to wriggle beneath her weight, to scrape along the landing as if crawling her to safety.

I tried to buck then, realizing I might be the stronger, that my surprise and fear had been her real weapons. So far.

I was trying to overturn us, put myself on top, when another weapon intruded.

A gun was pressed stock and barrel against my face. I stopped moving. The gun barrel was cold, almost felt wet. It turned painfully, digging into my flesh until the opening was braced against my cheekbone.

The body on top of me heaved as if to catch its breath. Heaved like a panting bird, bony and small and light, smelling faintly of shampoo and antiseptic.

She wore a prison shift to protect her business suit from blowback or dirt from a possible scuffle.

Connie Gold was a real mensch, I guess, to return to work three days after she'd been shot, to come in on the weekend. And then I suppose she'd gotten a phone call: as soon as I withdrew as Rommel's counsel, the twittering judge had phoned Gold, looking for reassurance she'd done the right thing.

Gold must have realized what it meant. I'd been to see

Rommel; he'd signed the affidavit allowing me to withdraw. I'd used my arrest as a pretext; but Gold and I both knew she had no evidence against me, that the charges would be dropped. I hadn't withdrawn for Brad's benefit—I'd renounced my obligation to serve his interests. I'd figured out the truth.

My next step would be to contact the San Francisco police and tell them what I knew about Gold and Rommel's bargain. I'd lulled Rommel with vague talk about the lawyer-client privilege, but Gold knew its limits. Gold knew how little protection it offered them.

Gold saw that it was now or never. If she didn't kill me now, I'd open the whole can of worms. The sheriff here might think me hysterical; but he knew nothing of the deal I was on my way to San Francisco to describe. In the city, I'd be taken seriously.

Gold had to stop me. Here, where no one believed I'd seen her in the woods.

She had to stop me now. Stop me, and get back to her office with no sign of tussle or blood on her clothing; with her prison shift stuffed down some garbage chute they'd never check.

The authorities might conclude I'd been right about being the target of earlier shootings. But they'd have no reason to suspect Gold, busy at work but for a brief break no one noticed. She'd get away with everything if she could kill me now. And she'd get away with killing me if she was fast enough. If she could jam the elevator and run upstairs to meet me in this untrafficked place.

Earlier, she'd been cautious, making a pact with someone else to do the work—her own ''designer crime.'' But she no longer had that luxury. To save herself, she had to kill me right now, kill me fast.

I lay motionless beneath her, fighting every impulse to rear back and become a hydra of outraged fists and profanities. I lay motionless because her finger was on the trigger of a gun. With not even a millimeter between me and the cold barrel, the least disturbance could mean death.

But so could lying here doing nothing. Gold had already proved she wouldn't be drawn into chatter. She brought a cold professionalism to her vengeance. She might be driven by her passions, but she didn't let them taint her behavior; she didn't let them make her stupid.

I squirmed beneath my hopeless choices. She would kill me if I moved, kill me if I didn't, kill me if I tried to stall by talking.

She would kill me. I tried to push away the thought, tried to cope with the gun against my cheek. I could sense that Gold, catching her breath astride me, waited only for equilibrium before pulling the trigger.

I considered gambits: pretend I didn't know her and offer my wallet, offer to protect her for Rommel's sake, feign sympathy and ask her to explain, try to barter, plead. They might work on someone else. Ironically, begrudgingly, I respected Gold's intelligence too much to bother with them.

Seconds ticked away. Gold was more comfortably positioned now. She would shoot me any instant. I had only one real choice: to die struggling or to take the bullet with dignity.

I bucked as extravagantly as I could. I let the stifled anger explode out of me like a tidal wave. I jerked and twisted and screamed out my rage.

A shot echoed in the cement cavern of the stairwell. I heard it at the very instant I threw Gold off, shucking her like a ratty cape. I rose to my knees with a feral roar, wheeling toward her.

I'd heard the shot, but my body didn't care. I was consumed by anger, choking on acrid smoke; not even a bullet could slow me down.

Vision blurred and rage wakening every primal part of my (dying?) body, I faced Gold. She lay as if tossed against the wall, a rag doll in gray prison garb, a red stain spreading across her chest. Only her eyes burned through my fury: she stared at me with a hollowness, a nothingness that made no sense to me.

I raised both arms to pummel her, to save myself, though it might be too late, though I might already be shot. But her eyes were wet and empty, sightlessly fixed on some spot behind me.

I let my arms fall to my sides. Her eyes were devoid of intelligence, empty of feeling. The stain on her prison shift spread slowly, very slowly.

A voice behind me said, "I just needed you to put a little space between you, that's all. Get a little distance, so I could take a shot."

I turned to see Jay Bartoli a half-dozen steps below me, his gun still poised. He was as pale as ice, with the same clammy sheen. He stared round-eyed at Connie Gold, at the gun still in her delicate hand.

He lowered his arm, glancing at me. "They told me you said Connie shot at you in the woods. They didn't believe you."

I backed away from her body, backed toward the door, heaving, feeling as if my heart would come up my throat.

"But I talked to Linda Leiden after she got Connie's message last night. I checked on Brad Rommel—saw he was still in jail, knew there was some kind of mix-up. I went out to his cabin, thinking you'd go there, wanting to set you straight. I heard you screaming. I fired a shot in case you needed to find me. Then I saw you with your detective friend, safe and lovey-dovey. I figured you'd spooked yourself somehow. That you were okay." His voice deepened. "I should have talked to you. I didn't want to with him there, I guess. I didn't see Connie." His head quivered as if he suppressed a shudder. "But later when I heard what you'd told Turitte, I thought about it. I thought about Rommel. About everything that's happened. When I heard that you withdrew as his lawyer, I went to see Connie. I knew she was here today, but she was out of her office. And the elevator—that's what tipped me off. There was a book jamming the door. I was afraid of what I'd find on the stairs. I didn't want to believe it, but I knew. I think I knew what I'd find.''

I scrambled as far away from Gold as I could, bracing my back against the closed door.

Bartoli sank to a squat on the stairs beneath her body. He covered his eyes with his left hand, gun trembling in the other.

"I should have had it sooner," he whispered. "That night in your cell, I could see you didn't know about the phone number in your jacket. I got pissed off by your attitude— you never gave me a chance to get near you, not since high school. But I could see you were telling the truth. And I didn't put that paper in your pocket. It had to have been Connie at the hospital. She's the one who supposedly found it there. I knew how much all this hurt her—the bad publicity, the State Bar, getting sued." He began to sob. "How could she? Actually try to murder— Oh God," he moaned, "I've killed Connie."

I began to shake. I hugged myself on the cold concrete, closing my eyes as Jay Bartoli wept.

He'd saved my life. I tried to get it together to say thank you: Thank you for believing me over someone you work with. Thank you for trusting an old high school friend—as I'd trusted Brad Rommel.

But I wasn't able to speak. And he wasn't listening.

CHAPTER

Forty-one

I SAT FACING MARYANNE MORE ACROSS HER DESK. SHE looked pale and pinched, worse than she had the day I'd broken the news to her. Worse than she had during subsequent encounters at the Hall of Justice, where we had again described the shooting of Jocelyn Kinsley, with renewed focus on the clothing and body type of the masked man. Of Brad Rommel.

Maryanne More, in the chiaroscuro of intense sun half obscured by rain clouds, resembled one of the masterpieces on her office wall. Without makeup or fussy styling, she had the rare elegance of good sense and good intentions.

She said, "I hope you've been well?"

"Yes, I've been coming to terms with it." I'd learned some difficult lessons, especially about my so-called "instincts."

My instincts hadn't warned me Brad Rommel could slice Cathy Piatti in a rage of rejection, collecting her spurting blood in a bucket to minimize his cleanup. Jay Bartoli believed Brad had neglected the bucket by the wayside in his rush to get Piatti's belongings onto his boat. Considering the number of things Brad had to dump at sea, it was impressive that only the bucket and skirt remained to incriminate him. I hadn't believed those pieces of evidence important, but of course they told most of the story.

The one thing Brad hadn't lugged to his boat for disposal was Cathy Piatti's body. Because he was afraid to be spotted with something he couldn't explain away? He'd buried it instead. Later, he or Gold found a way to use it as the clincher in favor of dropping charges against him.

I hoped Brad Rommel hired a good lawyer and got a fair trial. But for once, I'd work as closely with the DA as I was allowed.

I felt a little guilty facing Maryanne More. Rommel could have shot me anywhere, but I'd come here and he'd followed. Maybe he'd seized the opportunity to look like yet another office sniper. Maybe he'd decided to do it that afternoon, no matter where. But the fact remained: my client killed More's partner. "This must make it harder for you."

"Not harder." The delicate skin beneath her eyes seemed to swell. "It's always better to know the facts, no matter how brutal they are. It's worse to wonder. To blame the randomness of fate. That's much scarier than any actual reason."

I nodded. "I'd rather see the sense in something, too— even if it depends on a psychotic context. I'm not comfortable writing things off as bad luck."

"You get used to taking responsibility when you have your own practice."

"That's why I'm here." I'd waited awhile, giving her time to sort things out. I'd waited until charges against me were dropped, until Brad Rommel was indicted for Kinsley's murder as well as Piatti's.

But I could wait no longer. I'd have to drum up business if I wanted to keep my office open. I'd have to make the rounds of charity dinners and political fundraisers and company seminars. When, frankly, I didn't care about the work. Bank and corporate clients didn't need me; they got what they deserved in Steve Sayres.

It was the thought of Sayres that most disturbed me. In my determination to be as important a player, I'd nearly become him. I'd undermined Connie Gold's reputation to shore up my own—exactly what Sayres had done to me. I needed to back away from the corporate mirror before it pulled me in. I needed to get some perspective.

I knew my strengths. I was a good strategist and a good advocate, not easily rattled and never deterred by bad publicity. I wanted to represent clients who required talent, not just competence. I wanted to work for people who deserved to beat the odds.

"You asked me two weeks ago if I'd like to take on Jocelyn Kinsley's caseload. You were under a lot of stress. And neither of us realized then she'd be alive if it weren't for me. That might change things."

Maryanne More scooted back a few inches in her chair, hand fluttering to her collar.

"I'm asking if the offer still stands." I tried not to care too much. Either way, my transition would be difficult. Either way, I'd have a lot of work ahead.

"Yes," she said. "It does stand. I'm completely overloaded here."

"There are a lot of good labor lawyers out there." I wanted her to be sure.

"This isn't about a legal specialty." She pulled her chair forward, watching me intently. "It's not a particularly complicated area of practice. What makes it complex is the emotions of the clients, how much they have at stake, how pronounced the power imbalance is."

"I understand that."

"I'm sure you can do the work. What's most important is whether we can work together."

At White, Sayres & Speck I'd been fired for being a

"lone wolf." For refusing to abandon a criminal case that mattered to me in favor of corporate motions that didn't.

"I would like to work with you and learn from you. I understand the importance of your practice to your clients. I'd do everything in my power to keep you afloat—and to expand the practice eventually. There's no other lawyer I could say that to."

A bit of color suffused her pale cheeks. "And I know your background. I've followed your cases. I admire you. I trust you to do your share. And I'd hope, as the practice broadened to include criminal matters, to learn from you, too." She smiled. "I'm a little stunned. We're partners." She looked uncertain. "Is that right?"

I smiled, too. "Yes. With one possible glitch."

She leaned toward me, a slight frown creasing her forehead. "Go on."

"I'd like to speak privately with your paralegal. With Hester Donne."

"Hester?" She blinked, looking confused. "She's one in a million. You'd have no complaints with her, believe me."

"I do believe you. But I wouldn't enter into a partnership without speaking to the office manager." I felt guilty beginning our relationship with a lie of omission.

"All right. If you'd like to wait here, I'll go get myself a brioche. You two can sit in my office and get acquainted."

"Thank you."

Passing my chair, she turned. I'd risen in anticipation, offering my hand as she offered hers. We hung on longer than was strictly polite. We had higher hopes than a mere handshake could express.

A moment after Maryanne left, Hester entered the room. I was still standing. As she moved closer, I grew conscious of craning my neck. She was a good eight inches taller than me. She stood close, feet apart as if preparing for battle, shoulders squared, plain features locked in a martial scowl.

"You've been listening to the conversation. You know what's been said here," I began.

She shook her head slightly.

"You have a listening device planted in this office and another one in Jocelyn Kinsley's. You even bugged Maryanne's purse to hear a conversation in my office."

Hester crossed her arms. Her lips set in a stubborn line.

"It could only be you or Maryanne. And Maryanne wouldn't have offered to make me her partner if she was involved in Designer Crimes."

Hester remained silent.

"I understand your motives." I meant it; I hoped she knew that. "So many clients here have terrible problems with no legal remedy. You've been listening to their consultations, choosing the best candidates. Fixing things for them extralegally."

"Do you expect me to admit something like that?"

I had to smile. "You're not the only one who can get into a computer system. I found Jocelyn Kinsley's file—the one hidden in the shovelware—before you copied it. Before you burned it. Her password was 'designer.' For Designer Crimes."

She blanched. I hoped she didn't ask me anything technical, anything revealing I'd had help. I wouldn't implicate Sandy.

"You weren't careful enough," I hurried on. "You made Kinsley suspicious." Although she seemed to suspect Maryanne, not Hester. "She started keeping notes on what you'd been doing."

A glint of tears appeared in her eyes. It must have shocked her to find the hidden file.

"No one was sorrier than me when Jocelyn died." Her voice was deep and distant. "I'd have been a million times happier with her confronting me than with losing her."

"I believe that. And I understand how your feelings for certain clients—" I pulled an old *Wall Street Journal* out of my briefcase. "Super Prime. They fired workers so they could make their product shoddy without anyone blowing the whistle."

"The law offered those employees zero protection! Even in a situation where machines will rust and cost other businesses money, no one's willing to side with labor—to say, Let's make these bastards give some kind of reason for throwing eight fine people out of work!"

"Did you set off the alarm the night Sandy and I were outside the plant?"

"One of the workers, someone acting as a spotter: Arkelett's license plate was on her list. He'd been nosing around; I didn't trust him. When she saw his car, she hit the alarm to warn ... well, to warn some other people not to come back."

"You'd already contaminated the primer?"

"Yes."

"What else were you planning to do?"

"It doesn't matter; it didn't happen. Luckily, the primer was enough." Her brows sank. "At the very least, let me protect my people."

I stuffed the newspaper into the outer flap of my case.

"I've never done anything an employer didn't have coming," she insisted. "I've never done *as much* as an employer had coming."

"I understand," I repeated. "Your motives don't conflict with the work you do here. But still—"

"I was afraid you'd figured it out! I got everyone else to believe Joss said, 'It's a sign of the times.' But you wouldn't let go of it."

"When you heard Maryanne offer me Kinsley's office, you tried to save mine. You'd been researching Steve Sayres since you heard me complain to Kinsley about him. Just in case you needed to offer me your services; in case you needed to bribe me with them."

But I'd been partly mistaken about Sayres. I'd confronted

Perry Verhoeven again, forcing him to lay it on the line. This time he'd made it clear: criminal lawyers represented scum, and he didn't want one representing him.

"Rather than have me join this firm, you tried to save my practice. You'd been scrutinizing Sayres's clients; you had the information you needed. You put together a RICO brief to make him look bad."

She shrugged. "I had to work fast. If he wasn't so sloppy . . ."

"I'm impressed. Truly." Though I doubted she'd worked on it alone. She'd mentioned having employees—presumably ones she treated well. "And I'm certainly not sorry for Sayres. He is sloppy; I'm glad he got called on it. But Designer Crimes is something else."

Playing by traditional rules wasn't always effective, wasn't usually fair. That's why Connie Gold had tried to bend them.

"I believe there's intrinsic value in behaving professionally," I told her. "There are too many unintended consequences, if you don't." Maybe I had been a lone wolf. But I regretted my detours off the high road.

She tilted her head, watching me, waiting for the other shoe to drop.

"You heard me accept the partnership offer."

"Yes." Anxiety skated the surface now.

"I'm not blind to what I owe you." I took a small step closer. "I know you eavesdropped on my cordless phone conversations. You heard me arrange to meet Brad Rommel. I don't know why you followed me there, but if your car hadn't come out of nowhere, he might have killed me."

She nodded. "When you hit the disconnect button on your phone, he didn't. He stayed on the line for a few seconds, very upset, just muttering, really."

"What did he say?" I could feel my flesh crawl.

"I'd never admit any of this—" she warned, "the eavesdropping, any of it—in court."

When I'd gone to meet Brad Rommel, he'd struggled to make me believe his story. So that he could avoid killing me? Try to welch on his deal?

But he'd killed Jocelyn Kinsley; Connie Gold had powerful ammunition.

"It was the way he sounded: fretful, wild. I was afraid for you." Hester's cheeks flamed. "Considering the shooting here. And that he was wanted for killing someone. I followed you, just sat there with my lights off, watching. And when you went leaping out of your car, I thought he must have drawn a gun or something. I couldn't think what to do. I hit your car door because it was the only thing that came to mind. All I could think of to give you time to get away."

She'd thought fast that night, trying to save me. She was a woman of action, clearly; a woman who took things upon herself. A woman capable of conceiving and running Designer Crimes.

"I'm grateful to you for saving my life. That's why I'm talking to you, not the police." Nevertheless, "I can't work here unless I'm confident I have privacy. You can understand that, I hope."

"I've been here since the office opened," she said.

"I'm aware of that. And also that I owe you a favor." I sighed. "I won't turn you in; that's a given. And I won't do anything about it if I hear of other 'designer crimes.' If you choose to continue your illegal operation, I'll be as blind to it as I can possibly be."

I hoped she wasn't recording this. I hoped reluctance to incriminate herself and her "people" would prevent her from blackmailing me. Her heart might be in the right place, but I'd never trust her.

"I've accepted the offer of a partnership. I'll start on Monday. Within a week, I'd like you to find an excuse to give notice. I don't care what it is—you can say you hate working with me, if you like. But I won't have a loose cannon in my office. And I won't worry about having my privacy invaded."

"Do you use a computer?" she asked.

"Of course."

"Then you have no privacy, not really."

We stared at one another.

I reiterated, "I won't tell the police. And you'll leave— and stay out of my computer. That's the deal."

"All right." She turned away. She hesitated a moment. But she had an enterprise to protect.

She walked out, closing the door behind her.

I checked my watch. In half an hour I was meeting Sandy. We were spending the weekend together. I was nervous, determined not to let embarrassment keep me from apologizing for four lost years.

I crossed to the window, staring down at the colorful bustle of the financial district. I'd found my way back.

LIA MATERA

DESIGNER CRIMES

00196-5/$5.99

FACE VALUE

88840-4/$5.99

☆A LAURA DI PALMA MYSTERY☆

"Di Palma is one of the smartest, most open-minded sleuths in the lawyering trade...."
—Marilyn Stasio, *The New York Times Book Review*

Available from Pocket Books